CHARLES BROCKDEN BROWN (1771–1810) became America's first professional writer. Born into a Quaker merchant family in Philadelphia, he was such a voracious reader that he came to be regarded as a literary prodigy. At the time authorship was not considered a serious profession, and Brown took up the study of law; but in 1793, just as he was about to begin practice, he gave up his law career and made the unprecedented resolve to earn his living as a writer. He took up residence in New York, where he found a place in a congenial literary circle, and in 1797 published his first complete work, a dialogue on the rights of women. During the next few years he worked furiously and produced his four most important novels: WIELAND, *Ormond, Edgar Huntly,* and *Arthur Mervyn.* Two more novels followed in 1801. But despite his output, Brown was unable to earn much money. To support himself he edited the *Monthly Magazine and North American Review,* and when the magazine failed he returned to Philadelphia and joined his brothers' mercantile firm. During his last years he continued his literary activity, abandoning fiction for historical writing and magazine work.

WIELAND;

or,

The Transformation

An American Tale

CHARLES BROCKDEN BROWN

From Virtue's blissful paths away
The double-tongued are sure to stray;
Good is a forth-right journey still,
And mazy paths but lead to ill.

Anchor Books
Anchor Press/Doubleday
Garden City, New York

Anchor Books edition: 1973

Printed in the United States of America

ADVERTISEMENT

The following work is delivered to the world as the first of a series of performances, which the favourable reception of this will induce the writer to publish. His purpose is neither selfish nor temporary, but aims at the illustration of some important branches of the moral constitution of man. Whether this tale will be classed with the ordinary or frivolous sources of amusement, or be ranked with the few productions whose usefulness secures to them a lasting reputation, the reader must be permitted to decide. *authority rests with people*

The incidents related are extraordinary and rare. Some of them, perhaps, approach as nearly to the nature of miracles as can be done by that which is not truly miraculous. It is hoped that intelligent readers will not disapprove of the manner in which appearances are solved, but that the solution will be found to correspond with the known principles of human nature. The power which the principal person is said to possess can scarcely be denied to be real. It must be acknowledged to be extremely rare; but no fact, equally uncommon, is supported by the same strength of historical evidence.

Some readers may think the conduct of the younger Wieland impossible. In support of its possibility the writer must appeal to physicians, and to men conversant with the latent springs and occasional perversions of the human mind. It will not be objected that the instances of similar delusion are rare, because it is the business of moral painters to exhibit their subject in its most instructive and memorable forms. If history furnishes one parallel fact, it is a sufficient vindication of the writer; but most readers will probably recollect an authentic case, remarkably similar to that of Wieland.

It will be necessary to add, that this narrative is addressed, in an epistolary form, by the lady whose story it contains, to a small number of friends, whose curiosity, with regard to it, had been greatly awakened. It may likewise be mentioned, that these events took place between the conclusion of the French and the beginning of the Revolutionary War. The memoirs of Carwin, alluded to at the conclusion of the work, will be published or suppressed according to the reception which is given to the present attempt.

C. B. B.

September 3, 1798.

WIELAND

CHAPTER I

I feel little reluctance in complying with your request. You know not fully the cause of my sorrows. You are a stranger to the depth of my distresses. Hence your efforts at consolation must necessarily fail. Yet the tale that I am going to tell is not intended as a claim upon your sympathy. In the midst of my despair, I do not disdain to contribute what little I can to the benefit of mankind. I acknowledge your right to be informed of the events that have lately happened in my family. Make what use of the tale you shall think proper. If it be communicated to the world, it will inculcate the duty of avoiding deceit. It will exemplify the force of early impressions, and show the immeasurable evils that flow from an erroneous or imperfect discipline.

My state is not destitute of tranquillity. The sentiment that dictates my feelings is not hope. Futurity has no power over my thoughts. To all that is to come I am perfectly indifferent. With regard to myself, I have nothing more to fear. Fate has done its worst. Henceforth, I am callous to misfortune.

I address no supplication to the Deity. The power that governs the course of human affairs has chosen his path. The decree that ascertained the condition of my life admits of no recall. No doubt it squares with the maxims of eternal equity. That is neither to be questioned nor denied by me. It suffices that the past is exempt from mutation. The storm that tore up our happiness, and changed into dreariness and desert the blooming scene of our existence, is lulled into grim repose; but not until the victim was transfixed and mangled; till every obstacle was dissipated by its rage; till every remnant of good was wrested from our grasp and exterminated.

How will your wonder, and that of your companions, be excited by my story! Every sentiment will yield to your amazement. If my testimony were without corroborations, you would reject it as incredible. The experience of no human being can furnish a parallel: that I, beyond the rest of mankind, should be reserved for a destiny without alleviation and without example! Listen to my narrative, and then say what it is that has made me deserve to be placed on this dreadful eminence, if, indeed, every faculty be not suspended in wonder that I am still alive and am able to relate it.

My father's ancestry was noble on the paternal side; but his mother was the daughter of a merchant. My grandfather was a younger brother, and a native of Saxony. He was placed, when he had reached the suitable age, at a German college. During the vacations, he employed himself in traversing the neighbouring territory. On one occasion it was his fortune to visit Hamburg. He formed an acquaintance with Leonard Weise, a merchant of that city, and was a frequent guest at his house. The merchant had an only daughter, for whom his guest speedily contracted an affection; and, in spite of parental menaces and prohibitions, he, in due season, became her husband.

By this act he mortally offended his relations. Thenceforward he was entirely disowned and rejected by them. They refused to contribute any thing to his support. All intercourse ceased, and he received from

them merely that treatment to which an absolute
stranger, or detested enemy, would be entitled.

He found an asylum in the house of his new father,
whose temper was kind, and whose pride was flattered
by this alliance. The nobility of his birth was put in the
balance against his poverty. Weise conceived himself,
on the whole, to have acted with the highest discretion
in thus disposing of his child. My grandfather found it
incumbent on him to search out some mode of independent subsistence. His youth had been eagerly devoted to literature and music. These had hitherto been
cultivated merely as sources of amusement. They were
now converted into the means of gain. At this period
there were few works of taste in the Saxon dialect. My
ancestor may be considered as the founder of the German Theatre. The modern poet of the same name is
sprung from the same family, and, perhaps, surpasses
but little, in the fruitfulness of his invention, or the
soundness of his taste, the elder Wieland. His life was
spent in the composition of sonatas and dramatic
pieces. They were not unpopular, but merely afforded
him a scanty subsistence. He died in the bloom of his
life, and was quickly followed to the grave by his wife.
Their only child was taken under the protection of the
merchant. At an early age he was apprenticed to a
London trader, and passed seven years of mercantile
servitude.

My father was not fortunate in the character of him
under whose care he was now placed. He was treated
with rigour, and full employment was provided for
every hour of his time. His duties were laborious and
mechanical. He had been educated with a view to this
profession, and, therefore, was not tormented with un-
satisfied desires. He did not hold his present occupations in abhorrence because they withheld him from
paths more flowery and more smooth, but he found in

unintermitted labour, and in the sternness of his master, sufficient occasions for discontent. No opportunities of recreation were allowed him. He spent all his time pent up in a gloomy apartment, or traversing narrow and crowded streets. His food was coarse, and his lodging humble.

His heart gradually contracted a habit of morose and gloomy reflection. He could not accurately define what was wanting to his happiness. He was not tortured by comparisons drawn between his own situation and that of others. His state was such as suited his age and his views as to fortune. He did not imagine himself treated with extraordinary or unjustifiable rigour. In this respect he supposed the condition of others, bound like himself to mercantile service, to resemble his own; yet every engagement was irksome, and every hour tedious in its lapse.

In this state of mind he chanced to light upon a book written by one of the teachers of the Albigenses, or French Protestants. He entertained no relish for books, and was wholly unconscious of any power they possessed to delight or instruct. This volume had lain for years in a corner of his garret, half buried in dust and rubbish. He had marked it as it lay; had thrown it, as his occasions required, from one spot to another; but had felt no inclination to examine its contents, or even to inquire what was the subject of which it treated.

One Sunday afternoon, being induced to retire for a few minutes to his garret, his eye was attracted by a page of this book, which, by some accident, had been opened and placed full in his view. He was seated on the edge of his bed, and was employed in repairing a rent in some part of his clothes. His eyes were not confined to his work, but, occasionally wandering, lighted at length upon the page. The words "Seek and ye shall find," were those that first offered themselves to his notice. His curiosity was roused by these so far as to prompt him to proceed. As soon as he finished his work, he took up the book and turned to the first page. The further he read, the more inducement he found to continue, and he regretted the decline of the light which obliged him for the present to close it.

The book contained an exposition of the doctrine of the sect of Camisards, and an historical account of its origin. His mind was in a state peculiarly fitted for the reception of devotional sentiments. The craving which had haunted him was now supplied with an object. His mind was at no loss for a theme of meditation. On days of business, he rose at the dawn, and retired to his chamber not till late at night. He now supplied himself with candles, and employed his nocturnal and Sunday hours in studying this book. It, of course, abounded with allusions to the Bible. All its conclusions were deduced from the sacred text. This was the fountain, beyond which it was unnecessary to trace the stream of religious truth; but it was his duty to trace it thus far.

A Bible was easily procured, and he ardently entered on the study of it. His understanding had received a particular direction. All his reveries were fashioned in the same mould. His progress towards the formation of his creed was rapid. Every fact and sentiment in this book were viewed through a medium which the writings of the Camisard apostle had suggested. His constructions of the text were hasty, and formed on a narrow scale. Every thing was viewed in a disconnected position. One action and one precept were not employed to illustrate and restrict the meaning of another. Hence arose a thousand scruples to which he had hitherto been a stranger. He was alternately agitated by fear and by ecstasy. He imagined himself beset by the snares of a spiritual foe, and that his security lay in ceaseless watchfulness and prayer.

His morals, which had never been loose, were now modelled by a stricter standard. The empire of religious duty extended itself to his looks, gestures, and phrases. All levities of speech, and negligences of behaviour, were proscribed. His air was mournful and contemplative. He laboured to keep alive a sentiment of fear, and a belief of the awe-creating presence of the Deity. Ideas foreign to this were sedulously excluded. To suffer their intrusion was a crime against the Divine Majesty, inexpiable but by days and weeks of the keenest agonies.

No material variation had occurred in the lapse of two years. Every day confirmed him in his present modes of thinking and acting. It was to be expected that the tide of his emotions would sometimes recede, that intervals of despondency and doubt would occur; but these gradually were more rare, and of shorter duration; and he, at last, arrived at a state considerably uniform in this respect.

His apprenticeship was now almost expired. On his arrival at age he became entitled, by the will of my grandfather, to a small sum. This sum would hardly suffice to set him afloat as a trader in his present situation, and he had nothing to expect from the generosity of his master. Residence in England had, besides, become almost impossible, on account of his religious tenets. In addition to these motives for seeking a new habitation, there was another of the most imperious and irresistible necessity. He had imbibed an opinion that it was his duty to disseminate the truths of the gospel among the unbelieving nations. He was terrified at first by the perils and hardships to which the life of a missionary is exposed. This cowardice made him diligent in the invention of objections and excuses; but he found it impossible wholly to shake off the belief that such was the injunction of his duty. The belief, after every new conflict with his passions, acquired new strength; and, at length, he formed a resolution of complying with what he deemed the will of heaven.

The North American Indians naturally presented themselves as the first objects for this species of benevolence. As soon as his servitude expired, he converted his little fortune into money, and embarked for Philadelphia. Here his fears were revived, and a nearer survey of savage manners once more shook his resolution. For a while he relinquished his purpose, and, purchasing a farm on the Schuylkill, within a few miles of the city, set himself down to the cultivation of it. The cheapness of land, and the service of African slaves, which were then in general use, gave him, who was poor in Europe, all the advantages of wealth. He passed fourteen years in a thrifty and laborious manner. In this time new objects, new employments, and new associates appeared to have nearly obliterated the devout impressions of his youth. He now became acquainted with a woman of a meek and quiet disposition, and of slender acquirements like himself. He proffered his hand and was accepted.

His previous industry had now enabled him to dispense with personal labour, and direct attention to his own concerns. He enjoyed leisure, and was visited afresh by devotional contemplation. The reading of the Scriptures, and other religious books, became once more his favourite employment. His ancient belief relative to the conversion of the savage tribes was revived with uncommon energy. To the former obstacles were now added the pleadings of parental and conjugal love. The struggle was long and vehement; but his sense of duty would not be stifled or enfeebled, and finally triumphed over every impediment.

His efforts were attended with no permanent success. His exhortations had sometimes a temporary power, but more frequently were repelled with insult and derision. In pursuit of this object he encountered the most imminent perils, and underwent incredible fatigues, hunger, sickness, and solitude. The license of savage passion, and the artifices of his depraved countrymen, all opposed themselves to his progress. His courage did not forsake him till there appeared no reasonable ground to hope for success. He desisted not till his heart was relieved from the supposed obligation to persevere. With a constitution somewhat decayed, he at length returned to his family. An interval of tranquillity succeeded. He was frugal, regular, and strict in the performance of domestic duties. He allied himself with no sect, because he perfectly agreed with none. Social worship is that by which they are all distinguished; but this article found no place in his creed. He rigidly interpreted that precept which enjoins us, when we worship, to retire into solitude, and shut out every species of society. According to him, devotion was not only a silent office, but must be performed alone. An hour at noon and an hour at midnight were thus appropriated.

At the distance of three hundred yards from his house, on the top of a rock whose sides were steep, rugged, and encumbered with dwarf cedars and stony asperities, he built what to a common eye would have seemed a summer-house. The eastern verge of this precipice was sixty feet above the river which flowed at its foot. The view before it consisted of a transparent current, fluctuating and rippling in a rocky channel, and bounded by a rising scene of cornfields and orchards. The edifice was slight and airy. It was no more than a circular area, twelve feet in diameter, whose flooring was the rock, cleared of moss and shrubs, and exactly levelled, edged by twelve Tuscan columns, and covered by an undulating dome. My father furnished the dimensions and outlines, but allowed the artist, whom he employed, to complete the structure on his own plan. It was without seat, table, or ornament of any kind.

This was the temple of his Deity. Twice in twenty-four hours he repaired hither, unaccompanied by any human being. Nothing but physical inability to move was allowed to obstruct or postpone this visit. He did not exact from his family compliance with his example. Few men, equally sincere in their faith, were as sparing in their censures and restrictions, with respect to the conduct of others, as my father. The character of my mother was no less devout; but her education had habituated her to a different mode of worship. The loneliness of their dwelling prevented her from joining any established congregation; but she was punctual in the offices of prayer, and in the performance of hymns to her Saviour, after the manner of the disciples of Zinzendorf. My father refused to interfere in her arrangements. His own system was embraced not, accurately speaking, because it was the best, but because it had been expressly prescribed to him. Other modes, if practised by other persons, might be equally acceptable.

His deportment to others was full of charity and mildness. A sadness perpetually overspread his features, but was unmingled with sternness or discontent. The tones of his voice, his gestures, his steps, were all in tranquil uniform. His conduct was characterized by a certain forbearance and humility, which secured the esteem of those to whom his tenets were most obnoxious. They might call him a fanatic and a dreamer, but they could not deny their veneration to his invincible candour and invariable integrity. His own belief of rectitude was the foundation of his happiness. This, however, was destined to find an end.

Suddenly the sadness that constantly attended him was deepened. Sighs, and even tears, sometimes escaped him. To the expostulations of his wife he seldom answered any thing. When he designed to be communicative, he hinted that his peace of mind was flown, in consequence of deviation from his duty. A command had been laid upon him, which he had delayed to perform. He felt as if a certain period of hesitation and reluctance had been allowed him, but that this period was passed. He was no longer permitted to obey. The duty assigned to him was transferred, in consequence of his disobedience, to another, and all that remained was to endure the penalty.

He did not describe this penalty. It appeared to be nothing more for some time than a sense of wrong. This was sufficiently acute, and was aggravated by the belief that his offence was incapable of expiation. No one could contemplate the agonies which he seemed to suffer without the deepest compassion. Time, instead of lightening the burden, appeared to add to it. At length he hinted to his wife that his end was near. His imagination did not prefigure the mode or the time of his decease, but was fraught with an incurable persuasion that his death was at hand. He was likewise haunted by the belief that the kind of death that awaited him was strange and terrible. His anticipations were thus far vague and indefinite; but they sufficed to poison every moment of his being and devote him to ceaseless anguish.

CHAPTER II

Early in the morning of a sultry day in August he left Mettingen to go to the city. He had seldom passed a day from home since his return from the shores of the Ohio. Some urgent engagements at this time existed, which would not admit of further delay. He returned in the evening, but appeared to be greatly oppressed with fatigue. His silence and dejection were likewise in a more than ordinary degree conspicuous. My mother's brother, whose profession was that of a surgeon, chanced to spend this night at our house. It was from him that I have frequently received an exact account of the mournful catastrophe that followed.

As the evening advanced, my father's inquietudes increased. He sat with his family as usual, but took no part in their conversation. He appeared fully engrossed by his own reflections. Occasionally his countenance exhibited tokens of alarm; he gazed steadfastly and wildly at the ceiling; and the exertions of his companions were scarcely sufficient to interrupt his reverie. On recovering from these fits, he expressed no surprise, but, pressing his hand to his head, complained, in a tremulous and terrified tone, that his brain was scorched to cinders. He would then betray marks of insupportable anxiety.

My uncle perceived by his pulse that he was indisposed, but in no alarming degree, and ascribed appearances chiefly to the workings of his mind. He exhorted him to recollection and composure, but in vain. At the hour of repose he readily retired to his chamber. At the persuasion of my mother he even undressed and went to bed. Nothing could abate his restlessness. He checked her tender expostulations with some sternness. "Be silent," said he; "for that which I feel there is but one cure, and that will shortly come. You can help me nothing. Look to your own condition, and pray to God to strengthen you under the calamities that await you." "What am I to fear?" she answered. "What terrible disaster is it that you think of?" "Peace!—as yet I know it not myself, but come it will, and shortly." She repeated her inquiries and doubts; but he suddenly put an end to the discourse, by a stern command to be silent.

She had never before known him in this mood. Hitherto all was benign in his deportment. Her heart was pierced with sorrow at the contemplation of this change. She was utterly unable to account for it, or to figure to herself the species of disaster that was menaced.

Contrary to custom, the lamp, instead of being placed on the hearth, was left upon the table. Over it, against the wall, there hung a small clock, so contrived as to strike a very hard stroke at the end of every sixth hour. That which was now approaching was the signal for retiring to the fane at which he addressed his devotions. Long habit had occasioned him to be always awake at this hour, and the toll was instantly obeyed.

Now frequent and anxious glances were cast at the clock. Not a single movement of the index appeared to escape his notice. As the hour verged towards twelve, his anxiety visibly augmented. The trepidations of my mother kept pace with those of her husband; but she was intimidated into silence. All that was left to her was to watch every change of his features and give vent to her sympathy in tears.

At length the hour was spent, and the clock tolled. The sound appeared to communicate a shock to every

part of my father's frame. He rose immediately, and
threw over himself a loose gown. Even this office was
performed with difficulty, for his joints trembled and
his teeth chattered with dismay. At this hour his duty
called him to the rock, and my mother naturally concluded that it was thither he intended to repair. Yet
these incidents were so uncommon as to fill her with
astonishment and foreboding. She saw him leave the
room, and heard his steps as they hastily descended
the stairs. She half resolved to rise and pursue him, but
the wildness of the scheme quickly suggested itself.
He was going to a place whither no power on earth
could induce him to suffer an attendant.

The window of her chamber looked towards the
rock. The atmosphere was clear and calm, but the edifice could not be discovered at that distance through
the dusk. My mother's anxiety would not allow her to
remain where she was. She rose, and seated herself at
the window. She strained her sight to get a view of the
dome, and of the path that led to it. The first painted
itself with sufficient distinctness on her fancy, but was
undistinguishable by the eye from the rocky mass on
which it was erected. The second could be imperfectly
seen; but her husband had already passed, or had
taken a different direction.

What was it that she feared? Some disaster impended over her husband or herself. He had predicted
evils, but professed himself ignorant of what nature
they were. When were they to come? Was this night,
or this hour, to witness the accomplishment? She was
tortured with impatience and uncertainty. All her fears
were at present linked to his person, and she gazed at
the clock, with nearly as much eagerness as my father
had done, in expectation of the next hour.

A half hour passed away in this state of suspense.
Her eyes were fixed upon the rock; suddenly it was

illuminated. A light proceeding from the edifice made
every part of the scene visible. A gleam diffused itself
over the intermediate space, and instantly a loud report, like the explosion of a mine, followed. She uttered an involuntary shriek, but the new sounds that
greeted her ear quickly conquered her surprise. They
were piercing shrieks, and uttered without intermis-
sion. The gleams, which had diffused themselves far
and wide, were in a moment withdrawn; but the interior of the edifice was filled with rays.

The first suggestion was that a pistol was discharged,
and that the structure was on fire. She did not allow
herself time to meditate a second thought, but rushed
into the entry and knocked loudly at the door of her
brother's chamber. My uncle had been previously
roused by the noise, and instantly flew to the window.
He also imagined what he saw to be fire. The loud and
vehement shrieks which succeeded the first explosion
seemed to be an invocation of succour. The incident
was inexplicable; but he could not fail to perceive the
propriety of hastening to the spot. He was unbolting
the door, when his sister's voice was heard on the outside conjuring him to come forth.

He obeyed the summons with all the speed in his
power. He stopped not to question her, but hurried
down-stairs and across the meadow which lay between
the house and the rock. The shrieks were no longer to
be heard; but a blazing light was clearly discernible
between the columns of the temple. Irregular steps,
hewn in the stone, led him to the summit. On three
sides this edifice touched the very verge of the cliff.
On the fourth side, which might be regarded as the
front, there was an area of small extent, to which the
rude staircase conducted you. My uncle speedily
gained this spot. His strength was for a moment exhausted by his haste. He paused to rest himself. Mean-

while he bent the most vigilant attention towards the object before him.

Within the columns he beheld what he could no better describe than by saying that it resembled a cloud impregnated with light. It had the brightness of flame, but was without its upward motion. It did not occupy the whole area, and rose but a few feet above the floor. No part of the building was on fire. This appearance was astonishing. He approached the temple. As he went forward the light retired, and, when he put his feet within the apartment, utterly vanished. The suddenness of this transition increased the darkness that succeeded in a tenfold degree. Fear and wonder rendered him powerless. An occurrence like this, in a place assigned to devotion, was adapted to intimidate the stoutest heart.

His wandering thoughts were recalled by the groans of one near him. His sight gradually recovered its power, and he was able to discern my father stretched on the floor. At that moment my mother and servants arrived, with a lantern, and enabled my uncle to examine more closely this scene. My father, when he left the house, besides a loose upper vest and slippers, wore a shirt and drawers. Now he was naked; his skin throughout the greater part of his body was scorched and bruised. His right arm exhibited marks as of having been struck by some heavy body. His clothes had been removed, and it was not immediately perceived that they were reduced to ashes. His slippers and his hair were untouched.

He was removed to his chamber, and the requisite attention paid to his wounds, which gradually became more painful. A mortification speedily showed itself in the arm, which had been most hurt. Soon after, the other wounded parts exhibited the like appearance.

Immediately subsequent to this disaster, my father

seemed nearly in a state of insensibility. He was passive under every operation. He scarcely opened his
eyes, and was with difficulty prevailed upon to answer
the questions that were put to him. By his imperfect
account, it appeared, that while engaged in silent ori-
sons, with thoughts full of confusion and anxiety, a
faint gleam suddenly shot athwart the apartment. His
fancy immediately pictured to itself a person bearing
a lamp. It seemed to come from behind. He was in the
act of turning to examine the visitant, when his right
arm received a blow from a heavy club. At the same
instant, a very bright spark was seen to light upon his
clothes. In a moment, the whole was reduced to ashes.
This was the sum of the information which he chose to
give. There was somewhat in his manner that indicated an imperfect tale. My uncle was inclined to believe that half the truth had been suppressed.

Meanwhile, the disease thus wonderfully generated
betrayed more terrible symptoms. Fever and delirium
terminated in lethargic slumber, which, in the course
of two hours, gave place to death; yet not till insupportable exhalations and crawling putrefaction had
driven from his chamber and the house every one
whom their duty did not detain.

Such was the end of my father. None, surely, was
ever more mysterious. When we recollect his gloomy
anticipations and unconquerable anxiety, the security
from human malice which his character, the place, and
the condition of the times might be supposed to confer,
the purity and cloudlessness of the atmosphere, which
rendered it impossible that lightning was the cause,
what are the conclusions that we must form?

The prelusive gleam, the blow upon his arm, the
fatal spark, the explosion heard so far, the fiery cloud
that environed him, without detriment to the structure, though composed of combustible materials, the

sudden vanishing of this cloud at my uncle's approach: —what is the inference to be drawn from these facts? Their truth cannot be doubted. My uncle's testimony is peculiarly worthy of credit, because no man's temper is more skeptical, and his belief is unalterably attached to natural causes. *

I was at this time a child of six years of age. The impressions that were then made upon me can never be effaced. I was ill qualified to judge respecting what was then passing; but, as I advanced in age and became more fully acquainted with these facts, they oftener became the subject of my thoughts. Their resemblance to recent events revived them with new force in my memory, and made me more anxious to explain them. Was this the penalty of disobedience?—this the stroke of a vindictive and invisible hand? Is it a fresh proof that the Divine Ruler interferes in human affairs, meditates an end, selects and commissions his agents, and enforces, by unequivocal sanctions, submission to his will? Or was it merely the irregular expansion of the fluid that imparts warmth to our heart and our blood, caused by the fatigue of the preceding day, or flowing, by established laws, from the condition of his thoughts.

CHAPTER III

The shock which this disastrous occurrence occasioned to my mother was the foundation of a disease which

* A case in its symptoms exactly parallel to this is published in one of the Journals of Florence. See, likewise, similar cases reported by Messrs. Merrille and Muraire, in the "Journal de Medicine" for February and May, 1783. The researches of Maffei and Fontana have thrown some light upon this subject.

carried her, in a few months, to the grave. My brother
and myself were children at this time, and were now
reduced to the condition of orphans. The property
which our parents left was by no means inconsidera-
ble. It was intrusted to faithful hands till we should
arrive at a suitable age. Meanwhile our education was
assigned to a maiden aunt who resided in the city, and
whose tenderness made us in a short time cease to regret that we had lost a mother.

The years that succeeded were tranquil and happy.
Our lives were molested by few of those cares that are
incident to childhood. By accident more than design,
the indulgence and yielding temper of our aunt was
mingled with resolution and steadfastness. She seldom
deviated into either extreme of rigour or lenity. Our
social pleasures were subject to no unreasonable restraints. We were instructed in most branches of useful
knowledge, and were saved from the corruption and
tyranny of colleges and boarding-schools.

Our companions were chiefly selected from the children of our neighbours. Between one of these and my
brother there quickly grew the most affectionate intimacy. Her name was Catharine Pleyel. She was rich,
beautiful, and contrived to blend the most bewitching
softness with the most exuberant vivacity. The tie by
which my brother and she were united seemed to add
force to the love which I bore her, and which was amply returned. Between her and myself there was every
circumstance tending to produce and foster friendship. Our sex and age were the same. We lived within
sight of each other's abode. Our tempers were remarkably congenial, and the superintendents of our education not only prescribed to us the same pursuits, but
allowed us to cultivate them together.

Every day added strength to the triple bonds that
united us. We gradually withdrew ourselves from the

society of others, and found every moment irksome that was not devoted to each other. My brother's advance in age made no change in our situation. It was determined that his profession should be agriculture. His fortune exempted him from the necessity of personal labour. The task to be performed by him was nothing more than superintendence. The skill that was demanded by this was merely theoretical, and was furnished by casual inspection, or by closet study. The attention that was paid to this subject did not seclude him for any long time from us, on whom time had no other effect than to augment our impatience in the absence of each other and of him. Our tasks, our walks, our music, were seldom performed but in each other's company.

It was easy to see that Catharine and my brother were born for each other. The passion which they mutually entertained quickly broke those bounds which extreme youth had set to it; confessions were made or extorted, and their union was postponed only till my brother had passed his minority. The previous lapse of two years was constantly and usefully employed.

Oh, my brother! But the task I have set myself let me perform with steadiness. The felicity of that period was marred by no gloomy anticipations. The future, like the present, was serene. Time was supposed to have only new delights in store. I mean not to dwell on previous incidents longer than is necessary to illustrate or explain the great events that have since happened. The nuptial day at length arrived. My brother took possession of the house in which he was born, and here the long-protracted marriage was solemnized.

My father's property was equally divided between us. A neat dwelling, situated on the bank of the river, three-quarters of a mile from my brother's, was now occupied by me. These domains were called, from the

name of the first possessor, Mettingen. I can scarcely
account for my refusing to take up my abode with him,
unless it were from a disposition to be an economist
of pleasure. Self-denial, seasonably exercised, is one
means of enhancing our gratifications. I was, besides,
desirous of administering a fund and regulating a
household of my own. The short distance allowed us
to exchange visits as often as we pleased. The walk
from one mansion to the other was no undelightful
prelude to our interviews. I was sometimes their visitant, and they as frequently were my guests.

Our education had been modelled by no religious
standard. We were left to the guidance of our own understanding and the casual impressions which society
might make upon us. My friends' temper, as well as my
own, exempted us from much anxiety on this account.
It must not be supposed that we were without religion;
but with us it was the product of lively feelings, excited
by reflection on our own happiness, and by the grandeur of external nature. We sought not a basis for our
faith in the weighing of proofs and the dissection of
creeds. Our devotion was a mixed and casual sentiment, seldom verbally expressed, or solicitously sought,
or carefully retained. In the midst of present enjoyment, no thought was bestowed on the future. As a
consolation in calamity, religion is dear. But calamity
was yet at a distance; and its only tendency was to
heighten enjoyments which needed not this addition
to satisfy every craving.

My brother's situation was somewhat different. His
deportment was grave, considerate, and thoughtful. I
will not say whether he was indebted to sublimer views
for this disposition. Human life, in his opinion, was
made up of changeable elements, and the principles of
duty were not easily unfolded. The future, either as
anterior or subsequent to death, was a scene that re-

quired some preparation and provision to be made for it. These positions we could not deny; but what distinguished him was a propensity to ruminate on these truths. The images that visited us were blithesome and gay, but those with which he was most familiar were of an opposite hue. They did not generate affliction and fear, but they diffused over his behaviour a certain air of forethought and sobriety. The principal effect of this temper was visible in his features and tones. These, in general, bespoke a sort of thrilling melancholy. I scarcely ever knew him to laugh. He never accompanied the lawless mirth of his companions with more than a smile, but his conduct was the same as ours.

He partook of our occupations and amusements with a zeal not less than ours, but of a different kind. The diversity in our temper was never the parent of discord, and was scarcely a topic of regret. The scene was variegated but not tarnished or disordered by it. It hindered the element in which we moved from stagnating. Some agitation and concussion is requisite to the due exercise of human understanding. In his studies, he pursued an austerer and more arduous path. He was much conversant with the history of religious opinions, and took pains to ascertain their validity. He deemed it indispensable to examine the ground of his belief, to settle the relation between motives and actions, the criterion of merit, and the kinds and properties of evidence.

There was an obvious resemblance between him and my father in their conceptions of the importance of certain topics, and in the light in which the vicissitudes of human life were accustomed to be viewed. Their characters were similar; but the mind of the son was enriched by science and embellished with literature.

The temple was no longer assigned to its ancient

use. From an Italian adventurer, who erroneously imagined that he could find employment for his skill and sale for his sculptures in America, my brother had purchased a bust of Cicero. He professed to have copied this piece from an antique dug up with his own hands in the environs of Modena. Of the truth of his assertions we were not qualified to judge; but the marble was pure and polished, and we were contented to admire the performance, without waiting for the sanction of connoisseurs. We hired the same artist to hew a suitable pedestal from a neighbouring quarry. This was placed in the temple, and the bust rested upon it. Opposite to this was a harpsichord, sheltered by a temporary roof from the weather. This was the place of resort in the evenings of summer. Here we sung, and talked, and read, and occasionally banqueted. Every joyous and tender scene most dear to my memory is connected with this edifice. Here the performances of our musical and poetical ancestors were rehearsed. Here my brother's children received the rudiments of their education; here a thousand conversations, pregnant with delight and improvement, took place; and here the social affections were accustomed to expand, and the tear of delicious sympathy to be shed.

My brother was an indefatigable student. The authors whom he read were numerous; but the chief object of his veneration was Cicero. He was never tired of conning and rehearsing his productions. To understand them was not sufficient. He was anxious to discover the gestures and cadences with which they ought to be delivered. He was very scrupulous in selecting a true scheme of pronunciation for the Latin tongue, and in adapting it to the words of his darling writer. His favourite occupation consisted in embellishing his rhetoric with all the proprieties of gesticulation and utterance.

Not contented with this, he was diligent in settling and restoring the purity of the text. For this end, he collected all the editions and commentaries that could be procured, and employed months of severe study in exploring and comparing them. He never betrayed more satisfaction than when he made a discovery of this kind.

It was not till the addition of Henry Pleyel, my friend's only brother, to our society, that his passion for Roman eloquence was countenanced and fostered by a sympathy of tastes. This young man had been some years in Europe. We had separated at a very early age, and he was now returned to spend the remainder of his days among us.

Our circle was greatly enlivened by the accession of a new member. His conversation abounded with novelty. His gayety was almost boisterous, but was capable of yielding to a grave deportment when the occasion required it. His discernment was acute; but he was prone to view every object merely as supplying materials for mirth. His conceptions were ardent but ludicrous, and his memory, aided, as he honestly acknowledged, by his invention, was an inexhaustible fund of entertainment.

His residence was at the same distance below the city as ours was above, but there seldom passed a day without our being favoured with a visit. My brother and he were endowed with the same attachment to the Latin writers; and Pleyel was not behind his friend in his knowledge of the history and metaphysics of religion. Their creeds, however, were in many respects opposite. Where one discovered only confirmations of his faith, the other could find nothing but reasons for doubt. Moral necessity and Calvinistic inspiration were

the props on which my brother thought proper to repose. Pleyel was the champion of intellectual liberty,
and rejected all guidance but that of his reason. Their
discussions were frequent, but, being managed with
candour as well as with skill, they were always listened
to by us with avidity and benefit.

Pleyel, like his new friends, was fond of music and
poetry. Henceforth our concerts consisted of two vio-
lins, a harpsichord, and three voices. We were frequently reminded how much happiness depends upon
society. This new friend, though before his arrival we
were sensible of no vacuity, could not now be spared.
His departure would occasion a void which nothing
could fill, and which would produce insupportable regret. Even my brother, though his opinions were hourly
assailed, and even the divinity of Cicero contested, was
captivated with his friend, and laid aside some part of
his ancient gravity at Pleyel's approach.

CHAPTER IV

Six years of uninterrupted happiness had rolled away
since my brother's marriage. The sound of war had
been heard, but it was at such a distance as to enhance
our enjoyment by affording objects of comparison.
The Indians were repulsed on the one side, and Canada was conquered on the other. Revolutions and bat-
tles, however calamitous to those who occupied the
scene, contributed in some sort to our happiness,
by agitating our minds with curiosity and furnishing
causes of patriotic exultation. Four children, three of
whom were of an age to compensate, by their personal

and mental progress, the cares of which they had been, at a more helpless age, the objects, exercised my brother's tenderness. The fourth was a charming babe that promised to display the image of her mother, and enjoyed perfect health. To these were added a sweet girl fourteen years old, who was loved by all of us with an affection more than parental.

Her mother's story was a mournful one. She had come hither from England when this child was an infant, alone, without friends, and without money. She appeared to have embarked in a hasty and clandestine manner. She passed three years of solitude and anguish under my aunt's protection, and died a martyr to woe the source of which she could by no importunities be prevailed upon to unfold. Her education and manners bespoke her to be of no mean birth. Her last moments were rendered serene by the assurances she received from my aunt that her daughter should experience the same protection that had been extended to herself.

On my brother's marriage it was agreed that she should make a part of his family. I cannot do justice to the attractions of this girl. Perhaps the tenderness she excited might partly originate in her personal resemblance to her mother, whose character and misfortunes were still fresh in our remembrance. She was habitually pensive, and this circumstance tended to remind the spectator of her friendless condition; and yet that epithet was surely misapplied in this case. This being was cherished with unspeakable fondness by those with whom she now resided. Every exertion was made to enlarge and improve her mind. Her safety was the object of a solicitude that almost exceeded the bounds of discretion. Our affection, indeed, could scarcely transcend her merits. She never met my eye or occurred to my reflections without exciting a kind of enthusiasm. Her softness, her intelligence, her equa-

nimity, never shall I see surpassed. I have often shed
tears of pleasure at her approach and pressed her to
my bosom in an agony of fondness.

While every day was adding to the charms of her
person and the stores of her mind, there occurred an
event which threatened to deprive us of her. An officer of some rank, who had been disabled by a wound
at Quebec, had employed himself, since the ratification
of peace, in travelling through the colonies. He remained a considerable period at Philadelphia, but was
at last preparing for his departure. No one had been
more frequently honoured with his visits than Mrs.
Baynton, a worthy lady with whom our family were
intimate. He went to her house with a view to perform
a farewell visit, and was on the point of taking his leave
when I and my young friend entered the apartment.
It is impossible to describe the emotions of the stranger
when he fixed his eyes upon my companion. He was
motionless with surprise. He was unable to conceal his
feelings, but sat silently gazing at the spectacle before
him. At length he turned to Mrs. Baynton, and, more
by his looks and gestures than by words, besought her
for an explanation of the scene. He seized the hand of
the girl, who, in her turn, was surprised by his behaviour, and, drawing her forward, said, in an eager and
faltering tone, "Who is she? whence does she come?
what is her name?"

The answers that were given only increased the confusion of his thoughts. He was successively told that
she was the daughter of one whose name was Louisa
Conway, who arrived among us at such a time, who
sedulously concealed her parentage and the motives of
her flight, whose incurable griefs had finally destroyed
her, and who had left this child under the protection
of her friends. Having heard the tale, he melted into
tears, eagerly clasped the young lady in his arms, and

called himself her father. When the tumults excited in his breast by this unlooked-for meeting were somewhat subsided, he gratified our curiosity by relating the following incidents:—

"Miss Conway was the only daughter of a banker in London, who discharged towards her every duty of an affectionate father. He had chanced to fall into her company, had been subdued by her attractions, had tendered her his hand, and been joyfully accepted both by parent and child. His wife had given him every proof of the fondest attachment. Her father, who possessed immense wealth, treated him with distinguished respect, liberally supplied his wants, and had made one condition of his consent to their union a resolution to take up their abode with him.

"They had passed three years of conjugal felicity, which had been augmented by the birth of this child, when his professional duty called him into Germany. It was not without an arduous struggle that she was persuaded to relinquish the design of accompanying him through all the toils and perils of war. No parting was ever more distressful. They strove to alleviate, by frequent letters, the evils of their lot. Those of his wife breathed nothing but anxiety for his safety and impatience of his absence. At length a new arrangement was made, and he was obliged to repair from Westphalia to Canada. One advantage attended this change: it afforded him an opportunity of meeting his family. His wife anticipated this interview with no less rapture than himself. He hurried to London, and, the moment he alighted from the stage-coach, ran with all speed to Mr. Conway's house.

"It was a house of mourning. His father was overwhelmed with grief and incapable of answering his inquiries. The servants, sorrowful and mute, were equally refractory. He explored the house, and called on the names of his wife and daughter; but his summons were fruitless. At length this new disaster was explained. Two days before his arrival, his wife's chamber was found empty. No search, however diligent and anxious, could trace her steps. No cause could be assigned for her disappearance. The mother and child had fled away together.

"New exertions were made; her chamber and cabinets were ransacked; but no vestige was found serving to inform them as to the motives of her flight, whether it had been voluntary or otherwise, and in what corner of the kingdom or of the world she was concealed. Who shall describe the sorrow and amazement of the husband,—his restlessness, his vicissitudes of hope and fear, and his ultimate despair? His duty called him to America. He had been in this city, and had frequently passed the door of the house in which his wife at that moment resided. Her father had not remitted his exertions to elucidate this painful mystery; but they had failed. This disappointment hastened his death; in consequence of which Louisa's father became possessor of his immense property."

This tale was a copious theme of speculation. A thousand questions were started and discussed in our domestic circle respecting the motives that influenced Mrs. Stuart to abandon her country. It did not appear that her proceeding was involuntary. We recalled and reviewed every particular that had fallen under our own observation. By none of these were we furnished with a clue. Her conduct, after the most rigorous scrutiny, still remained an impenetrable secret. On a nearer view, Major Stuart proved himself a man of most amiable character. His attachment to Louisa appeared hourly to increase. She was no stranger to the sentiments suitable to her new character. She could not but readily embrace the scheme which was proposed to her,—to return with her father to England. This scheme his regard for her induced him, however, to postpone. Some time was necessary to prepare her for so great a change and enable her to think without agony of her separation from us.

I was not without hopes of prevailing on her father entirely to relinquish this unwelcome design. Meanwhile, he pursued his travels through the southern colonies, and his daughter continued with us. Louisa and my brother frequently received letters from him which indicated a mind of no common order. They were filled with amusing details and profound reflections. While here, he often partook of our evening conversations at the temple; and since his departure his correspondence had frequently supplied us with topics of discourse.

One afternoon in May, the blandness of the air and brightness of the verdure induced us to assemble earlier than usual in the temple. We females were busy at the needle, while my brother and Pleyel were bandying quotations and syllogisms. The point discussed was the merit of the oration for Cluentius, as descriptive, first, of the genius of the speaker, and, secondly, of the manners of the times. Pleyel laboured to extenuate both these species of merit, and tasked his ingenuity to show that the orator had embraced a bad cause, or, at least, a doubtful one. He urged that to rely on the exaggerations of an advocate, or to make the picture of a single family a model from which to sketch the condition of a nation, was absurd. The controversy was suddenly diverted into a new channel, by a misquotation. Pleyel accused his companion of saying *"polliciatur"* when he should have said *"polliceretur."* Nothing would decide the contest but an appeal to the volume. My brother was returning to the house for this purpose, when a servant met him with a letter from Major Stuart. He immediately returned to read it in our company.

Besides affectionate compliments to us and paternal
benedictions on Louisa, his letter contained a description of a waterfall on the Monongahela. A sudden gust
of rain falling, we were compelled to remove to the
house. The storm passed away, and a radiant moonlight succeeded. There was no motion to resume our
seats in the temple. We therefore remained where we
were, and engaged in sprightly conversation. The letter
lately received naturally suggested the topic. A parallel was drawn between the cataract there described
and one which Pleyel had discovered among the Alps
of Glarus. In the state of the former, some particular
was mentioned the truth of which was questionable.
To settle the dispute which thence arose, it was proposed to have recourse to the letter. My brother
searched for it in his pocket. It was nowhere to be
found. At length he remembered to have left it in the
temple, and he determined to go in search for it. His
wife, Pleyel, Louisa, and myself, remained where we
were.

In a few minutes he returned. I was somewhat interested in the dispute, and was therefore impatient for
his return; yet, as I heard him ascending the stairs, I
could not but remark that he had executed his intention with remarkable despatch. My eyes were fixed
upon him on his entrance. Methought he brought with
him looks considerably different from those with which
he departed. Wonder and a slight portion of anxiety
were mingled in them. His eyes seemed to be in search
of some object. They passed quickly from one person
to another, till they rested on his wife. She was seated
in a careless attitude on the sofa, in the same spot as
before. She had the same muslin in her hand by which
her attention was chiefly engrossed.

The moment he saw her, his perplexity visibly increased. He quietly seated himself, and, fixing his eyes

on the floor, appeared to be absorbed in meditation. These singularities suspended the inquiry which I was preparing to make respecting the letter. In a short time, the company relinquished the subject which engaged them, and directed their attention to Wieland. They thought that he only waited for a pause in the discourse to produce the letter. The pause was uninterrupted by him. At length Pleyel said, "Well, I suppose you have found the letter?"

"No," said he, without any abatement of his gravity, and looking steadfastly at his wife; "I did not mount the hill."—"Why not?"—"Catharine, have you not moved from that spot since I left the room?"—She was affected with the solemnity of his manner, and, laying down her work, answered, in a tone of surprise, "No. Why do you ask that question?"—His eyes were again fixed upon the floor, and he did not immediately answer. At length he said, looking round upon us, "Is it true that Catharine did not follow me to the hill?— that she did not just now enter the room?" We assured him, with one voice, that she had not been absent for a moment, and inquired into the motive of his questions.

"Your assurances," said he, "are solemn and unanimous; and yet I must deny credit to your assertions, or disbelieve the testimony of my senses, which informed me, when I was half-way up the hill, that Catharine was at the bottom."

We were confounded at this declaration. Pleyel rallied him with great levity on his behaviour. He listened to his friend with calmness, but without any relaxation of features.

"One thing," said he, with emphasis, "is true: either I heard my wife's voice at the bottom of the hill, or I do not hear your voice at present."

"Truly," returned Pleyel, "it is a sad dilemma to

which you have reduced yourself. Certain it is, if our
eyes can give us certainty, that your wife has been sit-
ting in that spot during every moment of your absence.
You have heard her voice, you say, upon the hill. In
general, her voice, like her temper, is all softness. To
be heard across the room, she is obliged to exert herself. While you were gone, if I mistake not, she did not
utter a word. Clara and I had all the talk to ourselves.
Still, it may be that she held a whispering conference
with you on the hill; but tell us the particulars."

"The conference," said he, "was short, and far from
being carried on in a whisper. You know with what intention I left the house. Half-way to the rock, the moon
was for a moment hidden from us by a cloud. I never
knew the air to be more bland and more calm. In this
interval I glanced at the temple, and thought I saw a
glimmering between the columns. It was so faint that
it would not perhaps have been visible if the moon had
not been shrouded. I looked again, but saw nothing. I
never visit this building alone, or at night, without being reminded of the fate of my father. There was nothing wonderful in this appearance; yet it suggested
something more than mere solitude and darkness in the
same place would have done.

"I kept on my way. The images that haunted me
were solemn; and I entertained an imperfect curiosity,
but no fear, as to the nature of this object. I had ascended the hill little more than half way, when a voice
called me from behind. The accents were clear, distinct, powerful, and were uttered, as I fully believed,
by my wife. Her voice is not commonly so loud. She
has seldom occasion to exert it; but, nevertheless, I
have sometimes heard her call with force and eagerness. If my ear was not deceived, it was her voice
which I heard:—

"'Stop! go no farther. There is danger in your path.'

The suddenness and unexpectedness of this warning, the tone of alarm with which it was given, and, above all, the persuasion that it was my wife who spoke, were enough to disconcert and make me pause. I turned, and listened to assure myself that I was not mistaken. The deepest silence succeeded. At length I spoke in my turn:—'Who calls? Is it you, Catharine?' I stopped, and presently received an answer:—'Yes, it is I; go not up; return instantly; you are wanted at the house.' Still the voice was Catharine's, and still it proceeded from the foot of the stairs.

"What could I do? The warning was mysterious. To be uttered by Catharine at a place and on an occasion like this enhanced the mystery. I could do nothing but obey. Accordingly, I trod back my steps, expecting that she waited for me at the bottom of the hill. When I reached the bottom, no one was visible. The moonlight was once more universal and brilliant, and yet, as far as I could see, no human or moving figure was discernible. If she had returned to the house, she must have used wondrous expedition to have passed already beyond the reach of my eye. I exerted my voice, but in vain. To my repeated exclamations no answer was returned.

"Ruminating on these incidents, I returned hither. There was no room to doubt that I had heard my wife's voice; attending incidents were not easily explained; but you now assure me that nothing extraordinary has happened to urge my return, and that my wife has not moved from her seat."

Such was my brother's narrative. It was heard by us with different emotions. Pleyel did not scruple to regard the whole as a deception of the senses. Perhaps a voice had been heard; but Wieland's imagination had misled him in supposing a resemblance to that of his wife and giving such a signification to the sounds.

According to his custom, he spoke what he thought. Sometimes he made it the theme of grave discussion, but more frequently treated it with ridicule. He did not believe that sober reasoning would convince his friend; and gayety, he thought, was useful to take away the solemnities which, in a mind like Wieland's, an accident of this kind was calculated to produce.

Pleyel proposed to go in search of the letter. He went, and speedily returned, bearing it in his hand. He had found it open on the pedestal; and neither voice nor visage had risen to impede his design.

Catharine was endowed with an uncommon portion of good sense; but her mind was accessible, on this quarter, to wonder and panic. That her voice should be thus inexplicably and unwarrantably assumed was a source of no small disquietude. She admitted the plausibility of the arguments by which Pleyel endeavoured to prove that this was no more than an auricular deception; but this conviction was sure to be shaken when she turned her eyes upon her husband and perceived that Pleyel's logic was far from having produced the same effect upon him.

As to myself, my attention was engaged by this occurrence. I could not fail to perceive a shadowy resemblance between it and my father's death. On the latter event I had frequently reflected; my reflections never conducted me to certainty, but the doubts that existed were not of a tormenting kind. I could not deny that the event was miraculous, and yet I was invincibly averse to that method of solution. My wonder was excited by the inscrutableness of the cause, but my wonder was unmixed with sorrow or fear. It begat in me a thrilling and not unpleasing solemnity. Similar to these were the sensations produced by the recent adventure.

But its effect upon my brother's imagination was of

chief moment. All that was desirable was that it should
be regarded by him with indifference. The worst effect
that could flow was not indeed very formidable. Yet I
could not bear to think that his senses should be the
victims of such delusion. It argued a diseased condition
of his frame, which might show itself hereafter in more
dangerous symptoms. The will is the tool of the understanding, which must fashion its conclusions on the notices of sense. If the senses be depraved, it is impossible
to calculate the evils that may flow from the consequent deductions of the understanding.

I said, This man is of an ardent and melancholy
character. Those ideas which, in others, are casual or
obscure, which are entertained in moments of abstrac-
tion and solitude and easily escape when the scene is
changed, have obtained an immovable hold upon his
mind. The conclusions which long habit have rendered
familiar and, in some sort, palpable to his intellect, are
drawn from the deepest sources. All his actions and
practical sentiments are linked with long and abstruse
deductions from the system of divine government and
the laws of our intellectual constitution. He is in some
respects an enthusiast, but is fortified in his belief by
innumerable arguments and subtleties.

His father's death was always regarded by him as
flowing from a direct and supernatural decree. It
visited his meditations oftener than it did mine. The
traces which it left were more gloomy and permanent.
This new incident had a visible effect in augmenting
his gravity. He was less disposed than formerly to con-
verse and reading. When we sifted his thoughts, they
were generally found to have a relation more or less
direct with this incident. It was difficult to ascertain
the exact species of impression which it made upon
him. He never introduced the subject into conversa-

tion, and listened with a silent and half-serious smile to the satirical effusions of Pleyel.

One evening we chanced to be alone together in the temple. I seized that opportunity of investigating the state of his thoughts. After a pause, which he seemed in no wise inclined to interrupt, I spoke to him:—"How almost palpable is this dark! yet a ray from above would dispel it." "Ay," said Wieland, with fervour; "not only the physical but moral night would be dispelled." "But why," said I, "must the divine will address its precepts to the eye?" He smiled significantly. "True," said he; "the understanding has other avenues." "You have never," said I, approaching nearer to the point,—"you have never told me in what way you considered the late extraordinary incident." "There is no determinate way in which the subject can be viewed. Here is an effect; but the cause is utterly inscrutable. To suppose a deception will not do. Such is possible, but there are twenty other suppositions more probable. They must all be set aside before we reach that point." "What are these twenty suppositions?" "It is needless to mention them. They are only less improbable than Pleyel's. Time may convert one of them into certainty. Till then, it is useless to expatiate on them."

CHAPTER V

Some time had elapsed when there happened another occurrence, still more remarkable. Pleyel, on his return from Europe, brought information of considerable importance to my brother. My ancestors were noble Saxons, and possessed large domains in Lusatia. The Prus-

sian wars had destroyed those persons whose right to
these estates precluded my brother's. Pleyel had been
exact in his inquiries, and had discovered that, by the
law of male-primogeniture, my brother's claims were
superior to those of any other person now living. Nothing was wanting but his presence in that country, and
a legal application, to establish his claim.

Pleyel strenuously recommended this measure. The
advantages he thought attending it were numerous,
and it would argue the utmost folly to neglect them.
Contrary to his expectation, he found my brother
averse to the scheme. Slight efforts, he at first thought,
would subdue his reluctance; but he found this aversion by no means slight. The interest that he took in the
happiness of his friend and his sister, and his own
partiality to the Saxon soil, from which he had likewise
sprung, and where he had spent several years of his
youth, made him redouble his exertions to win Wieland's consent. For this end he employed every argument that his invention could suggest. He painted, in
attractive colours, the state of manners and government in that country, the security of civil rights, and
the freedom of religious sentiments. He dwelt on the
privileges of wealth and rank, and drew from the ser-
vile condition of one class an argument in favour of his
scheme, since the revenue and power annexed to a
German principality afford so large a field for benevolence. The evil flowing from this power, in malignant
hands, was proportioned to the good that would arise
from the virtuous use of it. Hence, Wieland, in forbear-
ing to claim his own, withheld all the positive felicity
that would accrue to his vassals from his success, and
hazarded all the misery that would redound from a less
enlightened proprietor.

It was easy for my brother to repel these arguments,
and to show that no spot on the globe enjoyed equal

security and liberty to that which he at present inhabited:—that, if the Saxons had nothing to fear from misgovernment, the external causes of havoc and alarm were numerous and manifest. The recent devastations committed by the Prussians furnished a specimen of these. The horrors of war would always impend over them, till Germany were seized and divided by Austrian and Prussian tyrants; an event which he strongly suspected was at no great distance. But, setting these considerations aside, was it laudable to grasp at wealth and power even when they were within our reach? Were not these the two great sources of depravity? What security had he that in this change of place and condition he should not degenerate into a tyrant and voluptuary? Power and riches were chiefly to be dreaded on account of their tendency to deprave the possessor. He held them in abhorrence, not only as instruments of misery to others, but to him on whom they were conferred. Besides, riches were comparative; and was he not rich already? He lived at present in the bosom of security and luxury. All the instruments of pleasure on which his reason or imagination set any value were within his reach. But these he must forego, for the sake of advantages which, whatever were their value, were as yet uncertain. In pursuit of an imaginary addition to his wealth, he must reduce himself to poverty; he must exchange present certainties for what was distant and contingent; for who knows not that the law is a system of expense, delay, and uncertainty? If he should embrace this scheme, it would lay him under the necessity of making a voyage to Europe, and remaining for a certain period separate from his family. He must undergo the perils and discomforts of the ocean; he must divest himself of all domestic pleasures; he must deprive his wife of her companion, and his children of a father and instructor: and all for what? For the ambiguous advantages which overgrown wealth and flagitious tyranny have to bestow? For a precarious possession in a land of turbulence and war? Advantages which will not certainly be gained, and of which the acquisition, if it were sure, is necessarily distant.

Pleyel was enamoured of his scheme on account of its intrinsic benefits, but likewise for other reasons. His abode at Leipsic made that country appear to him like home. He was connected with this place by many social ties. While there, he had not escaped the amorous contagion. But the lady, though her heart was impressed in his favour, was compelled to bestow her hand upon another. Death had removed this impediment, and he was now invited by the lady herself to return. This he was of course determined to do, but was anxious to obtain the company of Wieland: he could not bear to think of an eternal separation from his present associates. Their interest, he thought, would be no less promoted by the change than his own. Hence he was importunate and indefatigable in his arguments and solicitations.

He knew that he could not hope for mine or his sister's ready concurrence in this scheme. Should the subject be mentioned to us, we should league our efforts against him and strengthen that reluctance in Wieland which already was sufficiently difficult to conquer. He therefore anxiously concealed from us his purpose. If Wieland were previously enlisted in his cause, he would find it a less difficult task to overcome our aversion. My brother was silent on this subject, because he believed himself in no danger of changing his opinion, and he was willing to save us from any uneasiness. The mere mention of such a scheme, and the possibility of his embracing it, he knew, would considerably impair our tranquillity.

One day, about three weeks subsequent to the mysterious call, it was agreed that the family should be my guests. Seldom had a day been passed by us of more serene enjoyment. Pleyel had promised us his company; but we did not see him till the sun had nearly declined. He brought with him a countenance that betokened disappointment and vexation. He did not wait for our inquiries, but immediately explained the cause. Two days before a packet had arrived from Hamburg, by which he had flattered himself with the expectation of receiving letters; but no letters had arrived. I never saw him so much subdued by an untoward event. His thoughts were employed in accounting for the silence of his friends. He was seized with the torments of jealousy, and suspected nothing less than the infidelity of her to whom he had devoted his heart. The silence must have been concerted. Her sickness, or absence, or death, would have increased the certainty of some one's having written. No supposition could be formed but that his mistress had grown indifferent, or that she had transferred her affections to another. The miscarriage of a letter was hardly within the reach of possibility. From Leipsic to Hamburg, and from Hamburg hither, the conveyance was exposed to no hazard.

He had been so long detained in America chiefly in consequence of Wieland's aversion to the scheme which he proposed. He now became more impatient than ever to return to Europe. When he reflected that by his delays he had probably forfeited the affections of his mistress, his sensations amounted to agony. It only remained by his speedy departure to repair, if possible, or prevent, so intolerable an evil. Already he had half resolved to embark in this very ship, which, he was informed, would set out in a few weeks on her return.

Meanwhile he determined to make a new attempt

to shake the resolution of Wieland. The evening was somewhat advanced when he invited the latter to walk abroad with him. The invitation was accepted, and they left Catharine, Louisa, and me, to amuse ourselves by the best means in our power. During this walk, Pleyel renewed the subject that was nearest his heart. He reurged all his former arguments and placed them in more forcible lights.

They promised to return shortly; but hour after hour passed, and they made not their appearance. Engaged in sprightly conversation, it was not till the clock struck twelve that we were reminded of the lapse of time. The absence of our friends excited some uneasy apprehensions. We were expressing our fears, and comparing our conjectures as to what might be the cause, when they entered together. There were indications in their countenances that struck me mute. These were unnoticed by Catharine, who was eager to express her surprise and curiosity at the length of their walk. As they listened to her, I remarked that their surprise was not less than ours. They gazed in silence on each other and on her. I watched their looks, but could not understand the emotions that were written in them.

These appearances diverted Catharine's inquiries into a new channel. What did they mean, she asked, by their silence, and by their thus gazing wildly at each other and at her? Pleyel profited by this hint, and, assuming an air of indifference, framed some trifling excuse, at the same time darting significant glances at Wieland, as if to caution him against disclosing the truth. My brother said nothing, but delivered himself up to meditation. I likewise was silent, but burned with impatience to fathom this mystery. Presently my brother, and his wife, and Louisa, returned home. Pleyel proposed, of his own accord, to be my guest for the night. This circumstance, in addition to those which preceded, gave new edge to my wonder.

As soon as we were left alone, Pleyel's countenance assumed an air of seriousness, and even consternation, which I had never before beheld in him. The steps with which he measured the floor betokened the trouble of his thoughts. My inquiries were suspended by the hope that he would give me the information that I wanted without the importunity of questions. I waited some time, but the confusion of his thoughts appeared in no degree to abate. At length I mentioned the apprehensions which their unusual absence had occasioned, and which were increased by their behaviour since their return, and solicited an explanation. He stopped when I began to speak, and looked steadfastly at me. When I had done, he said to me, in a tone which faltered through the vehemence of his emotions, "How were you employed during our absence?" "In turning over the Della Crusca dictionary and talking on different subjects; but just before your entrance we were tormenting ourselves with omens and prognostics relative to your absence." "Catharine was with you the whole time?" "Yes." "But are you sure?" "Most sure. She was not absent a moment." He stood, for a time, as if to assure himself of my sincerity. Then, clenching his hands and wildly lifting them above his head, "Lo," cried he, "I have news to tell you. The Baroness de Stolberg is dead!"

This was her whom he loved. I was not surprised at the agitation which he betrayed. "But how was the information procured? How was the truth of this news connected with the circumstance of Catharine's remaining in our company?" He was for some time inattentive to my questions. When he spoke, it seemed merely a continuation of the reverie into which he had been plunged.

"And yet it might be a mere deception. But could both of us in that case have been deceived? A rare and prodigious coincidence! Barely not impossible. And yet, if the accent be oracular, Theresa is dead. No, no!" continued he, covering his face with his hands, and in a tone half broken into sobs, "I cannot believe it. She has not written; but, if she were dead, the faithful Bertrand would have given me the earliest information. And yet, if he knew his master, he must have easily guessed at the effect of such tidings. In pity to me he was silent.

"Clara, forgive me; to you this behaviour is mysterious. I will explain as well as I am able. But say not a word to Catharine. Her strength of mind is inferior to yours. She will, besides, have more reason to be startled. She is Wieland's angel."

Pleyel proceeded to inform me, for the first time, of the scheme which he had pressed with so much earnestness on my brother. He enumerated the objections which had been made, and the industry with which he had endeavoured to confute them. He mentioned the effect upon his resolutions produced by the failure of a letter. "During our late walk," continued he, "I introduced the subject that was nearest my heart. I reurged all my former arguments, and placed them in more forcible lights. Wieland was still refractory. He expatiated on the perils of wealth and power, on the sacredness of conjugal and parental duties, and the happiness of mediocrity.

"No wonder that the time passed unperceived away. Our whole souls were engaged in this cause. Several times we came to the foot of the rock: as soon as we perceived it we changed our course, but never failed to terminate our circuitous and devious ramble at this spot. At length your brother observed, 'We seem to be led hither by a kind of fatality. Since we are so near,

let us ascend and rest ourselves a while. If you are not
weary of this argument we will resume it there.'

"I tacitly consented. We mounted the stairs, and,
drawing the sofa in front of the river, we seated ourselves upon it. I took up the thread of our discourse
where we had dropped it. I ridiculed his dread of the
sea, and his attachment to home. I kept on in this
strain, so congenial with my disposition, for some time,
uninterrupted by him. At length he said to me, 'Suppose, now, that I, whom argument has not convinced,
should yield to ridicule, and should agree that your
scheme is eligible: what will you have gained? Nothing. You have other enemies besides myself to encounter. When you have vanquished me, your toil has
scarcely begun. There are my sister and wife, with
whom it will remain for you to maintain the contest.
And, trust me, they are adversaries whom all your
force and stratagem will never subdue.' I insinuated
that they would model themselves by his will; that
Catharine would think obedience her duty. He answered, with some quickness, 'You mistake. Their concurrence is indispensable. It is not my custom to exact
sacrifices of this kind. I live to be their protector and
friend, and not their tyrant and foe. If my wife shall
deem her happiness and that of her children most con-
sulted by remaining where she is, here she shall remain.' 'But,' said I, 'when she knows your pleasure, will
she not conform to it?' Before my friend had time to
answer this question, a negative was clearly and distinctly uttered from another quarter. It did not come
from one side or the other, from before us or behind.
Whence then did it come? By whose organs was it
fashioned?

"If any uncertainty had existed with regard to these
particulars, it would have been removed by a deliberate and equally-distinct repetition of the same mono-

syllable, 'No.' The voice was my sister's. It appeared to come from the roof. I started from my seat. 'Catharine,' exclaimed I, 'where are you?' No answer was returned. I searched the room and the area before it, but in vain. Your brother was motionless in his seat. I returned to him, and placed myself again by his side. My astonishment was not less than his.

"'Well,' said he at length, 'what think you of this? This is the selfsame voice which I formerly heard: you are now convinced that my ears were well informed.'

"'Yes,' said I, 'this, it is plain, is no fiction of the fancy.' We again sunk into mutual and thoughtful silence. A recollection of the hour, and of the length of our absence, made me at last propose to return. We rose up for this purpose. In doing this, my mind reverted to the contemplation of my own condition. 'Yes,' said I, aloud, but without particularly addressing myself to Wieland, 'my resolution is taken. I cannot hope to prevail with my friends to accompany me. They may doze away their days on the banks of Schuylkill; but, as to me, I go in the next vessel; I will fly to her presence and demand the reason of this extraordinary silence.'

"I had scarcely finished the sentence, when the same mysterious voice exclaimed, 'You shall not go. The seal of death is on her lips. Her silence is the silence of the tomb.' Think of the effects which accents like these must have had upon me. I shuddered as I listened. As soon as I recovered from my first amazement, 'Who is it that speaks?' said I; 'whence did you procure these dismal tidings?' I did not wait long for an answer. 'From a source that cannot fail. Be satisfied. She is dead.' You may justly be surprised that, in the circumstances in which I heard the tidings, and notwithstanding the mystery which environed him by whom they were imparted, I could give an undivided attention to

the facts which were the subject of our dialogue. I
eagerly inquired, When and where did she die? What
was the cause of her death? Was her death absolutely
certain? An answer was returned only to the last of
these questions. 'Yes,' was pronounced by the same
voice; but it now sounded from a greater distance, and
the deepest silence was all the return made to my subsequent interrogatories.

"It was my sister's voice; but it could not be uttered
by her; and yet, if not by her, by whom was it uttered?
When we returned hither and discovered you together,
the doubt that had previously existed was removed. It
was manifest that the intimation came not from her.
Yet, if not from her, from whom could it come? Are the
circumstances attending the imparting of this news
proof that the tidings are true? God forbid that they
should be true!"

Here Pleyel sunk into anxious silence, and gave me
leisure to ruminate on this inexplicable event. I am at a
loss to describe the sensations that affected me. I am
not fearful of shadows. The tales of apparitions and enchantments did not possess that power over my belief
which could even render them interesting. I saw nothing in them but ignorance and folly, and was a stranger even to that terror which is pleasing. But this
incident was different from any that I had ever before
known. Here were proofs of a sensible and intelligent
existence, which could not be denied. Here was information obtained and imparted by means unquestionably superhuman.

That there are conscious beings besides ourselves in
existence, whose modes of activity and information surpass our own, can scarcely be denied. Is there a
glimpse afforded us into a world of these superior beings? My heart was scarcely large enough to give admittance to so swelling a thought. An awe, the sweetest

and most solemn that imagination can conceive, pervaded my whole frame. It forsook me not when I parted from Pleyel and retired to my chamber. An impulse was given to my spirits utterly incompatible with sleep. I passed the night wakeful and full of meditation. I was impressed with the belief of mysterious but not of malignant agency. Hitherto nothing had occurred to persuade me that this airy minister was busy to evil rather than to good purposes. On the contrary, the idea of superior virtue had always been associated in my mind with that of superior power. The warnings that had thus been heard appeared to have been prompted by beneficent intentions. My brother had been hindered by this voice from ascending the hill. He was told that danger lurked in his path, and his obedience to the intimation had perhaps saved him from a destiny similar to that of my father.

Pleyel had been rescued from tormenting uncertainty, and from the hazards and fatigues of a fruitless voyage, by the same interposition. It had assured him of the death of his Theresa.

This woman was, then, dead. A confirmation of the tidings, if true, would speedily arrive. Was this confirmation to be deprecated or desired? By her death, the tie that attached him to Europe was taken away. Henceforward every motive would combine to retain him in his native country, and we were rescued from the deep regrets that would accompany his hopeless absence from us. Propitious was the spirit that imparted these tidings. Propitious he would perhaps have been, if he had been instrumental in producing as well as in communicating the tidings of her death. Propitious to us, the friends of Pleyel, to whom has thereby been secured the enjoyment of his society; and not unpropitious to himself; for, though this object of his love be snatched away, is there not another who is able and willing to console him for her loss?

Twenty days after this, another vessel arrived from the same port. In this interval, Pleyel for the most part estranged himself from his old companions. He was become the prey of a gloomy and unsociable grief. His walks were limited to the bank of the Delaware. This bank is an artificial one. Reeds and the river are on one side, and a watery marsh on the other, in that part which bounded his lands, and which extended from the mouth of Hollander's Creek to that of Schuylkill. No scene can be imagined less enticing to a lover of the picturesque than this. The shore is deformed with mud and encumbered with a forest of reeds. The fields, in most seasons, are mire; but, when they afford a firm footing, the ditches by which they are bounded and intersected are mantled with stagnating green, and emit the most noxious exhalations. Health is no less a stranger to those seats than pleasure. Spring and autumn are sure to be accompanied with agues and bilious remittents.

The scenes which environed our dwellings at Mettingen constituted the reverse of this. Schuylkill was here a pure and translucid current broken into wild and ceaseless music by rocky points, murmuring on a sandy margin, and reflecting on its surface banks of all varieties of height and degrees of declivity. These banks were checkered by patches of dark verdure and shapeless masses of white marble, and crowned by copses of cedar, or by the regular magnificence of orchards, which, at this season, were in blossom, and were prodigal of odours. The ground which receded from the river was scooped into valleys and dales. Its beauties were enhanced by the horticultural skill of my brother, who bedecked this exquisite assemblage of slopes and risings with every species of vegetable ornament, from the giant arms of the oak to the clustering tendrils of the honeysuckle.

To screen him from the unwholesome airs of his own residence, it had been proposed to Pleyel to spend the months of spring with us. He had apparently acquiesced in this proposal; but the late event induced him to change his purpose. He was only to be seen by visiting him in his retirements. His gayety had flown, and every passion was absorbed in eagerness to procure tidings from Saxony. I have mentioned the arrival of another vessel from the Elbe. He described her early one morning as he was passing along the skirt of the river. She was easily recognised, being the ship in which he had performed his first voyage to Germany. He immediately went on board, but found no letters directed to him. This omission was in some degree compensated by meeting with an old acquaintance among the passengers, who had till lately been a resident in Leipsic. This person put an end to all suspense respecting the fate of Theresa, by relating the particulars of her death and funeral.

Thus was the truth of the former intimation attested. No longer devoured by suspense, the grief of Pleyel was not long in yielding to the influence of society. He gave himself up once more to our company. His vivacity had indeed been damped; but even in this respect he was a more acceptable companion than formerly, since his seriousness was neither incommunicative nor sullen.

These incidents for a time occupied all our thoughts. In me they produced a sentiment not unallied to pleasure, and more speedily than in the case of my friends were intermixed with other topics. My brother was particularly affected by them. It was easy to perceive that most of his meditations were tinctured from this source. To this was to be ascribed a design in which his pen was at this period engaged, of collecting and investigating the facts which relate to that mysterious personage, the Dæmon of Socrates.

My brother's skill in Greek and Roman learning was exceeded by that of few, and no doubt the world would have accepted a treatise upon this subject from his hand with avidity; but, alas! this and every other scheme of felicity and honour were doomed to sudden blast and hopeless extermination.

CHAPTER VI

I now come to the mention of a person with whose name the most turbulent sensations are connected. It is with a shuddering reluctance that I enter on the province of describing him. Now it is that I begin to perceive the difficulty of the task which I have undertaken; but it would be weakness to shrink from it. My blood is congealed and my fingers are palsied when I call up his image. Shame upon my cowardly and infirm heart! Hitherto I have proceeded with some degree of composure; but now I must pause. I mean not that dire remembrance shall subdue my courage or baffle my design; but this weakness cannot be immediately conquered. I must desist for a little while.

I have taken a few turns in my chamber, and have gathered strength enough to proceed. Yet have I not projected a task beyond my power to execute? If thus, on the very threshold of the scene, my knees falter and I sink, how shall I support myself when I rush into the midst of horrors such as no heart has hitherto conceived nor tongue related? I sicken and recoil at the prospect; and yet my irresolution is momentary. I have not formed this design upon slight grounds; and, though I may at times pause and hesitate, I will not be finally diverted from it.

And thou, O most fatal and potent of mankind, in what terms shall I describe thee? What words are adequate to the just delineation of thy character? How shall I detail the means which rendered the secrecy of thy purposes unfathomable? But I will not anticipate. Let me recover, if possible, a sober strain. Let me keep down the flood of passion that would render me precipitate or powerless. Let me stifle the agonies that are awakened by thy name. Let me for a time regard thee as a being of no terrible attributes. Let me tear myself from contemplation of the evils of which it is but too certain that thou wast the author, and limit my view to those harmless appearances which attended thy entrance on the stage.

One sunny afternoon I was standing in the door of my house, when I marked a person passing close to the edge of the bank that was in front. His pace was a careless and lingering one, and had none of that gracefulness and ease which distinguish a person with certain advantages of education from a clown. His gait was rustic and awkward. His form was ungainly and disproportioned. Shoulders broad and square, breast sunken, his head drooping, his body of uniform breadth, supported by long and lank legs, were the ingredients of his frame. His garb was not ill adapted to such a figure. A slouched hat, tarnished by the weather, a coat of thick gray cloth, cut and wrought, as it seemed, by a country tailor, blue worsted stockings, and shoes fastened by thongs and deeply discoloured by dust, which brush had never disturbed, constituted his dress.

There was nothing remarkable in these appearances: they were frequently to be met with on the road and in the harvest-field. I cannot tell why I gazed upon them, on this occasion, with more than ordinary attention, unless it were that such figures were seldom seen by me except on the road or field. This lawn was only traversed by men whose views were directed to the pleasures of the walk or the grandeur of the scenery.

He passed slowly along, frequently pausing, as if to examine the prospect more deliberately, but never turning his eye towards the house, so as to allow me a view of his countenance. Presently he entered a copse at a small distance, and disappeared. My eye followed him while he remained in sight. If his image remained for any duration in my fancy after his departure, it was because no other object occurred sufficient to expel it.

I continued in the same spot for half an hour, vaguely, and by fits, contemplating the image of this wanderer, and drawing from outward appearances those inferences, with respect to the intellectual history of this person, which experience affords us. I reflected on the alliance which commonly subsists between ignorance and the practice of agriculture, and indulged myself in airy speculations as to the influence of progressive knowledge in dissolving this alliance and embodying the dreams of the poets. I asked why the plough and the hoe might not become the trade of every human being, and how this trade might be made conducive to, or at least consistent with, the acquisition of wisdom and eloquence.

Weary with these reflections, I returned to the kitchen to perform some household office. I had usually but one servant, and she was a girl about my own age. I was busy near the chimney, and she was employed near the door of the apartment, when some one knocked. The door was opened by her, and she was immediately addressed with, "Pr'ythee, good girl, canst thou supply a thirsty man with a glass of buttermilk?"

She answered that there was none in the house. "Ay, but there is some in the dairy yonder. Thou knowest as well as I, though Hermes never taught thee, that, though every dairy be a house, every house is not a dairy." To this speech, though she understood only a part of it, she replied by repeating her assurances that she had none to give. "Well, then," rejoined the stranger, "for charity's sweet sake, hand me forth a cup of cold water." The girl said she would go to the spring and fetch it. "Nay, give me the cup, and suffer me to help myself. Neither manacled nor lame, I should merit burial in the maw of carrion-crows if I laid this task upon thee." She gave him the cup, and he turned to go to the spring.

I listened to this dialogue in silence. The words uttered by the person without affected me as somewhat singular; but what chiefly rendered them remarkable was the tone that accompanied them. It was wholly new. My brother's voice and Pleyel's were musical and energetic. I had fondly imagined that, in this respect, they were surpassed by none. Now my mistake was detected. I cannot pretend to communicate the impression that was made upon me by these accents, or to depict the degree in which force and sweetness were blended in them. They were articulated with a distinctness that was unexampled in my experience. But this was not all. The voice was not only mellifluent and clear, but the emphasis was so just, and the modulation so impassioned, that it seemed as if a heart of stone could not fail of being moved by it. It imparted to me an emotion altogether involuntary and incontrollable. When he uttered the words, "for charity's sweet sake," I dropped the cloth that I held in my hand; my heart overflowed with sympathy and my eyes with unbidden tears.

This description will appear to you trifling or incredible. The importance of these circumstances will be manifested in the sequel. The manner in which I was affected on this occasion was, to my own apprehension, a subject of astonishment. The tones were indeed such as I never heard before; but that they should in an instant, as it were, dissolve me in tears, will not easily be believed by others, and can scarcely be comprehended by myself.

It will be readily supposed that I was somewhat inquisitive as to the person and demeanour of our visitant. After a moment's pause, I stepped to the door and looked after him. Judge my surprise when I beheld the selfsame figure that had appeared a half-hour before upon the bank. My fancy had conjured up a very different image. A form and attitude and garb were instantly created worthy to accompany such elocution; but this person was, in all visible respects, the reverse of this phantom. Strange as it may seem, I could not speedily reconcile myself to this disappointment. Instead of returning to my employment, I threw myself in a chair that was placed opposite the door, and sunk into a fit of musing.

My attention was in a few minutes recalled by the stranger, who returned with the empty cup in his hand. I had not thought of the circumstance, or should certainly have chosen a different seat. He no sooner showed himself, than a confused sense of impropriety, added to the suddenness of the interview, for which, not having foreseen it, I had made no preparation, threw me into a state of the most painful embarrassment. He brought with him a placid brow; but no sooner had he cast his eyes upon me than his face was as glowingly suffused as my own. He placed the cup upon the bench, stammered out thanks, and retired.

It was some time before I could recover my wonted composure. I had snatched a view of the stranger's countenance. The impression that it made was vivid and indelible. His cheeks were pallid and lank, his eyes sunken, his forehead overshadowed by coarse straggling hairs, his teeth large and irregular, though sound and brilliantly white, and his chin discoloured by a tetter. His skin was of coarse grain and sallow hue. Every feature was wide of beauty, and the outline of his face reminded you of an inverted cone.

And yet his forehead, so far as shaggy locks would allow it to be seen, his eyes lustrously black, and possessing, in the midst of haggardness, a radiance inexpressibly serene and potent, and something in the rest of his features which it would be in vain to describe, but which served to betoken a mind of the highest order, were essential ingredients in the portrait. This, in the effects which immediately flowed from it, I count among the most extraordinary incidents of my life. This face, seen for a moment, continued for hours to occupy my fancy, to the exclusion of almost every other image. I had proposed to spend the evening with my brother; but I could not resist the inclination of forming a sketch upon paper of this memorable visage. Whether my hand was aided by any peculiar inspiration, or I was deceived by my own fond conceptions, this portrait, though hastily executed, appeared unexceptionable to my own taste.

I placed it at all distances and in all lights; my eyes were riveted upon it. Half the night passed away in wakefulness and in contemplation of this picture. So flexible, and yet so stubborn, is the human mind! So obedient to impulses the most transient and brief, and yet so unalterably observant of the direction which is given to it! How little did I then foresee the termination of that chain of which this may be regarded as the first link!

Next day arose in darkness and storm. Torrents of

rain fell during the whole day, attended with incessant
thunder, which reverberated in stunning echoes from
the opposite declivity. The inclemency of the air
would not allow me to walk out. I had, indeed, no inclination to leave my apartment. I betook myself to the
contemplation of this portrait, whose attractions time
had rather enhanced than diminished. I laid aside my
usual occupations, and, seating myself at a window,
consumed the day in alternately looking out upon the
storm and gazing at the picture which lay upon a table
before me. You will perhaps deem this conduct somewhat singular, and ascribe it to certain peculiarities of
temper. I am not aware of any such peculiarities. I can
account for my devotion to this image no otherwise
than by supposing that its properties were rare and
prodigious. Perhaps you will suspect that such were
the first inroads of a passion incident to every female
heart, and which frequently gains a footing by means
even more slight and more improbable than these. I
shall not controvert the reasonableness of the suspicion, but leave you at liberty to draw from my narrative what conclusions you please.

Night at length returned, and the storm ceased. The
air was once more clear and calm, and bore an affecting
contrast to that uproar of the elements by which it had
been preceded. I spent the darksome hours, as I spent
the day, contemplative and seated at the window.
Why was my mind absorbed in thoughts ominous and
dreary? Why did my bosom heave with sighs and my
eyes overflow with tears? Was the tempest that had
just passed a signal of the ruin which impended over
me? My soul fondly dwelt upon the images of my
brother and his children; yet they only increased the
mournfulness of my contemplations. The smiles of the
charming babes were as bland as formerly. The same
dignity sat on the brow of their father, and yet I

thought of them with anguish. Something whispered that the happiness we at present enjoyed was set on mutable foundations. Death must happen to all. Whether our felicity was to be subverted by it to-morrow, or whether it was ordained that we should lay down our heads full of years and of honour, was a question that no human being could solve. At other times these ideas seldom intruded. I either forbore to reflect upon the destiny that is reserved for all men, or the reflection was mixed up with images that disrobed it of terror; but now the uncertainty of life occurred to me without any of its usual and alleviating accompaniments. I said to myself, We must die. Sooner or later, we must disappear forever from the face of the earth. Whatever be the links that hold us to life, they must be broken. This scene of existence is, in all its parts, calamitous. The greater number is oppressed with immediate evils, and those the tide of whose fortunes is full, how small is their portion of enjoyment, since they know that it will terminate!

For some time I indulged myself, without reluctance, in these gloomy thoughts; but at length the dejection which they produced became insupportably painful. I endeavoured to dissipate it with music. I had all my grandfather's melody as well as poetry by rote. I now lighted by chance on a ballad which commemorated the fate of a German cavalier who fell at the siege of Nice under Godfrey of Bouillon. My choice was unfortunate; for the scenes of violence and carnage which were here wildly but forcibly portrayed only suggested to my thoughts a new topic in the horrors of war.

I sought refuge, but ineffectually, in sleep. My mind was thronged by vivid but confused images, and no effort that I made was sufficient to drive them away. In this situation I heard the clock, which hung in the room, give the signal for twelve. It was the same instrument which formerly hung in my father's chamber, and which, on account of its being his workmanship, was regarded by every one of our family with veneration. It had fallen to me in the division of his property, and was placed in this asylum. The sound awakened a series of reflections respecting his death. I was not allowed to pursue them; for scarcely had the vibrations ceased, when my attention was attracted by a whisper, which, at first, appeared to proceed from lips that were laid close to my ear.

No wonder that a circumstance like this startled me. In the first impulse of my terror, I uttered a slight scream and shrunk to the opposite side of the bed. In a moment, however, I recovered from my trepidation. I was habitually indifferent to all the causes of fear by which the majority are afflicted. I entertained no apprehension of either ghosts or robbers. Our security had never been molested by either, and I made use of no means to prevent or counterwork their machinations. My tranquillity on this occasion was quickly retrieved. The whisper evidently proceeded from one who was posted at my bedside. The first idea that suggested itself was that it was uttered by the girl who lived with me as a servant. Perhaps somewhat had alarmed her, or she was sick, and had come to request my assistance. By whispering in my ear she intended to rouse without alarming me.

Full of this persuasion, I called, "Judith," said I, "is it you? What do you want? Is there any thing the matter with you?" No answer was returned. I repeated my inquiry, but equally in vain. Cloudy as was the atmosphere, and curtained as my bed was, nothing was visible. I withdrew the curtain, and, leaning my head on my elbow, I listened with the deepest attention to catch some new sound. Meanwhile, I ran over in my thoughts every circumstance that could assist my conjectures.

My habitation was a wooden edifice, consisting of two stories. In each story were two rooms, separated by an entry, or middle passage, with which they communicated by opposite doors. The passage on the lower story had doors at the two ends, and a staircase. Windows answered to the doors on the upper story. Annexed to this, on the eastern side, were wings, divided in like manner into an upper and lower room; one of them comprised a kitchen, and chamber above it for the servant, and communicated on both stories with the parlour adjoining it below and the chamber adjoining it above. The opposite wing is of smaller dimensions, the rooms not being above eight feet square. The lower of these was used as a depository of household implements; the upper was a closet in which I deposited my books and papers. They had but one inlet, which was from the room adjoining. There was no window in the lower one, and in the upper a small aperture which communicated light and air, but would scarcely admit the body. The door which led into this was close to my bed-head, and was always locked but when I myself was within. The avenues below were accustomed to be closed and bolted at nights.

The maid was my only companion; and she could not reach my chamber without previously passing through the opposite chamber and the middle passage, of which, however, the doors were usually unfastened. If she had occasioned this noise, she would have answered my repeated calls. No other conclusion, therefore, was left me, but that I had mistaken the sounds, and that my imagination had transformed some casual noise into the voice of a human creature. Satisfied with this solution, I was preparing to relinquish my listening attitude, when my ear was again saluted with a new and yet louder whispering. It appeared, as before, to issue from lips that touched my pillow. A second effort of attention, however, clearly showed me that the sounds issued from within the closet, the door of which was not more than eight inches from my pillow.

This second interruption occasioned a shock less vehement than the former. I started, but gave no audible token of alarm. I was so much mistress of my feelings as to continue listening to what should be said. The whisper was distinct, hoarse, and uttered so as to show that the speaker was desirous of being heard by some one near, but, at the same time, studious to avoid being overheard by any other:—

"Stop! stop, I say, madman as you are! there are better means than that. Curse upon your rashness! There is no need to shoot."

Such were the words uttered, in a tone of eagerness and anger, within so small a distance of my pillow. What construction could I put upon them? My heart began to palpitate with dread of some unknown danger. Presently, another voice, but equally near me, was heard whispering in answer, "Why not? I will draw a trigger in this business; but perdition be my lot if I do more!" To this the first voice returned, in a tone which rage had heightened in a small degree above a whisper, "Coward! stand aside, and see me do it. I will grasp her throat; I will do her business in an instant; she shall not have time so much as to groan." What wonder that I was petrified by sounds so dreadful! Murderers lurked in my closet. They were planning the means of my destruction. One resolved to shoot, and the other menaced suffocation. Their means being chosen, they would forthwith break the door. Flight instantly suggested itself as most eligible in circumstances so perilous. I deliberated not a moment; but, fear adding wings to my speed, I leaped out of bed, and, scantily robed as I was, rushed out of the chamber, down-stairs, and into the open air. I can hardly recollect the process of turning keys and withdrawing bolts. My terrors urged me forward with almost a mechanical impulse. I stopped not till I reached my brother's door. I had not gained the threshold, when, exhausted by the violence of my emotions and by my speed, I sunk down in a fit.

How long I remained in this situation I know not. When I recovered, I found myself stretched on a bed, surrounded by my sister and her female servants. I was astonished at the scene before me, but gradually recovered the recollection of what had happened. I answered their importunate inquiries as well as I was able. My brother and Pleyel, whom the storm of the preceding day chanced to detain here, informing themselves of every particular, proceeded with lights and weapons to my deserted habitation. They entered my chamber and my closet, and found every thing in its proper place and customary order. The door of the closet was locked, and appeared not to have been opened in my absence. They went to Judith's apartment. They found her asleep and in safety. Pleyel's caution induced him to forbear alarming the girl; and, finding her wholly ignorant of what had passed, they directed her to return to her chamber. They then fastened the doors and returned.

My friends were disposed to regard this transaction as a dream. That persons should be actually immured in this closet, to which, in the circumstances of the time, access from without or within was apparently impossible, they could not seriously believe. That any human beings had intended murder, unless it were to cover a scheme of pillage, was incredible; but that no such design had been formed was evident from the security in which the furniture of the house and the closet remained.

I revolved every incident and expression that had occurred. My senses assured me of the truth of them; and yet their abruptness and improbability made me, in my turn, somewhat incredulous. The adventure had made a deep impression on my fancy; and it was not till after a week's abode at my brother's that I resolved to resume the possession of my own dwelling.

There was another circumstance that enhanced the mysteriousness of this event. After my recovery, it was obvious to inquire by what means the attention of the family had been drawn to my situation. I had fallen before I had reached the threshold or was able to give any signal. My brother related that, while this was transacting in my chamber, he himself was awake, in consequence of some slight indisposition, and lay, according to his custom, musing on some favourite topic. Suddenly the silence, which was remarkably profound, was broken by a voice of most piercing shrillness, that seemed to be uttered by one in the hall below his chamber. "Awake! arise!" it exclaimed; "hasten to succour one that is dying at your door!"

This summons was effectual. There was no one in the house who was not roused by it. Pleyel was the first to obey, and my brother overtook him before he reached the hall. What was the general astonishment when your friend was discovered stretched upon the grass before the door, pale, ghastly, and with every mark of death!

This was the third instance of a voice exerted for the benefit of this little community. The agent was no less inscrutable in this than in the former case. When I ruminated upon these events, my soul was suspended in wonder and awe. Was I really deceived in imagining that I heard the closet conversation? I was no longer at liberty to question the reality of those accents which had formerly recalled my brother from the hill, which had imparted tidings of the death of the German lady to Pleyel, and which had lately summoned them to my assistance.

But how was I to regard this midnight conversation? Hoarse and manlike voices conferring on the means of death, so near my bed, and at such an hour! How had my ancient security vanished! That dwelling which had hitherto been an inviolate asylum was now beset with danger to my life. That solitude formerly so dear to me could no longer be endured. Pleyel, who had consented to reside with us during the months of spring, lodged in the vacant chamber, in order to quiet my alarms. He treated my fears with ridicule, and in a short time very slight traces of them remained; but, as it was wholly indifferent to him whether his nights were passed at my house or at my brother's, this arrangement gave general satisfaction.

CHAPTER VII

I will enumerate the various inquiries and conjectures which these incidents occasioned. After all our efforts, we came no nearer to dispelling the mist in which they were involved; and time, instead of facilitating a solution, only accumulated our doubts.

In the midst of thoughts excited by these events, I was not unmindful of my interview with the stranger. I related the particulars, and showed the portrait to my friends. Pleyel recollected to have met with a figure resembling my description in the city; but neither his face or garb made the same impression upon him that it made upon me. It was a hint to rally me upon my prepossessions, and to amuse us with a thousand ludicrous anecdotes which he had collected in his travels. He made no scruple to charge me with being in love; and threatened to inform the swain, when he met him, of his good fortune.

Pleyel's temper made him susceptible of no durable impressions. His conversation was occasionally visited by gleams of his ancient vivacity; but, though his impetuosity was sometimes inconvenient, there was nothing to dread from his malice. I had no fear that my character or dignity would suffer in his hands, and was not heartily displeased when he declared his intention of profiting by his first meeting with the stranger to introduce him to our acquaintance.

Some weeks after this I had spent a toilsome day, and, as the sun declined, found myself disposed to seek relief in a walk. The river-bank is, at this part of it and for some considerable space upward, so rugged and steep as not to be easily descended. In a recess of this declivity, near the southern verge of my little demesne, was placed a slight building, with seats and lattices. From a crevice of the rock to which this edifice was attached there burst forth a stream of the purest water, which, leaping from ledge to ledge for the space of sixty feet, produced a freshness in the air, and a murmur, the most delicious and soothing imaginable. These, added to the odours of the cedars which embowered it, and of the honeysuckle which clustered among the lattices, rendered this my favourite retreat in summer.

On this occasion I repaired hither. My spirits drooped through the fatigue of long attention, and I threw myself upon a bench, in a state, both mentally and personally, of the utmost supineness. The lulling sounds of the waterfall, the fragrance, and the dusk, combined to becalm my spirits, and, in a short time, to sink me into sleep. Either the uneasiness of my posture, or some slight indisposition, molested my repose with dreams of no cheerful hue. After various incoherences had taken their turn to occupy my fancy, I at length imagined myself walking, in the evening twilight, to my brother's habitation. A pit, methought, had been dug in the path I had taken, of which I was not aware. As I carelessly pursued my walk, I thought I saw my brother standing at some distance before me, beckoning and calling me to make haste. He stood on the opposite edge of the gulf. I mended my pace, and one step more would have plunged me into this abyss, had not some one from behind caught suddenly my arm, and exclaimed, in a voice of eagerness and terror, "Hold! hold!"

The sound broke my sleep, and I found myself, at the next moment, standing on my feet, and surrounded by the deepest darkness. Images so terrific and forcible disabled me for a time from distinguishing between sleep and wakefulness, and withheld from me the knowledge of my actual condition. My first panic was succeeded by the perturbations of surprise to find myself alone in the open air and immersed in so deep a gloom. I slowly recollected the incidents of the afternoon, and how I came hither. I could not estimate the time, but saw the propriety of returning with speed to the house. My faculties were still too confused, and the darkness too intense, to allow me immediately to find my way up the steep. I sat down, therefore, to recover myself, and to reflect upon my situation.

This was no sooner done, than a low voice was heard from behind the lattice, on the side where I sat. Between the rock and the lattice was a chasm not wide enough to admit a human body; yet in this chasm he that spoke appeared to be stationed. "Attend! attend! but be not terrified."

I started, and exclaimed, "Good heavens! what is that? Who are you?"

"A friend; one come not to injure but to save you: fear nothing."

This voice was immediately recognised to be the same with one of those which I had heard in the closet; it was the voice of him who had proposed to shoot rather than to strangle his victim. My terror made me at once mute and motionless. He continued, "I leagued to murder you. I repent. Mark my bidding, and be safe. Avoid this spot. The snares of death encompass it. Elsewhere danger will be distant; but this spot, shun it as you value your life. Mark me further: profit by this warning, but divulge it not. If a syllable of what has passed escape you, your doom is sealed. Remember your father, and be faithful."

Here the accents ceased, and left me overwhelmed with dismay. I was fraught with the persuasion that during every moment I remained here my life was endangered; but I could not take a step without hazard of falling to the bottom of the precipice. The path leading to the summit was short, but rugged and intricate. Even starlight was excluded by the umbrage, and not the faintest gleam was afforded to guide my steps. What should I do? To depart or remain was equally and eminently perilous.

In this state of uncertainty, I perceived a ray flit across the gloom and disappear. Another succeeded, which was stronger, and remained for a passing moment. It glittered on the shrubs that were scattered at the entrance, and gleam continued to succeed gleam for a few seconds, till they finally give place to unintermitted darkness.

The first visitings of this light called up a train of

horrors in my mind; destruction impended over this spot; the voice which I had lately heard had warned me to retire, and had menaced me with the fate of my father if I refused. I was desirous, but unable to obey; these gleams were such as preluded the stroke by which he fell; the hour, perhaps, was the same. I shuddered as if I had beheld suspended over me the exterminating sword.

Presently a new and stronger illumination burst through the lattice on the right hand, and a voice from the edge of the precipice above called out my name. It was Pleyel. Joyfully did I recognise his accents; but such was the tumult of my thoughts that I had not power to answer him till he had frequently repeated his summons. I hurried at length from the fatal spot, and, directed by the lantern which he bore, ascended the hill.

Pale and breathless, it was with difficulty I could support myself. He anxiously inquired into the cause of my affright and the motive of my unusual absence. He had returned from my brother's at a late hour, and was informed by Judith that I had walked out before sunset and had not yet returned. This intelligence was somewhat alarming. He waited some time; but, my absence continuing, he had set out in search of me. He had explored the neighbourhood with the utmost care, but, receiving no tidings of me, he was preparing to acquaint my brother with this circumstance, when he recollected the summer-house on the bank, and conceived it possible that some accident had detained me there. He again inquired into the cause of this detention, and of that confusion and dismay which my looks testified.

I told him that I had strolled hither in the afternoon, that sleep had overtaken me as I sat, and that I had awakened a few minutes before his arrival. I could tell

him no more. In the present impetuosity of my
thoughts, I was almost dubious whether the pit into
which my brother had endeavoured to entice me, and
the voice that talked through the lattice, were not parts
of the same dream. I remembered, likewise, the charge
of secrecy, and the penalty denounced if I should
rashly divulge what I had heard. For these reasons I was
silent on that subject, and, shutting myself in my
chamber, delivered myself up to contemplation.

What I have related will, no doubt, appear to you a
fable. You will believe that calamity has subverted my
reason, and that I am amusing you with the chimeras of
my brain instead of facts that have really happened. I
shall not be surprised or offended if these be your suspicions. I know not, indeed, how you can deny them
admission. For, if to me, the immediate witness, they
were fertile of perplexity and doubt, how must they
affect another to whom they are recommended only
by my testimony? It was only by subsequent events
that I was fully and incontestably assured of the veracity of my senses.

Meanwhile, what was I to think? I had been assured
that a design had been formed against my life. The
ruffians had leagued to murder me. Whom had I offended? Who was there, with whom I had ever maintained intercourse, who was capable of harbouring
such atrocious purposes?

My temper was the reverse of cruel and imperious.
My heart was touched with sympathy for the children
of misfortune. But this sympathy was not a barren sentiment. My purse, scanty as it was, was ever open, and
my hands ever active, to relieve distress. Many were
the wretches whom my personal exertions had extricated from want and disease, and who rewarded me
with their gratitude. There was no face which lowered
at my approach, and no lips which uttered impreca-

tions in my hearing. On the contrary, there was none, over whose fate I had exerted any influence or to whom I was known by reputation, who did not greet me with smiles and dismiss me with proofs of veneration: yet did not my senses assure me that a plot was laid against my life?

I am not destitute of courage. I have shown myself deliberative and calm in the midst of peril. I have hazarded my own life for the preservation of another; but now was I confused and panic-struck. I have not lived so as to fear death; yet to perish by an unseen and secret stroke, to be mangled by the knife of an assassin, was a thought at which I shuddered: what had I done to deserve to be made the victim of malignant passions?

But soft! was I not assured that my life was safe in all places but one? And why was the treason limited to take effect in this spot? I was everywhere equally defenceless. My house and chamber were at all times accessible. Danger still impended over me; the bloody purpose was still entertained, but the hand that was to execute it was powerless in all places but one!

Here I had remained for the last four or five hours, without the means of resistance or defence; yet I had not been attacked. A human being was at hand, who was conscious of my presence, and warned me hereafter to avoid this retreat. His voice was not absolutely new, but had I never heard it but once before? But why did he prohibit me from relating this incident to others, and what species of death will be awarded if I disobey?

He talked of my father. He intimated that disclosure would pull upon my head the same destruction. Was then the death of my father, portentous and inexplicable as it was, the consequence of human machinations? It should seem that this being is apprized of the true

nature of this event, and is conscious of the means that
led to it. Whether it shall likewise fall upon me depends upon the observance of silence. Was it the infraction of a similar command that brought so horrible
a penalty upon my father?

Such were the reflections that haunted me during
the night, and which effectually deprived me of sleep.
Next morning, at breakfast, Pleyel related an event
which my disappearance had hindered him from mentioning the night before. Early the preceding morning,
his occasions called him to the city: he had stepped
into a coffeehouse to while away an hour; here he had
met a person whose appearance instantly bespoke him
to be the same whose hasty visit I have mentioned,
and whose extraordinary visage and tones had so powerfully affected me. On an attentive survey, however,
he proved, likewise, to be one with whom my friend
had had some intercourse in Europe. This authorized
the liberty of accosting him, and after some conversation, mindful, as Pleyel said, of the footing which this
stranger had gained in my heart, he had ventured to
invite him to Mettingen. The invitation had been
cheerfully accepted, and a visit promised on the afternoon of the next day.

This information excited no sober emotions in my
breast. I was, of course, eager to be informed as to the
circumstances of their ancient intercourse. When and
where had they met? What knew he of the life and
character of this man?

In answer to my inquiries, he informed me that,
three years before, he was a traveller in Spain. He had
made an excursion from Valencia to Murviedro, with
a view to inspect the remains of Roman magnificence
scattered in the environs of that town. While traversing
the site of the theatre of old Saguntum, he alighted
upon this man, seated on a stone, and deeply engaged

in perusing the work of the deacon Marti. A short conversation ensued, which proved the stranger to be English. They returned to Valencia together.

His garb, aspect, and deportment were wholly Spanish. A residence of three years in the country, indefatigable attention to the language, and a studious conformity with the customs of the people, had made him indistinguishable from a native when he chose to assume that character. Pleyel found him to be connected, on the footing of friendship and respect, with many eminent merchants in that city. He had embraced the Catholic religion, and adopted a Spanish name instead of his own, which was CARWIN, and devoted himself to the literature and religion of his new country. He pursued no profession, but subsisted on remittances from England.

While Pleyel remained in Valencia, Carwin betrayed no aversion to intercourse, and the former found no small attractions in the society of this new acquaintance. On general topics he was highly intelligent and communicative. He had visited every corner of Spain, and could furnish the most accurate details respecting its ancient and present state. On topics of religion and of his own history, previous to his *transformation* into a Spaniard, he was invariably silent. You could merely gather from his discourse that he was English, and that he was well acquainted with the neighbouring countries.

His character excited considerable curiosity in the observer. It was not easy to reconcile his conversion to the Romish faith with those proofs of knowledge and capacity that were exhibited by him on different occasions. A suspicion was sometimes admitted that his belief was counterfeited for some political purpose. The most careful observation, however, produced no discovery. His manners were at all times harmless and inartificial, and his habits those of a lover of contemplation and seclusion. He appeared to have contracted an affection for Pleyel, who was not slow to return it.

My friend, after a month's residence in this city, returned into France, and, since that period, had heard nothing concerning Carwin till his appearance at Mettingen.

On this occasion Carwin had received Pleyel's greeting with a certain distance and solemnity to which the latter had not been accustomed. He had waived noticing the inquiries of Pleyel respecting his desertion of Spain, in which he had formerly declared that it was his purpose to spend his life. He had assiduously diverted the attention of the latter to indifferent topics, but was still, on every theme, as eloquent and judicious as formerly. Why he had assumed the garb of a rustic Pleyel was unable to conjecture. Perhaps it might be poverty; perhaps he was swayed by motives which it was his interest to conceal, but which were connected with consequences of the utmost moment.

Such was the sum of my friend's information. I was not sorry to be left alone during the greater part of this day. Every employment was irksome which did not leave me at liberty to meditate. I had now a new subject on which to exercise my thoughts. Before evening I should be ushered into his presence, and listen to those tones whose magical and thrilling power I had already experienced. But with what new images would he then be accompanied?

Carwin was an adherent to the Romish faith, yet was an Englishman by birth, and, perhaps, a Protestant by education. He had adopted Spain for his country, and had intimated a design to spend his days there, yet now was an inhabitant of this district, and disguised by the habiliments of a clown! What could have obliterated the impressions of his youth and made him abjure his religion and his country? What subsequent events had introduced so total a change in his plans? In withdrawing from Spain, had he reverted to the religion of his ancestors? or was it true that his former conversion was deceitful, and that his conduct had been swayed by motives which it was prudent to conceal?

Hours were consumed in revolving these ideas. My meditations were intense; and, when the series was broken, I began to reflect with astonishment on my situation. From the death of my parents till the commencement of this year my life had been serene and blissful beyond the ordinary portion of humanity; but now my bosom was corroded by anxiety. I was visited by dread of unknown dangers, and the future was a scene over which clouds rolled and thunders muttered. I compared the cause with the effect, and they seemed disproportioned to each other. All unaware, and in a manner which I had no power to explain, I was pushed from my immovable and lofty station and cast upon a sea of troubles.

I determined to be my brother's visitant on this evening; yet my resolves were not unattended with wavering and reluctance. Pleyel's insinuations that I was in love affected in no degree my belief; yet the consciousness that this was the opinion of one who would probably be present at our introduction to each other would excite all that confusion which the passion itself is apt to produce. This would confirm him in his error and call forth new railleries. His mirth, when exerted upon this topic, was the source of the bitterest vexation. Had he been aware of its influence upon my happiness, his temper would not have allowed him to persist; but this influence it was my chief endeavour to conceal. That the belief of my having bestowed my heart upon another produced in my friend none but ludicrous sensations was the true cause of my distress; but if this had

been discovered by him my distress would have been
unspeakably aggravated.

CHAPTER VIII

As soon as evening arrived, I performed my visit. Carwin made one of the company into which I was ushered. Appearances were the same as when I before
beheld him. His garb was equally negligent and rustic.
I gazed upon his countenance with new curiosity. My
situation was such as to enable me to bestow upon it a
deliberate examination. Viewed at more leisure, it lost
none of its wonderful properties. I could not deny my
homage to the intelligence expressed in it, but was
wholly uncertain whether he were an object to be
dreaded or adored, and whether his powers had been
exerted to evil or to good.

He was sparing in discourse; but whatever he said
was pregnant with meaning, and uttered with rectitude of articulation and force of emphasis of which I
had entertained no conception previously to my knowledge of him. Notwithstanding the uncouthness of his
garb, his manners were not unpolished. All topics were
handled by him with skill, and without pedantry or af-
fectation. He uttered no sentiment calculated to produce a disadvantageous impression; on the contrary,
his observations denoted a mind alive to every generous and heroic feeling. They were introduced without
parade, and accompanied with that degree of earnestness which indicates sincerity.

He parted from us not till late, refusing an invitation
to spend the night here, but readily consented to re-

peat his visit. His visits were frequently repeated. Each day introduced us to a more intimate acquaintance with his sentiments, but left us wholly in the dark concerning that about which we were most inquisitive. He studiously avoided all mention of his past or present situation. Even the place of his abode in the city he concealed from us.

Our sphere in this respect being somewhat limited, and the intellectual endowments of this man being indisputably great, his deportment was more diligently marked and copiously commented on by us than you, perhaps, will think the circumstances warranted. Not a gesture, or glance, or accent, that was not, in our private assemblies, discussed, and inferences deduced from it. It may well be thought that he modelled his behaviour by an uncommon standard, when, with all our opportunities and accuracy of observation, we were able for a long time to gather no satisfactory information. He afforded us no ground on which to build even a plausible conjecture.

There is a degree of familiarity which takes place between constant associates, that justifies the negligence of many rules of which, in an earlier period of their intercourse, politeness requires the exact observance. Inquiries into our condition are allowable when they are prompted by a disinterested concern for our welfare; and this solicitude is not only pardonable, but may justly be demanded from those who choose us for their companions. This state of things was more slow to arrive at on this occasion than on most others, on account of the gravity and loftiness of this man's behaviour.

Pleyel, however, began at length to employ regular means for this end. He occasionally alluded to the circumstances in which they had formerly met, and remarked the incongruousness between the religion and habits of a Spaniard with those of a native of Britain.

He expressed his astonishment at meeting our guest in this corner of the globe, especially as, when they parted in Spain, he was taught to believe that Carwin should never leave that country. He insinuated that a change so great must have been prompted by motives of a singular and momentous kind.

No answer, or an answer wide of the purpose, was generally made to these insinuations. Britons and Spaniards, he said, are votaries of the same Deity, and square their faith by the same precepts; their ideas are drawn from the same fountains of literature, and they speak dialects of the same tongue; their government and laws have more resemblances than differences; they were formerly provinces of the same civil, and, till lately, of the same religious, empire.

As to the motives which induce men to change the place of their abode, these must unavoidably be fleeting and mutable. If not bound to one spot by conjugal or parental ties, or by the nature of that employment to which we are indebted for subsistence, the inducements to change are far more numerous and powerful than opposite inducements.

He spoke as if desirous of showing that he was not aware of the tendency of Pleyel's remarks; yet certain tokens were apparent that proved him by no means wanting in penetration. These tokens were to be read in his countenance, and not in his words. When any thing was said indicating curiosity in us, the gloom of his countenance was deepened, his eyes sunk to the ground, and his wonted air was not resumed without visible struggle. Hence, it was obvious to infer that some incidents of his life were reflected on by him with regret; and that, since these incidents were carefully concealed, and even that regret which flowed from them laboriously stifled, they had not been merely disastrous. The secrecy that was observed appeared not designed to provoke or baffle the inquisitive, but was prompted by the shame or by the prudence of guilt.

These ideas, which were adopted by Pleyel and my brother as well as myself, hindered us from employing more direct means for accomplishing our wishes. Questions might have been put in such terms that no room should be left for the pretence of misapprehension; and, if modesty merely had been the obstacle, such questions would not have been wanting; but we considered that, if the disclosure were productive of pain or disgrace, it was inhuman to extort it.

Amidst the various topics that were discussed in his presence, allusions were, of course, made to the inexplicable events that had lately happened. At those times the words and looks of this man were objects of my particular attention. The subject was extraordinary; and any one whose experience or reflections could throw any light upon it was entitled to my gratitude. As this man was enlightened by reading and travel, I listened with eagerness to the remarks which he should make.

At first I entertained a kind of apprehension that the tale would be heard by him with incredulity and secret ridicule. I had formerly heard stories that resembled this in some of their mysterious circumstances; but they were commonly heard by me with contempt. I was doubtful whether the same impression would not now be made on the mind of our guest; but I was mistaken in my fears.

He heard them with seriousness, and without any marks either of surprise or incredulity. He pursued with visible pleasure that kind of disquisition which was naturally suggested by them. His fancy was eminently vigorous and prolific; and, if he did not persuade us that human beings are sometimes admitted to a sensible intercourse with the Author of nature, he at least won over our inclination to the cause. He merely deduced, from his own reasonings, that such intercourse was probable, but confessed that, though he was acquainted with many instances somewhat similar to those which had been related by us, none of them were perfectly exempted from the suspicion of human agency.

On being requested to relate these instances, he amused us with many curious details. His narratives were constructed with so much skill, and rehearsed with so much energy, that all the effects of a dramatic exhibition were frequently produced by them. Those that were most coherent and most minute, and, of consequence, least entitled to credit, were yet rendered probable by the exquisite art of this rhetorician. For every difficulty that was suggested a ready and plausible solution was furnished. Mysterious voices had always a share in producing the catastrophe; but they were always to be explained on some known principles, either as reflected into a focus or communicated through a tube. I could not but remark that his narratives, however complex or marvellous, contained no instance sufficiently parallel to those that had befallen ourselves, and in which the solution was applicable to our own case.

My brother was a much more sanguine reasoner than our guest. Even in some of the facts which were related by Carwin, he maintained the probability of celestial interference, when the latter was disposed to deny it, and had found, as he imagined, footsteps of a human agent. Pleyel was by no means equally credulous. He scrupled not to deny faith to any testimony but that of his senses, and allowed the facts which had lately been supported by this testimony not to mould his belief, but merely to give birth to doubts.

It was soon observed that Carwin adopted, in some

degree, a similar distinction. A tale of this kind, related
by others, he would believe, provided it was explicable
upon known principles; but that such notices were actually communicated by beings of a higher order he
would believe only when his own ears were assailed in
a manner which could not be otherwise accounted for.
Civility forbade him to contradict my brother or myself, but his understanding refused to acquiesce in
our testimony. Besides, he was disposed to question
whether the voices heard in the temple, at the foot of
the hill, and in my closet, were not really uttered by
human organs. On this supposition he was desired to
explain how the effect was produced.

He answered that the power of mimicry was very
common. Catharine's voice might easily be imitated by
one at the foot of the hill, who would find no difficulty
in eluding by flight the search of Wieland. The tidings
of the death of the Saxon lady were uttered by one
near at hand, who overheard the conversation, who
conjectured her death, and whose conjecture happened to accord with the truth. That the voice appeared to come from the ceiling was to be considered
as an illusion of the fancy. The cry for help, heard in
the hall on the night of my adventure, was to be
ascribed to a human creature, who actually stood in the
hall when he uttered it. It was of no moment, he said,
that we could not explain by what motives he that
made the signal was led hither. How imperfectly acquainted were we with the condition and designs of
the beings that surrounded us! The city was near at
hand, and thousands might there exist whose powers
and purposes might easily explain whatever was mysterious in this transaction. As to the closet dialogue, he
was obliged to adopt one of two suppositions, and af-
firm either that it was fashioned in my own fancy, or

that it actually took place between two persons in the closet.

Such was Carwin's mode of explaining these appearances. It is such, perhaps, as would commend itself as most plausible to the most sagacious minds; but it was insufficient to impart conviction to us. As to the treason that was meditated against me, it was doubtless just to conclude that it was either real or imaginary; but that it was real was attested by the mysterious warning in the summer-house, the secret of which I had hitherto locked up in my own breast.

A month passed away in this kind of intercourse. As to Carwin, our ignorance was in no degree enlightened respecting his genuine character and views. Appearances were uniform. No man possessed a larger store of knowledge, or a greater degree of skill in the communication of it to others; hence he was regarded as an inestimable addition to our society. Considering the distance of my brother's house from the city, he was frequently prevailed upon to pass the night where he spent the evening. Two days seldom elapsed without a visit from him; hence he was regarded as a kind of inmate of the house. He entered and departed without ceremony. When he arrived he received an unaffected welcome, and when he chose to retire no importunities were used to induce him to remain.

The temple was the principal scene of our social enjoyments; yet the felicity that we tasted when assembled in this asylum was but the gleam of a former sunshine. Carwin never parted with his gravity. The inscrutableness of his character, and the uncertainty whether his fellowship tended to good or to evil, were seldom absent from our minds. This circumstance powerfully contributed to sadden us.

My heart was the seat of growing disquietudes. This change in one who had formerly been characterized by all the exuberances of soul could not fail to be remarked by my friends. My brother was always a pattern of solemnity. My sister was clay, moulded by the circumstances in which she happened to be placed. There was but one whose deportment remains to be described as being of importance to our happiness. Had Pleyel likewise dismissed his vivacity?

He was as whimsical and jestful as ever, but he was not happy. The truth in this respect was of too much importance to me not to make me a vigilant observer. His mirth was easily perceived to be the fruit of exertion. When his thoughts wandered from the company, an air of dissatisfaction and impatience stole across his features. Even the punctuality and frequency of his visits were somewhat lessened. It may be supposed that my own uneasiness was heightened by these tokens; but, strange as it may seem, I found, in the present state of my mind, no relief but in the persuasion that Pleyel was unhappy.

That unhappiness, indeed, depended for its value in my eyes on the cause that produced it. It did not arise from the death of the Saxon lady; it was not a contagious emanation from the countenances of Wieland or Carwin. There was but one other source whence it could flow. A nameless ecstasy thrilled through my frame when any new proof occurred that the ambiguousness of my behaviour was the cause.

CHAPTER IX

My brother had received a new book from Germany. It was a tragedy, and the first attempt of a Saxon poet

of whom my brother had been taught to entertain the
highest expectations. The exploits of Zisca, the Bohe-
mian hero, were woven into a dramatic series and connection. According to German custom, it was minute
and diffuse, and dictated by an adventurous and
lawless fancy. It was a chain of audacious acts and
unheard-of disasters. The moated fortress and the
thicket, the ambush and the battle, and the conflict of
headlong passions, were portrayed in wild numbers
and with terrific energy. An afternoon was set apart to
rehearse this performance. The language was familiar
to all of us but Carwin, whose company, therefore, was
tacitly dispensed with.

The morning previous to this intended rehearsal I
spent at home. My mind was occupied with reflections
relative to my own situation. The sentiment which
lived with chief energy in my heart was connected
with the image of Pleyel. In the midst of my anguish,
I had not been destitute of consolation. His late deportment had given spring to my hopes. Was not the hour
at hand which should render me the happiest of human
creatures? He suspected that I looked with favourable
eyes upon Carwin. Hence arose disquietudes which he
struggled in vain to conceal. He loved me, but was
hopeless that his love would be compensated. Is it not
time, said I, to rectify this error? But by what means is
this to be effected? It can only be done by a change of
deportment in me; but how must I demean myself for
this purpose?

I must not speak. Neither eyes nor lips must impart
the information. He must not be assured that my heart
is his, previous to the tender of his own; but he must
be convinced that it has not been given to another; he
must be supplied with space whereon to build a doubt
as to the true state of my affections; he must be
prompted to avow himself. The line of delicate pro-

priety,—how hard it is not to fall short, and not to over-leap it!

This afternoon we shall meet at the temple. We shall not separate till late. It will be his province to accompany me home. The airy expanse is without a speck. This breeze is usually steadfast, and its promise of a bland and cloudless evening may be trusted. The moon will rise at eleven, and at that hour we shall wind along this bank. Possibly that hour may decide my fate. If suitable encouragement be given, Pleyel will reveal his soul to me; and I, ere I reach this threshold, will be made the happiest of beings.

And is this good to be mine? Add wings to thy speed, sweet evening; and thou, moon, I charge thee, shroud thy beams at the moment when my Pleyel whispers love. I would not for the world that the burning blushes and the mounting raptures of that moment should be visible.

But what encouragement is wanting? I must be regardful of insurmountable limits. Yet, when minds are imbued with a genuine sympathy, are not words and looks superfluous? Are not motion and touch sufficient to impart feelings such as mine? Has he not eyed me at moments when the pressure of his hand has thrown me into tumults, and was it impossible that he mistook the impetuosities of love for the eloquence of indignation?

But the hastening evening will decide. Would it were come! And yet I shudder at its near approach. An interview that must thus terminate is surely to be wished for by me; and yet it is not without its terrors. Would to heaven it were come and gone!

I feel no reluctance, my friends, to be thus explicit. Time was, when these emotions would be hidden with immeasurable solicitude from every human eye. Alas! these airy and fleeting impulses of shame are gone. My

scruples were preposterous and criminal. They are
bred in all hearts by a perverse and vicious education,
and they would still have maintained their place in my
heart, had not my portion been set in misery. My errors
have taught me thus much wisdom:—that those sentiments which we ought not to disclose it is criminal to
harbour.

It was proposed to begin the rehearsal at four
o'clock. I counted the minutes as they passed; their
flight was at once too rapid and too slow: my sensations
were of an excruciating kind; I could taste no food, nor
apply to any task, nor enjoy a moment's repose; when
the hour arrived I hastened to my brother's.

Pleyel was not there. He had not yet come. On ordinary occasions he was eminent for punctuality. He had
testified great eagerness to share in the pleasures of this
rehearsal. He was to divide the task with my brother,
and in tasks like these he always engaged with peculiar zeal. His elocution was less sweet than sonorous,
and, therefore, better adapted than the mellifluences of
his friend to the outrageous vehemence of this drama.

What could detain him? Perhaps he lingered
through forgetfulness. Yet this was incredible. Never
had his memory been known to fail upon even more
trivial occasions. Not less impossible was it that the
scheme had lost its attractions, and that he stayed because his coming would afford him no gratification. But
why should we expect him to adhere to the minute?

A half-hour elapsed, but Pleyel was still at a distance. Perhaps he had misunderstood the hour which
had been proposed. Perhaps he had conceived that to-
morrow, and not to-day, had been selected for this purpose; but no. A review of preceding circumstances
demonstrated that such misapprehension was impossible; for he had himself proposed this day, and this
hour. This day his attention would not otherwise be

occupied; but to-morrow an indispensable engagement was foreseen, by which all his time would be engrossed; his detention, therefore, must be owing to some unforeseen and extraordinary event. Our conjectures were vague, tumultuous, and sometimes fearful. His sickness and his death might possibly have detained him.

Tortured with suspense, we sat gazing at each other, and at the path which led from the road. Every horseman that passed was, for a moment, imagined to be him. Hour succeeded hour, and the sun, gradually declining, at length disappeared. Every signal of his coming proved fallacious, and our hopes were at length dismissed. His absence affected my friends in no insupportable degree. They should be obliged, they said, to defer this undertaking till the morrow; and perhaps their impatient curiosity would compel them to dispense entirely with his presence. No doubt some harmless occurrence had diverted him from his purpose; and they trusted that they should receive a satisfactory account of him in the morning.

It may be supposed that this disappointment affected me in a very different manner. I turned aside my head to conceal my tears. I fled into solitude, to give vent to my reproaches without interruption or restraint. My heart was ready to burst with indignation and grief. Pleyel was not the only object of my keen but unjust upbraiding. Deeply did I execrate my own folly. Thus fallen into ruins was the gay fabric which I had reared! Thus had my golden vision melted into air!

How fondly did I dream that Pleyel was a lover! If he were, would he have suffered any obstacle to hinder his coming? "Blind and infatuated man!" I exclaimed. "Thou sportest with happiness. The good that is offered thee thou hast the insolence and folly to refuse.

Well, I will henceforth intrust my felicity to no one's keeping but my own."

The first agonies of this disappointment would not allow me to be reasonable or just. Every ground on which I had built the persuasion that Pleyel was not unimpressed in my favour appeared to vanish. It seemed as if I had been misled into this opinion by the most palpable illusions.

I made some trifling excuse, and returned, much earlier than I expected, to my own house. I retired early to my chamber, without designing to sleep. I placed myself at a window, and gave the reins to reflection.

The hateful and degrading impulses which had lately controlled me were, in some degree, removed. New dejection succeeded, but was now produced by contemplating my late behaviour. Surely that passion is worthy to be abhorred which obscures our understanding and urges us to the commission of injustice. What right had I to expect his attendance? Had I not demeaned myself like one indifferent to his happiness, and as having bestowed my regards upon another? His absence might be prompted by the love which I considered his absence as a proof that he wanted. He came not because the sight of me, the spectacle of my coldness or aversion, contributed to his despair. Why should I prolong, by hypocrisy or silence, his misery as well as my own? Why not deal with him explicitly, and assure him of the truth?

You will hardly believe that, in obedience to this suggestion, I rose for the purpose of ordering a light, that I might instantly make this confession in a letter. A second thought showed me the rashness of this scheme, and I wondered by what infirmity of mind I could be betrayed into a momentary approbation of it. I saw with the utmost clearness that a confession like that would be the most remediless and unpardonable outrage upon the dignity of my sex, and utterly unworthy of that passion which controlled me.

I resumed my seat and my musing. To account for the absence of Pleyel became once more the scope of my conjectures. How many incidents might occur to raise an insuperable impediment in his way! When I was a child, a scheme of pleasure, in which he and his sister were parties, had been in like manner frustrated by his absence; but his absence, in that instance, had been occasioned by his falling from a boat into the river, in consequence of which he had run the most imminent hazard of being drowned. Here was a second disappointment endured by the same persons, and produced by his failure. Might it not originate in the same cause? Had he not designed to cross the river that morning to make some necessary purchases in New Jersey? He had preconcerted to return to his own house to dinner; but perhaps some disaster had befallen him. Experience had taught me the insecurity of a canoe, and that was the only kind of boat which Pleyel used; I was, likewise, actuated by an hereditary dread of water. These circumstances combined to bestow considerable plausibility on this conjecture; but the consternation with which I began to be seized was allayed by reflecting that, if this disaster had happened, my brother would have received the speediest information of it. The consolation which this idea imparted was ravished from me by a new thought. This disaster might have happened, and his family not be apprized of it. The first intelligence of his fate may be communicated by the livid corpse which the tide may cast, many days hence, upon the shore.

Thus was I distressed by opposite conjectures; thus was I tormented by phantoms of my own creation. It was not always thus. I can ascertain the date when my mind became the victim of this imbecility; perhaps it was coeval with the inroad of a fatal passion,—a passion that will never rank me in the number of its eulogists; it was alone sufficient to the extermination of my peace; it was itself a plenteous source of calamity, and needed not the concurrence of other evils to take away the attractions of existence and dig for me an untimely grave.

The state of my mind naturally introduced a train of reflections upon the dangers and cares which inevitably beset a human being. By no violent transition was I led to ponder on the turbulent life and mysterious end of my father. I cherished with the utmost veneration the memory of this man, and every relic connected with his fate was preserved with the most scrupulous care. Among these was to be numbered a manuscript containing memoirs of his own life. The narrative was by no means recommended by its eloquence; but neither did all its value flow from my relationship to the author. Its style had an unaffected and picturesque simplicity. The great variety and circumstantial display of the incidents, together with their intrinsic importance as descriptive of human manners and passions, made it the most useful book in my collection. It was late: but, being sensible of no inclination to sleep, I resolved to betake myself to the perusal of it.

To do this, it was requisite to procure a light. The girl had long since retired to her chamber: it was therefore proper to wait upon myself. A lamp, and the means of lighting it, were only to be found in the kitchen. Thither I resolved forthwith to repair; but the light was of use merely to enable me to read the book. I knew the shelf and the spot where it stood. Whether I took down the book, or prepared the lamp in the first place, appeared to be a matter of no moment. The latter was preferred, and, leaving my seat, I approached the closet in which, as I mentioned formerly, my books and papers were deposited.

Suddenly the remembrance of what had lately passed in this closet occurred. Whether midnight was approaching, or had passed, I knew not. I was, as then, alone and defenceless. The wind was in that direction in which, aided by the deathlike repose of nature, it brought to me the murmur of the waterfall. This was mingled with that solemn and enchanting sound which a breeze produces among the leaves of pines. The words of that mysterious dialogue, their fearful import, and the wild excess to which I was transported by my terrors, filled my imagination anew. My steps faltered, and I stood a moment to recover myself.

I prevailed on myself at length to move towards the closet. I touched the lock, but my fingers were powerless; I was visited afresh by unconquerable apprehensions. A sort of belief darted into my mind that some being was concealed within whose purposes were evil. I began to contend with those fears, when it occurred to me that I might, without impropriety, go for a lamp previously to opening the closet. I receded a few steps; but before I reached the chamber door my thoughts took a new direction. Motion seemed to produce a mechanical influence upon me. I was ashamed of my weakness. Besides, what aid could be afforded me by a lamp?

My fears had pictured to themselves no precise object. It would be difficult to depict in words the ingredients and hues of that phantom which haunted me. A hand invisible and of preternatural strength, lifted by human passions, and selecting my life for its aim, were parts of this terrific image. All places were alike accessible to this foe; or, if his empire were restricted by local bounds, those bounds were utterly inscrutable by me. But had I not been told, by some one in league with this enemy, that every place but the recess in the bank was exempt from danger?

I returned to the closet, and once more put my hand upon the lock. Oh, may my ears lose their sensibility ere they be again assailed by a shriek so terrible! Not merely my understanding was subdued by the sound; it acted on my nerves like an edge of steel. It appeared to cut asunder the fibres of my brain and rack every joint with agony.

The cry, loud and piercing as it was, was nevertheless human. No articulation was ever more distinct. The breath which accompanied it did not fan my hair, yet did every circumstance combine to persuade me that the lips which uttered it touched my very shoulder.

"Hold! hold!" were the words of this tremendous prohibition, in whose tone the whole soul seemed to be wrapped up, and every energy converted into eagerness and terror.

Shuddering, I dashed myself against the wall, and, by the same involuntary impulse, turned my face backward to examine the mysterious monitor. The moonlight streamed into each window, and every corner of the room was conspicuous, and yet I beheld nothing!

The interval was too brief to be artificially measured, between the utterance of these words and my scrutiny directed to the quarter whence they came. Yet, if a human being had been there, could he fail to have been visible? Which of my senses was the prey of a fatal illusion? The shock which the sound produced was still felt in every part of my frame. The sound, therefore, could not but be a genuine commotion. But that I had heard it was not more true than that the being who uttered it was stationed at my right ear; yet my attendant was invisible.

I cannot describe the state of my thoughts at that mo-

ment. Surprise had mastered my faculties. My frame
shook, and the vital current was congealed. I was conscious only to the vehemence of my sensations. This
condition could not be lasting. Like a tide, which suddenly mounts to an overwhelming height and then
gradually subsides, my confusion slowly gave place to
order, and my tumults to a calm. I was able to deliberate and move. I resumed my feet, and advanced into
the midst of the room. Upward, and behind, and on
each side, I threw penetrating glances. I was not satisfied with one examination. He that hitherto refused to
be seen might change his purpose, and on the next
survey be clearly distinguishable.

Solitude imposes least restraint upon the fancy. Dark
is less fertile of images than the feeble lustre of the
moon. I was alone, and the walls were checkered by
shadowy forms. As the moon passed behind a cloud
and emerged, these shadows seemed to be endowed
with life, and to move. The apartment was open to the
breeze, and the curtain was occasionally blown from
its ordinary position. This motion was not unaccompanied with sound. I failed not to snatch a look and
to listen when this motion and this sound occurred. My
belief that my monitor was posted near was strong, and
instantly converted these appearances to tokens of his
presence; and yet I could discern nothing.

When my thoughts were at length permitted to re-
vert to the past, the first idea that occurred was the
resemblance between the words of the voice which I
had just heard and those which had terminated my
dream in the summer-house. There are means by
which we are able to distinguish a substance from a
shadow, a reality from the phantom of a dream. The
pit, my brother beckoning me forward, the seizure of
my arm, and the voice behind, were surely imaginary.
That these incidents were fashioned in my sleep is sup-

ported by the same indubitable evidence that compels me to believe myself awake at present; yet the words and the voice were the same. Then, by some inexplicable contrivance, I was aware of the danger, while my actions and sensations were those of one wholly unacquainted with it. Now, was it not equally true that my actions and persuasions were at war? Had not the belief that evil lurked in the closet gained admittance, and had not my actions betokened an unwarrantable security? To obviate the effects of my infatuation, the same means had been used.

In my dream, he that tempted me to my destruction was my brother. Death was ambushed in my path. From what evil was I now rescued? What minister or implement of ill was shut up in this recess? Who was it whose suffocating grasp I was to feel should I dare to enter it? What monstrous conception is this? My brother?

No; protection, and not injury, is his province. Strange and terrible chimera! Yet it would not be suddenly dismissed. It was surely no vulgar agency that gave this form to my fears. He to whom all parts of time are equally present, whom no contingency approaches, was the author of that spell which now seized upon me. Life was dear to me. No consideration was present that enjoined me to relinquish it. Sacred duty combined with every spontaneous sentiment to endear to me my being. Should I not shudder when my being was endangered? But what emotion should possess me when the arm lifted against me was Wieland's?

Ideas exist in our minds that can be accounted for by no established laws. Why did I dream that my brother was my foe? Why but because an omen of my fate was ordained to be communicated? Yet what salutary end did it serve? Did it arm me with caution to elude or fortitude to bear the evils to which I was reserved? My present thoughts were, no doubt, indebted for their hue to the similitude existing between these incidents and those of my dream. Surely it was frenzy that dictated my deed. That a ruffian was hidden in the closet was an idea the genuine tendency of which was to urge me to flight. Such had been the effect formerly produced. Had my mind been simply occupied with this thought at present, no doubt the same impulse would have been experienced; but now it was my brother whom I was irresistibly persuaded to regard as the contriver of that ill of which I had been forewarned. This persuasion did not extenuate my fears or my danger. Why then did I again approach the closet and withdraw the bolt? My resolution was instantly conceived, and executed without faltering.

The door was formed of light materials. The lock, of simple structure, easily forewent its hold. It opened into the room, and commonly moved upon its hinges, after being unfastened, without any effort of mine. This effort, however, was bestowed upon the present occasion. It was my purpose to open it with quickness; but the exertion which I made was ineffectual. It refused to open.

At another time, this circumstance would not have looked with a face of mystery. I should have supposed some casual obstruction and repeated my efforts to surmount it. But now my mind was accessible to no conjecture but one. The door was hindered from opening by human force. Surely, here was a new cause for affright. This was confirmation proper to decide my conduct. Now was all ground of hesitation taken away. What could be supposed but that I deserted the chamber and the house? that I at least endeavoured no longer to withdraw the door?

Have I not said that my actions were dictated by frenzy? My reason had forborne, for a time, to suggest or to sway my resolves. I reiterated my endeavours. I exerted all my force to overcome the obstacle, but in vain. The strength that was exerted to keep it shut was superior to mine.

A casual observer might, perhaps, applaud the audaciousness of this conduct. Whence, but from a habitual defiance of danger, could my perseverance arise? I have already assigned, as distinctly as I am able, the cause of it. The frantic conception that my brother was within, that the resistance made to my design was exerted by him, had rooted itself in my mind. You will comprehend the height of this infatuation, when I tell you that, finding all my exertions vain, I betook myself to exclamations. Surely I was utterly bereft of understanding.

Now I had arrived at the crisis of my fate. "Oh, hinder not the door to open," I exclaimed, in a tone that had less of fear than of grief in it. "I know you well. Come forth, but harm me not. I beseech you, come forth."

I had taken my hand from the lock and removed to a small distance from the door. I had scarcely uttered these words, when the door swung upon its hinges and displayed to my view the interior of the closet. Whoever was within was shrouded in darkness. A few seconds passed without interruption of the silence. I knew not what to expect or to fear. My eyes would not stray from the recess. Presently, a deep sigh was heard. The quarter from which it came heightened the eagerness of my gaze. Some one approached from the farther end. I quickly perceived the outlines of a human figure. Its steps were irresolute and slow. I recoiled as it advanced.

By coming at length within the verge of the room, his form was clearly distinguishable. I had prefigured to myself a very different personage. The face that presented itself was the last that I should desire to meet at an hour and in a place like this. My wonder was stifled by my fears. Assassins had lurked in this recess. Some divine voice warned me of danger that at this moment awaited me. I had spurned the intimation, and challenged my adversary.

I recalled the mysterious countenance and dubious character of Carwin. What motive but atrocious ones could guide his steps hither? I was alone. My habit suited the hour, and the place, and the warmth of the season. All succour was remote. He had placed himself between me and the door. My frame shook with the vehemence of my apprehensions.

Yet I was not wholly lost to myself; I vigilantly marked his demeanour. His looks were grave, but not without perturbation. What species of inquietude it betrayed the light was not strong enough to enable me to discover. He stood still; but his eyes wandered from one object to another. When these powerful organs were fixed upon me, I shrunk into myself. At length he broke silence. Earnestness, and not embarrassment, was in his tone. He advanced close to me while he spoke:—

"What voice was that which lately addressed you?"

He paused for an answer; but, observing my trepidation, he resumed, with undiminished solemnity, "Be not terrified. Whoever he was, he has done you an important service. I need not ask you if it were the voice of a companion. That sound was beyond the compass of human organs. The knowledge that enabled him to tell you who was in the closet was obtained by incomprehensible means.

"You knew that Carwin was there. Were you not apprized of his intents? The same power could impart the one as well as the other. Yet, knowing these, you persisted. Audacious girl! But perhaps you confided in his guardianship. Your confidence was just. With succour like this at hand you may safely defy me.

"He is my eternal foe; the baffler of my best-concerted schemes. Twice have you been saved by his accursed interposition. But for him I should long ere now have borne away the spoils of your honour."

He looked at me with greater steadfastness than before. I became every moment more anxious for my safety. It was with difficulty I stammered out an entreaty that he would instantly depart, or suffer me to do so. He paid no regard to my request, but proceeded in a more impassioned manner:—

"What is it you fear? Have I not told you you are safe? Has not one in whom you more reasonably place trust assured you of it? Even if I execute my purpose, what injury is done? Your prejudices will call it by that name, but it merits it not.

"I was impelled by a sentiment that does you honour; a sentiment that would sanctify my deed; but, whatever it be, you are safe. Be this chimera still worshipped; I will do nothing to pollute it." There he stopped.

The accents and gestures of this man left me drained of all courage. Surely, on no other occasion should I have been thus pusillanimous. My state I regarded as a hopeless one. I was wholly at the mercy of this being. Whichever way I turned my eyes, I saw no avenue by which I might escape. The resources of my personal strength, my ingenuity, and my eloquence, I estimated at nothing. The dignity of virtue and the force of truth I had been accustomed to celebrate, and had frequently vaunted of the conquests which I should make with their assistance.

I used to suppose that certain evils could never befall a being in possession of a sound mind; that true virtue supplies us with energy which vice can never

resist; that it was always in our power to obstruct, by
his own death, the designs of an enemy who aimed at
less than our life. How was it that a sentiment like despair had now invaded me, and that I trusted to the
protection of chance, or to the pity of my persecutor?

His words imparted some notion of the injury which
he had meditated. He talked of obstacles that had
risen in his way. He had relinquished his design. These
sources supplied me with slender consolation. There
was no security but in his absence. When I looked at
myself, when I reflected on the hour and the place, I
was overpowered by horror and dejection.

He was silent, museful, and inattentive to my situation, yet made no motion to depart. I was silent in my
turn. What could I say? I was confident that reason in
this contest would be impotent. I must owe my safety
to his own suggestions. Whatever purpose brought him
hither, he had changed it. Why then did he remain?
His resolutions might fluctuate, and the pause of a few
minutes restore to him his first resolutions.

Yet was not this the man whom we had treated with
unwearied kindness? whose society was endeared to us
by his intellectual elevation and accomplishments?
who had a thousand times expatiated on the usefulness
and beauty of virtue? Why should such a one be
dreaded? If I could have forgotten the circumstances
in which our interview had taken place, I might have
treated his words as jests. Presently, he resumed:—

"Fear me not: the space that severs us is small, and
all visible succour is distant. You believe yourself com-
pletely in my power; that you stand upon the brink of
ruin. Such are your groundless fears. I cannot lift a fin-
ger to hurt you. Easier would it be to stop the moon in
her course than to injure you. The power that protects
you would crumble my sinews and reduce me to a heap

of ashes in a moment, if I were to harbour a thought
hostile to your safety.

"Thus are appearances at length solved. Little did I
expect that they originated hence. What a portion is
assigned to you! Scanned by the eyes of this intelligence, your path will be without pits to swallow or
snares to entangle you. Environed by the arms of this
protection, all artifices will be frustrated and all malice
repelled."

Here succeeded a new pause. I was still observant
of every gesture and look. The tranquil solemnity that
had lately possessed his countenance gave way to a
new expression. All now was trepidation and anxiety.

"I must be gone," said he, in a faltering accent.
"Why do I linger here? I will not ask your forgiveness.
I see that your terrors are invincible. Your pardon will
be extorted by fear, and not dictated by compassion. I
must fly from you forever. He that could plot against
your honour must expect from you and your friends
persecution and death. I must doom myself to endless
exile."

Saying this, he hastily left the room. I listened while
he descended the stairs, and, unbolting the outer door,
went forth. I did not follow him with my eyes, as the
moonlight would have enabled me to do. Relieved by
his absence, and exhausted by the conflict of my fears,
I threw myself on a chair, and resigned myself to those
bewildering ideas which incidents like these could not
fail to produce.

CHAPTER X

Order could not readily be introduced into my thoughts. The voice still rung in my ears. Every accent that was uttered by Carwin was fresh in my remembrance. His unwelcome approach, the recognition of his person, his hasty departure, produced a complex impression on my mind which no words can delineate. I strove to give a slower motion to my thoughts, and to regulate a confusion which became painful; but my efforts were nugatory. I covered my eyes with my hand, and sat, I know not how long, without power to arrange or utter my conceptions.

I had remained for hours, as I believed, in absolute solitude. No thought of personal danger had molested my tranquillity. I had made no preparation for defence. What was it that suggested the design of perusing my father's manuscript? If, instead of this, I had retired to bed and to sleep, to what fate might I not have been reserved. The ruffian, who must almost have suppressed his breathings to screen himself from discovery, would have noticed this signal, and I should have awakened only to perish with affright, and to abhor myself. Could I have remained unconscious of my danger? Could I have tranquilly slept in the midst of so deadly a snare?

And who was he that threatened to destroy me? By what means could he hide himself in this closet? Surely he is gifted with supernatural power. Such is the enemy of whose attempts I was forewarned. Daily I had seen him and conversed with him. Nothing could be discerned through the impenetrable veil of his duplicity. When busied in conjectures as to the author of the evil that was threatened, my mind did not light for a moment upon his image. Yet has he not avowed himself my enemy? Why should he be here if he had not meditated evil?

He confesses that this has been his second attempt. What was the scene of his former conspiracy? Was it not he whose whispers betrayed him? Am I deceived? or was there not a faint resemblance between the voice of this man and that which talked of grasping my throat and extinguishing my life in a moment? Then he had a colleague in his crime; now he is alone. Then death was the scope of his thoughts; now an injury unspeakably more dreadful. How thankful should I be to the power that has interposed to save me!

That power is invisible. It is subject to the cognizance of one of my senses. What are the means that will inform me of what nature it is? He has set himself to counterwork the machinations of this man, who had menaced destruction to all that is dear to me, and whose coming had surmounted every human impediment. There was none to rescue me from his grasp. My rashness even hastened the completion of his scheme, and precluded him from the benefits of deliberation. I had robbed him of the power to repent and forbear. Had I been apprized of the danger, I should have regarded my conduct as the means of rendering my escape from it impossible. Such, likewise, seem to have been the fears of my invisible protector. Else why that startling entreaty to refrain from opening the closet? By what inexplicable infatuation was I compelled to proceed?

Yet my conduct was wise. Carwin, unable to comprehend my folly, ascribed my behaviour to my knowledge. He conceived himself previously detected, and, such detection being possible to flow only from *my* heavenly friend and *his* enemy, his fears acquired additional strength.

He is apprized of the nature and intentions of this being. Perhaps he is a human agent. Yet on that supposition his achievements are incredible. Why should I be selected as the object of his care? or, if a mere mortal, should I not recognise some one whom benefits imparted and received had prompted to love me? What were the limits and duration of his guardianship? Was the genius of my birth intrusted by divine benignity with this province? Are human faculties adequate to receive stronger proofs of the existence of unfettered and beneficent intelligences than I have received?

But who was this man's coadjutor? The voice that acknowledged an alliance in treachery with Carwin warned me to avoid the summer-house. He assured me that there only my safety was endangered. His assurance, as it now appears, was fallacious. Was there not deceit in his admonition? Was his compact really annulled? Some purpose was, perhaps, to be accomplished by preventing my future visits to that spot. Why was I enjoined silence to others on the subject of this admonition, unless it were for some unauthorized and guilty purpose?

No one but myself was accustomed to visit it. Backward it was hidden from distant view by the rock, and in front it was screened from all examination by creeping plants and the branches of cedars. What recess could be more propitious to secrecy? The spirit which haunted it formerly was pure and rapturous. It was a fane sacred to the memory of infantile days, and to blissful imaginations of the future! What a gloomy reverse had succeeded since the ominous arrival of this stranger! Now, perhaps, it is the scene of his meditations. Purposes fraught with horror, that shun the light and contemplate the pollution of innocence, are here engendered, and fostered, and reared to maturity.

Such were the ideas that, during the night, were tumultuously revolved by me. I reviewed every conversation in which Carwin had borne a part. I studied to discover the true inferenced deducible from his deportment and words with regard to his former adventures and actual views. I pondered on the comments which he made on the relation which I had given of the closet dialogue. No new ideas suggested themselves in the course of this review. My expectation had, from the first, been disappointed on the small degree of surprise which this narrative excited in him. He never explicitly declared his opinion as to the nature of those voices, or decided whether they were real or visionary. He recommended no measures of caution or prevention.

But what measures were now to be taken? Was the danger which threatened me at an end? Had I nothing more to fear? I was lonely, and without means of defence. I could not calculate the motives and regulate the footsteps of this person. What certainty was there that he would not reassume his purposes and swiftly return to the execution of them?

This idea covered me once more with dismay. How deeply did I regret the solitude in which I was placed, and how ardently did I desire the return of day! But neither of these inconveniences were susceptible of remedy. At first it occurred to me to summon my servant and make her spend the night in my chamber; but the inefficacy of this expedient to enhance my safety was easily seen. Once I resolved to leave the house and retire to my brother's, but was deterred by reflecting on the unseasonableness of the hour, on the alarm which my arrival and the account which I should be obliged to give might occasion, and on the danger to which I might expose myself in the way thither. I began, likewise, to consider Carwin's return to molest me as exceedingly improbable. He had relinquished, of his own accord, his design, and departed without compulsion.

"Surely," said I, "there is omnipotence in the cause that changed the views of a man like Carwin. The divinity that shielded me from his attempts will take suitable care of my future safety. Thus to yield to my fears is to deserve that they should be real."

Scarcely had I uttered these words, when my attention was startled by the sound of footsteps. They denoted some one stepping into the piazza in front of my house. My new-born confidence was extinguished in a moment. Carwin, I thought, had repented his departure, and was hastily returning. The possibility that his return was prompted by intentions consistent with my safety found no place in my mind. Images of violation and murder assailed me anew, and the terrors which succeeded almost incapacitated me from taking any measures for my defence. It was an impulse of which I was scarcely conscious that made me fasten the lock and draw the bolts of my chamber door. Having done this, I threw myself on a seat; for I trembled to a degree which disabled me from standing, and my soul was so perfectly absorbed in the act of listening, that almost the vital motions were stopped.

The door below creaked on its hinges. It was not again thrust to, but appeared to remain open. Footsteps entered, traversed the entry, and began to mount the stairs. How I detested the folly of not pursuing the man when he withdrew, and bolting after him the outer door! Might he not conceive this omission to be a proof that my angel had deserted me, and be thereby fortified in guilt?

Every step on the stairs which brought him nearer
to my chamber added vigour to my desperation. The
evil with which I was menaced was to be at any rate
eluded. How little did I preconceive the conduct
which, in an exigence like this, I should be prone to
adopt! You will suppose that deliberation and despair
would have suggested the same course of action, and
that I should have unhesitatingly resorted to the best
means of personal defence within my power. A penknife lay open upon my table. I remembered that it
was there, and seized it. For what purpose you will
scarcely inquire. It will be immediately supposed that
I meant it for my last refuge, and that, if all other
means should fail, I should plunge it into the heart of
my ravisher.

I have lost all faith in the steadfastness of human
resolves. It was thus that in periods of calm I had determined to act. No cowardice had been held by me in
greater abhorrence than that which prompted an injured female to destroy, not her injurer ere the injury
was perpetrated, but herself when it was without remedy. Yet now this penknife appeared to me of no other
use than to baffle my assailant and prevent the crime
by destroying myself. To deliberate at such a time was
impossible; but, among the tumultuous suggestions of
the moment, I do not recollect that it once occurred
to me to use it as an instrument of direct defence.

The steps had now reached the second floor. Every
footfall accelerated the completion without augmenting the certainty of evil. The consciousness that the
door was fast, now that nothing but that was interposed between me and danger, was a source of some
consolation. I cast my eye towards the window. This,
likewise, was a new suggestion. If the door should give
way, it was my sudden resolution to throw myself from
the window. Its height from the ground, which was

covered beneath by a brick pavement, would insure my destruction; but I thought not of that.

When opposite to my door the footsteps ceased. Was he listening whether my fears were allayed and my caution were asleep? Did he hope to take me by surprise? Yet, if so, why did he allow so many noisy signals to betray his approach? Presently the steps were again heard to approach the door. A hand was laid upon the lock, and the latch pulled back. Did he imagine it possible that I should fail to secure the door? A slight effort was made to push it open, as if, all bolts being withdrawn, a slight effort only was required.

I no sooner perceived this than I moved swiftly towards the window. Carwin's frame might be said to be all muscle. His strength and activity had appeared, in various instances, to be prodigious. A slight exertion of his force would demolish the door. Would not that exertion be made? Too surely it would; but, at the same moment that this obstacle should yield and he should enter the apartment, my determination was formed to leap from the window. My senses were still bound to this object. I gazed at the door in momentary expectation that the assault would be made. The pause continued. The person without was irresolute and motionless.

Suddenly it occurred to me that Carwin might conceive me to have fled. That I had not betaken myself to flight was, indeed, the least probable of all conclusions. In this persuasion he must have been confirmed on finding the lower door unfastened and the chamber door locked. Was it not wise to foster this persuasion? Should I maintain deep silence, this, in addition to other circumstances, might encourage the belief, and he would once more depart. Every new reflection added plausibility to this reasoning. It was presently more strongly enforced when I noticed footsteps withdrawing from the door. The blood once more flowed back to my heart, and a dawn of exultation began to rise; but my joy was short-lived. Instead of descending the stairs, he passed to the door of the opposite chamber, opened it, and, having entered, shut it after him with a violence that shook the house.

How was I to interpret this circumstance? For what end could he have entered this chamber? Did the violence with which he closed the door testify the depth of his vexation? This room was usually occupied by Pleyel. Was Carwin aware of his absence on this night? Could he be suspected of a design so sordid as pillage? If this were his view, there were no means in my power to frustrate it. It behooved me to seize the first opportunity to escape; but, if my escape were supposed by my enemy to have been already effected, no asylum was more secure than the present. How could my passage from the house be accomplished without noises that might incite him to pursue me?

Utterly at a loss to account for his going into Pleyel's chamber, I waited in instant expectation of hearing him come forth. All, however, was profoundly still. I listened in vain for a considerable period to catch the sound of the door when it should again be opened. There was no other avenue by which he could escape, but a door which led into the girl's chamber. Would any evil from this quarter befall the girl?

Hence arose a new train of apprehensions. They merely added to the turbulence and agony of my reflections. Whatever evil impended over her, I had no power to avert it. Seclusion and silence were the only means of saving myself from the perils of this fatal night. What solemn vows did I put up, that, if I should once more behold the light of day, I would never trust myself again within the threshold of this dwelling!

Minute lingered after minute, but no token was

given that Carwin had returned to the passage. What, I again asked, could detain him in this room? Was it possible that he had returned, and glided unperceived away? I was speedily aware of the difficulty that attended an enterprise like this; and yet, as if by that means I were capable of gaining any information on that head, I cast anxious looks from the window.

The object that first attracted my attention was a human figure standing on the edge of the bank. Perhaps my penetration was assisted by my hopes. Be that as it will, the figure of Carwin was clearly distinguishable. From the obscurity of my station, it was impossible that I should be discerned by him; and yet he scarcely suffered me to catch a glimpse of him. He turned and went down the steep, which in this part was not difficult to be scaled.

My conjecture, then, had been right. Carwin had softly opened the door, descended the stairs, and issued forth. That I should not have overheard his steps was only less incredible than that my eyes had deceived me. But what was now to be done? The house was at length delivered from this detested inmate. By one avenue might he again re-enter. Was it not wise to bar the lower door? Perhaps he had gone out by the kitchen door. For this end, he must have passed through Judith's chamber. These entrances being closed and bolted, as great security was gained as was compatible with my lonely condition.

The propriety of these measures was too manifest not to make me struggle successfully with my fears. Yet I opened my own door with the utmost caution, and descended as if I were afraid that Carwin had been still immured in Pleyel's chamber. The outer door was ajar. I shut it with trembling eagerness, and drew every bolt that appended to it. I then passed with light and less cautious steps through the parlour, but was surprised to discover that the kitchen door was secure. I was compelled to acquiesce in the first conjecture that Carwin had escaped through the entry.

My heart was now somewhat eased of the load of apprehension. I returned once more to my chamber, the door of which I was careful to lock. It was no time to think of repose. The moonlight began already to fade before the light of the day. The approach of morning was betokened by the usual signals. I mused upon the events of this night, and determined to take up my abode henceforth at my brother's. Whether I should inform him of what had happened was a question which seemed to demand some consideration. My safety unquestionably required that I should abandon my present habitation.

As my thoughts began to flow with fewer impediments, the image of Pleyel, and the dubiousness of his condition, again recurred to me. I again ran over the possible causes of his absence on the preceding day. My mind was attuned to melancholy. I dwelt, with an obstinacy for which I could not account, on the idea of his death. I painted to myself his struggles with the billows, and his last appearance. I imagined myself a midnight wanderer on the shore, and to have stumbled on his corpse, which the tide had cast up. These dreary images affected me even to tears. I endeavoured not to restrain them. They imparted a relief which I had not anticipated. The more copiously they flowed, the more did my general sensations appear to subside into calm, and a certain restlessness give way to repose.

Perhaps, relieved by this effusion, the slumber so much wanted might have stolen on my senses, had there been no new cause of alarm.

CHAPTER XI

I was aroused from this stupor by sounds that evidently arose in the next chamber. Was it possible that I had been mistaken in the figure which I had seen on the bank? or had Carwin, by some inscrutable means, penetrated once more into this chamber? The opposite door opened; footsteps came forth, and the person, advancing to mine, knocked.

So unexpected an incident robbed me of all presence of mind, and, starting up, I involuntarily exclaimed, "Who is there?" An answer was immediately given. The voice, to my inexpressible astonishment, was Pleyel's.

"It is I. Have you risen? If you have not, make haste; I want three minutes' conversation with you in the parlour. I will wait for you there." Saying this, he retired from the door.

Should I confide in the testimony of my ears? If that were true, it was Pleyel that had been hitherto immured in the opposite chamber; he whom my rueful fancy had depicted in so many ruinous and ghastly shapes; he whose footsteps had been listened to with such inquietude! What is man, that knowledge is so sparingly conferred upon him! that his heart should be wrung with distress, and his frame be exanimated with fear, though his safety be encompassed with impregnable walls! What are the bounds of human imbecility! He that warned me of the presence of my foe refused the intimation by which so many racking fears would have been precluded.

Yet who would have imagined the arrival of Pleyel at such an hour? His tone was desponding and anxious. Why this unseasonable summons? and why this hasty departure? Some tidings he, perhaps, bears of mysterious and unwelcome import.

My impatience would not allow me to consume much time in deliberation; I hastened down. Pleyel I found standing at a window, with eyes cast down as in meditation, and arms folded on his breast. Every line in his countenance was pregnant with sorrow. To this was added a certain wanness and air of fatigue. The last time I had seen him appearances had been the reverse of these. I was startled at the change. The first impulse was to question him as to the cause. This impulse was supplanted by some degree of confusion, flowing from a consciousness that love had too large, and, as it might prove, a perceptible, share in creating this impulse. I was silent.

Presently he raised his eyes and fixed them upon me. I read in them an anguish altogether ineffable. Never had I witnessed a like demeanour in Pleyel. Never, indeed, had I observed a human countenance in which grief was more legibly inscribed. He seemed struggling for utterance; but, his struggles being fruitless, he shook his head and turned away from me.

My impatience would not allow me to be longer silent. "What," said I, "for heaven's sake, my friend,—what is the matter?"

He started at the sound of my voice. His looks, for a moment, became convulsed with an emotion very different from grief. His accents were broken with rage:—

"The matter! O wretch!—thus exquisitely fashioned,—on whom nature seemed to have exhausted all her graces; with charms so awful and so pure! how art thou fallen! From what height fallen! A ruin so complete,—so unheard-of!"

His words were again choked by emotion. Grief and pity were again mingled in his features. He resumed, in a tone half suffocated by sobs:—

"But why should I upbraid thee? Could I restore to thee what thou hast lost, efface this cursed stain, snatch thee from the jaws of this fiend, I would do it. Yet what will avail my efforts? I have not arms with which to contend with so consummate, so frightful a depravity.

"Evidence less than this would only have excited resentment and scorn. The wretch who should have breathed a suspicion injurious to thy honour would have been regarded without anger: not hatred or envy could have prompted him; it would merely be an argument of madness. That my eyes, that my ears, should bear witness to thy fall! By no other way could detestable conviction be imparted.

"Why do I summon thee to this conference? Why expose myself to thy derision? Here admonition and entreaty are vain. Thou knowest him already for a murderer and thief. I had thought to have been the first to disclose to thee his infamy; to have warned thee of the pit to which thou art hastening; but thy eyes are open in vain. Oh, foul and insupportable disgrace!

"There is but one path. I know you will disappear together. In thy ruin, how will the felicity and honour of multitudes be involved! But it must come. This scene shall not be blotted by his presence. No doubt thou wilt shortly see thy detested paramour. This scene will be again polluted by a midnight assignation. Inform him of his dangers; tell him that his crimes are known; let him fly far and instantly from this spot, if he desires to avoid the fate which menaced him in Ireland.

"And wilt thou not stay behind? But shame upon my weakness! I know not what I would say. I have done what I purposed. To stay longer, to expostulate, to beseech, to enumerate the consequences of thy act, —what end can it serve but to blazon thy infamy and embitter our woes? And yet, oh, think—think ere it be too late—on the distresses which thy flight will entail upon us; on the base, grovelling, and atrocious character of the wretch to whom thou hast sold thy honour. But what is this? Is not thy effrontery impenetrable and thy heart thoroughly cankered? Oh, most specious and most profligate of women!"

Saying this, he rushed out of the house. I saw him in a few moments hurrying along the path which led to my brother's. I had no power to prevent his going, or to recall or to follow him. The accents I had heard were calculated to confound and bewilder. I looked around me, to assure myself that the scene was real. I moved, that I might banish the doubt that I was awake. Such enormous imputations from the mouth of Pleyel! To be stigmatized with the names of wanton and profligate! To be charged with the sacrifice of honour! with midnight meetings with a wretch known to be a murderer and thief! with an intention to fly in his company!

What I had heard was surely the dictate of frenzy, or it was built upon some fatal, some incomprehensible mistake. After the horrors of the night, after undergoing perils so imminent from this man, to be summoned to an interview like this!—to find Pleyel fraught with a belief that, instead of having chosen death as a refuge from the violence of this man, I had hugged his baseness to my heart, had sacrificed for him my purity, my spotless name, my friendships, and my fortune! That even madness could engender accusations like these was not to be believed.

What evidence could possibly suggest conceptions so wild? After the unlooked-for interview with Carwin in my chamber, he retired. Could Pleyel have observed his exit? It was not long after that Pleyel himself entered. Did he build on this incident his odious conclusions? Could the long series of my actions and sentiments grant me no exemption from suspicions so foul? Was it not more rational to infer that Carwin's designs had been illicit? that my life had been endangered by the fury of one whom, by some means, he had discovered to be an assassin and robber? that my honour had been assailed, not by blandishments, but by violence?

He has judged me without hearing. He has drawn from dubious appearances conclusions the most improbable and unjust. He has loaded me with all outrageous epithets. He has ranked me with prostitutes and thieves. I cannot pardon thee, Pleyel, for this injustice. Thy understanding must be hurt. If it be not, —if thy conduct was sober and deliberate,—I can never forgive an outrage so unmanly and so gross.

These thoughts gradually gave place to others. Pleyel was possessed by some momentary frenzy; appearances had led him into palpable errors. Whence could his sagacity have contracted this blindness? Was it not love? Previously assured of my affection for Carwin, distracted with grief and jealousy, and impelled hither at that late hour by some unknown instigation, his imagination transformed shadows into monsters, and plunged him into these deplorable errors.

This idea was not unattended with consolation. My soul was divided between indignation at his injustice and delight on account of the source from which I conceived it to spring. For a long time they would allow admission to no other thoughts. Surprise is an emotion that enfeebles, not invigorates. All my meditations were accompanied with wonder. I rambled with vagueness, or clung to one image with an obstinacy which sufficiently testified the maddening influence of late transactions.

Gradually I proceeded to reflect upon the consequences of Pleyel's mistake, and on the measures I should take to guard myself against future injury from Carwin. Should I suffer this mistake to be detected by time? When his passion should subside, would he not perceive the flagrancy of his injustice and hasten to atone for it? Did it not become my character to testify resentment for language and treatment so opprobrious? Wrapt up in the consciousness of innocence, and confiding in the influence of time and reflection to confute so groundless a charge, it was my province to be passive and silent.

As to the violences meditated by Carwin, and the means of eluding them, the path to be taken by me was obvious. I resolved to tell the tale to my brother and regulate myself by his advice. For this end, when the morning was somewhat advanced, I took the way to his house. My sister was engaged in her customary occupations. As soon as I appeared, she remarked a change in my looks. I was not willing to alarm her by the information which I had to communicate. Her health was in that condition which rendered a disastrous tale particularly unsuitable. I forbore a direct answer to her inquiries, and inquired, in my turn, for Wieland.

"Why," said she, "I suspect something mysterious and unpleasant has happened this morning. Scarcely had we risen when Pleyel dropped among us. What could have prompted him to make us so early and so unseasonable a visit I cannot tell. To judge from the disorder of his dress, and his countenance, something of an extraordinary nature has occurred. He permitted me merely to know that he had slept none, nor even undressed, during the past night. He took your brother to walk with him. Some topic must have deeply engaged them, for Wieland did not return till the break-fast-hour was passed, and returned alone. His disturb-ance was excessive; but he would not listen to my importunities, or tell me what had happened. I gath-ered, from hints which he let fall, that your situation was in some way the cause; yet he assured me that you were at your own house, alive, in good health, and in perfect safety. He scarcely ate a morsel, and immedi-ately after breakfast went out again. He would not in-form me whither he was going, but mentioned that he probably might not return before night."

I was equally astonished and alarmed by this infor-mation. Pleyel had told his tale to my brother, and had, by a plausible and exaggerated picture, instilled into him unfavourable thoughts of me. Yet would not the more correct judgment of Wieland perceive and ex-pose the fallacy of his conclusions? Perhaps his uneasi-ness might arise from some insight into the character of Carwin, and from apprehensions for my safety. The appearances by which Pleyel had been misled might induce him likewise to believe that I entertained an indiscreet though not dishonourable affection for Car-win. Such were the conjectures rapidly formed. I was inexpressibly anxious to change them into certainty. For this end an interview with my brother was desir-able. He was gone no one knew whither, and was not expected speedily to return. I had no clue by which to trace his footsteps.

My anxieties could not be concealed from my sister. They heightened her solicitude to be acquainted with the cause. There were many reasons persuading me to silence; at least, till I had seen my brother, it would be an act of inexcusable temerity to unfold what had lately passed. No other expedient for eluding her im-portunities occurred to me but that of returning to my own house. I recollected my determination to become a tenant of this roof. I mentioned it to her. She joyfully acceded to this proposal, and suffered me with less reluctance to depart when I told her that it was with a view to collect and send to my new dwelling what articles would be immediately useful to me.

Once more I returned to the house which had been the scene of so much turbulence and danger. I was at no great distance from it when I observed my brother coming out. On seeing me he stopped, and, after ascertaining, as it seemed, which way I was going, he returned into the house before me. I sincerely rejoiced at this event, and I hastened to set things, if possible, on their right footing.

His brow was by no means expressive of those vehement emotions with which Pleyel had been agitated. I drew a favourable omen from this circumstance. Without delay I began the conversation.

"I have been to look for you," said I, "but was told by Catharine that Pleyel had engaged you on some important and disagreeable affair. Before his interview with you he spent a few minutes with me. These minutes he employed in upbraiding me for crimes and intentions with which I am by no means chargeable. I believe him to have taken up his opinions on very insufficient grounds. His behaviour was in the highest degree precipitate and unjust, and, until I receive some atonement, I shall treat him, in my turn, with that contempt which he justly merits; meanwhile, I am fearful that he has prejudiced my brother against me. That is an evil which I most anxiously deprecate, and which I shall indeed exert myself to remove. Has he made me the subject of this morning's conversation?"

My brother's countenance testified no surprise at my address. The benignity of his looks was nowise diminished.

"It is true," said he, "your conduct was the subject of

our discourse. I am your friend as well as your brother.
There is no human being whom I love with more tenderness and whose welfare is nearer my heart. Judge,
then, with what emotions I listened to Pleyel's story.
I expect and desire you to vindicate yourself from aspersions so foul, if vindication be possible."

The tone with which he uttered the last words affected me deeply. "If vindication be possible!" repeated I. "From what you know, do you deem a formal
vindication necessary? Can you harbour for a moment
the belief of my guilt?"

He shook his head with an air of acute anguish. "I
have struggled," said he, "to dismiss that belief. You
speak before a judge who will profit by any pretence
to acquit you; who is ready to question his own senses
when they plead against you."

These words incited a new set of thoughts in my
mind. I began to suspect that Pleyel had built his accusations on some foundation unknown to me. "I may be
a stranger to the grounds of your belief. Pleyel loaded
me with indecent and virulent invectives, but he withheld from me the facts that generated his suspicions.
Events took place last night of which some of the circumstances were of an ambiguous nature. I conceived
that these might possibly have fallen under his cognizance, and that, viewed through the mists of prejudice
and passion, they supplied a pretence for his conduct,
but believed that your more unbiassed judgment
would estimate them at their just value. Perhaps his
tale has been different from what I suspect it to be.
Listen, then, to my narrative. If there be any thing in
his story inconsistent with mine, his story is false."

I then proceeded to a circumstantial relation of the
incidents of the last night. Wieland listened with deep
attention. Having finished, "This," continued I, "is the
truth. You see in what circumstances an interview took

place between Carwin and me. He remained for hours
in my closet, and for some minutes in my chamber.
He departed without haste or interruption. If Pleyel
marked him as he left the house, (and it is not impossible that he did,) inferences injurious to my character
might suggest themselves to him. In admitting them,
he gave proofs of less discernment and less candour
than I once ascribed to him."

"His proofs," said Wieland, after a considerable
pause, "are different. That he should be deceived is not
possible. That he himself is not the deceiver could not
be believed, if his testimony were not inconsistent with
yours; but the doubts which I entertained are now removed. Your tale, some parts of it, is marvellous; the
voice which exclaimed against your rashness in approaching the closet, your persisting, notwithstanding
that prohibition, your belief that I was the ruffian, and
your subsequent conduct, are believed by me, because
I have known you from childhood, because a thousand
instances have attested your veracity, and because
nothing less than my own hearing and vision would
convince me, in opposition to her own assertions, that
my sister had fallen into wickedness like this."

I threw my arms around him and bathed his cheek
with my tears. "That," said I, "is spoken like my
brother. But what are the proofs?"

He replied, "Pleyel informed me that, in going to
your house, his attention was attracted by two voices.
The persons speaking sat beneath the bank, out of
sight. These persons, judging by their voices, were Carwin and you. I will not repeat the dialogue. If my sister
was the female, Pleyel was justified in concluding you
to be indeed one of the most profligate of women.
Hence his accusations of you, and his efforts to obtain
my concurrence to a plan by which an eternal separa-

tion should be brought about between my sister and this man."

I made Wieland repeat this recital. Here indeed was a tale to fill me with terrible foreboding. I had vainly thought that my safety could be sufficiently secured by doors and bars, but this is a foe from whose grasp no power of divinity can save me! His artifices will ever lay my fame and happiness at his mercy. How shall I counterwork his plots or detect his coadjutor? He has taught some vile and abandoned female to mimic my voice. Pleyel's ears were the witnesses of my dishonour. This is the midnight assignation to which he alluded. Thus is the silence he maintained when attempting to open the door of my chamber, accounted for. He supposed me absent, and meant, perhaps, had my apartment been accessible, to leave in it some accusing memorial.

Pleyel was no longer equally culpable. The sincerity of his anguish, the depth of his despair, I remembered with some tendencies to gratitude. Yet was he not precipitate? Was the conjecture that my part was played by some mimic so utterly untenable? Instances of this faculty are common. The wickedness of Carwin must, in his opinion, have been adequate to such contrivances; and yet the supposition of my guilt was adopted in preference to that.

But how was this error to be unveiled? What but my own assertion had I to throw in the balance against it? Would this be permitted to outweigh the testimony of his senses? I had no witnesses to prove my existence in another place. The real events of that night are marvellous. Few to whom they should be related would scruple to discredit them. Pleyel is skeptical in a transcendent degree. I cannot summon Carwin to my bar, and make him the attester of my innocence and the accuser of himself.

My brother saw and comprehended my distress. He was unacquainted, however, with the full extent of it. He knew not by how many motives I was incited to retrieve the good opinion of Pleyel. He endeavoured to console me. Some new event, he said, would occur to disentangle the maze. He did not question the influence of my eloquence, if I thought proper to exert it. Why not seek an interview with Pleyel, and exact from him a minute relation, in which something may be met with serving to destroy the probability of the whole?

I caught with eagerness at this hope; but my alacrity was damped by new reflections. Should I, perfect in this respect, and unblemished as I was, thrust myself uncalled into his presence, and make my felicity depend upon his arbitrary verdict?

"If you choose to seek an interview," continued Wieland, "you must make haste; for Pleyel informed me of his intention to set out this evening or to-morrow on a long journey."

No intelligence was less expected or less welcome than this. I had thrown myself in a window-seat; but now, starting on my feet, I exclaimed, "Good heavens! what is it you say? A journey? Whither? when?"

"I cannot say whither. It is a sudden resolution, I believe. I did not hear of it till this morning. He promises to write to me as soon as he is settled."

I needed no further information as to the cause and issue of this journey. The scheme of happiness to which he had devoted his thoughts was blasted by the discovery of last night. My preference of another, and my unworthiness to be any longer the object of his adoration, were evinced by the same act and in the same moment. The thought of utter desertion, a desertion originating in such a cause, was the prelude to distraction. That Pleyel should abandon me forever, because I was blind to his excellence, because I coveted pollution and wedded infamy, when, on the contrary, my heart was the shrine of all purity, and beat only for his sake, was a destiny which, as long as my life was in my own hands, I would by no means consent to endure.

I remembered that this evil was still preventable; that this fatal journey it was still in my power to procrastinate, or, perhaps, to occasion it to be laid aside. There were no impediments to a visit; I only dreaded lest the interview should be too long delayed. My brother befriended my impatience, and readily consented to furnish me with a chaise and servant to attend me. My purpose was to go immediately to Pleyel's farm, where his engagements usually detained him during the day.

CHAPTER XII

My way lay through the city. I had scarcely entered it when I was seized with a general sensation of sickness. Every object grew dim and swam before my sight. It was with difficulty I prevented myself from sinking to the bottom of the carriage. I ordered myself to be carried to Mrs. Baynton's, in hope that an interval of repose would invigorate and refresh me. My distracted thoughts would allow me but little rest. Growing somewhat better in the afternoon, I resumed my journey.

My contemplations were limited to a few objects. I regarded my success in the purpose which I had in view as considerably doubtful. I depended, in some degree, on the suggestions of the moment, and on the materials which Pleyel himself should furnish me. When I reflected on the nature of the accusation, I burned with disdain. Would not truth, and the consciousness of innocence, render me triumphant? Should I not cast from me, with irresistible force, such atrocious imputations?

What an entire and mournful change has been effected in a few hours! The gulf that separates man from insects is not wider than that which severs the polluted from the chaste among women. Yesterday and to-day I am the same. There is a degree of depravity to which it is impossible for me to sink; yet, in the apprehension of another, my ancient and intimate associate, the perpetual witness of my actions and partaker of my thoughts, I had ceased to be the same. My integrity was tarnished and withered in his eyes. I was the colleague of a murderer and the paramour of a thief!

His opinion was not destitute of evidence; yet what proofs could reasonably avail to establish an opinion like this? If the sentiments corresponded not with the voice that was heard, the evidence was deficient; but this want of correspondence would have been supposed by me if I had been the auditor and Pleyel the criminal. But mimicry might still more plausibly have been employed to explain the scene. Alas! it is the fate of Clara Wieland to fall into the hands of a precipitate and inexorable judge.

But what, O man of mischief, is the tendency of thy thoughts? Frustrated in thy first design, thou wilt not forego the immolation of thy victim. To exterminate my reputation was all that remained to thee; and this my guardian has permitted. To dispossess Pleyel of this prejudice may be impossible; but, if that be effected, it cannot be supposed that thy wiles are exhausted;

thy cunning will discover innumerable avenues to the
accomplishment of thy malignant purpose.

Why should I enter the lists against thee? Would to
heaven I could disarm thy vengeance by my depreca-
tions!

When I think of all the resources with which nature
and education have supplied thee,—that thy form is a
combination of steely fibres and organs of exquisite
ductility and boundless compass, actuated by an intelligence gifted with infinite endowments and comprehending all knowledge,—I perceive that my doom is
fixed. What obstacle will be able to divert thy zeal or
repel thy efforts? That being who has hitherto pro-
tected me has borne testimony to the formidableness
of thy attempts, since nothing less than supernatural
interference could check thy career.

Musing on these thoughts, I arrived, towards the
close of the day, at Pleyel's house. A month before, I
had traversed the same path; but how different were
my sensations! Now I was seeking the presence of one
who regarded me as the most degenerate of human kind.
I was to plead the cause of my innocence against witnesses the most explicit and unerring of those which
support the fabric of human knowledge. The nearer I
approached the crisis, the more did my confidence decay. When the chaise stopped at the door, my strength
refused to support me, and I threw myself into the
arms of an ancient female domestic. I had not courage
to inquire whether her master was at home. I was tormented with fears that the projected journey was already undertaken. These fears were removed by her
asking me whether she should call her young master,
who had just gone into his own room. I was somewhat
revived by this intelligence, and resolved immediately
to seek him there.

In my confusion of mind, I neglected to knock at the

door, but entered his apartment without previous notice. This abruptness was altogether involuntary. Absorbed in reflections of such unspeakable moment, I
had no leisure to heed the niceties of punctilio. I discovered him standing with his back towards the entrance. A small trunk, with its lid raised, was before
him, in which it seemed as if he had been busy in pack-
ing his clothes. The moment of my entrance, he was
employed in gazing at something which he held in his
hand.

I imagined that I fully comprehended the scene.
The image which he held before him, and by which
his attention was so deeply engaged, I doubted not to
be my own. These preparations for his journey, the
cause to which it was to be imputed, the hopelessness
of success in the undertaking on which I had entered,
rushed at once upon my feelings, and dissolved me into
a flood of tears.

Startled by this sound, he dropped the lid of the
trunk and turned. The solemn sadness that previously
overspread his countenance gave sudden way to an
attitude and look of the most vehement astonishment.
Perceiving me unable to uphold myself, he stepped towards me without speaking, and supported me by
his arm. The kindness of this action called forth a new
effusion from my eyes. Weeping was a solace to which,
at that time, I had not grown familiar, and which,
therefore, was peculiarly delicious. Indignation was no
longer to be read in the features of my friend. They
were pregnant with a mixture of wonder and pity.
Their expression was easily interpreted. This visit, and
these tears, were tokens of my penitence. The wretch
whom he had stigmatized as incurably and obdurately
wicked now showed herself susceptible of remorse,
and had come to confess her guilt.

This persuasion had no tendency to comfort me. It

only showed me, with new evidence, the difficulty of the task which I had assigned myself. We were mutually silent. I had less power and less inclination than ever to speak. I extricated myself from his hold, and threw myself on a sofa. He placed himself by my side, and appeared to wait with impatience and anxiety for some beginning of the conversation. What could I say? If my mind had suggested any thing suitable to the occasion, my utterance was suffocated by tears.

Frequently he attempted to speak, but seemed deterred by some degree of uncertainty as to the true nature of the scene. At length, in faltering accents, he spoke:—

"My friend! would to heaven I were still permitted to call you by that name! The image that I once adored existed only in my fancy; but, though I cannot hope to see it realized, you may not be totally insensible to the horrors of that gulf into which you are about to plunge. What heart is forever exempt from the goadings of compunction and the influx of laudable propensities?

"I thought you accomplished and wise beyond the rest of women. Not a sentiment you uttered, not a look you assumed, that were not, in my apprehension, fraught with the sublimities of rectitude and the illuminations of genius. Deceit has some bounds. Your education could not be without influence. A vigorous understanding cannot be utterly devoid of virtue; but you could not counterfeit the powers of invention and reasoning. I was rash in my invectives. I will not but with life relinquish all hopes of you. I will shut out every proof that would tell me that your heart is incurably diseased.

"You come to restore me once more to happiness; to convince me that you have torn her mask from vice, and feel nothing but abhorrence for the part you have hitherto acted."

At these words my equanimity forsook me. For a moment I forgot the evidence from which Pleyel's opinions were derived, the benevolence of his remonstrances, and the grief which his accents bespoke; I was filled with indignation and horror at charges so black; I shrunk back and darted at him a look of disdain and anger. My passion supplied me with words:—

"What detestable infatuation was it that led me hither! Why do I patiently endure these horrible insults? My offences exist only in your own distempered imagination; you are leagued with the traitor who assailed my life; you have vowed the destruction of my peace and honour. I deserve infamy for listening to calumnies so base!"

These words were heard by Pleyel without visible resentment. His countenance relapsed into its former gloom; but he did not even look at me. The ideas which had given place to my angry emotions returned, and once more melted me into tears. "Oh!" I exclaimed, in a voice broken by sobs, "what a task is mine! Compelled to hearken to charges which I feel to be false, but which I know to be believed by him that utters them; believed, too, not without evidence, which, though fallacious, is not unplausible.

"I came hither not to confess, but to vindicate. I know the source of your opinions. Wieland has informed me on what your suspicions are built. These suspicions are fostered by you as certainties: the tenor of my life, of all my conversations and letters, affords me no security; every sentiment that my tongue and my pen have uttered bear testimony to the rectitude of my mind; but this testimony is rejected. I am condemned as brutally profligate; I am classed with the stupidly and sordidly wicked.

"And where are the proofs that must justify so foul and so improbable an accusation? You have overheard a midnight conference. Voices have saluted your ear, in which you imagine yourself to have recognised mine and that of a detected villain. The sentiments expressed were not allowed to outweigh the casual or concerted resemblance of voice,—sentiments the reverse of all those whose influence my former life had attested, denoting a mind polluted by grovelling vices and entering into compact with that of a thief and a murderer. The nature of these sentiments did not enable you to detect the cheat, did not suggest to you the possibility that my voice had been counterfeited by another.

"You were precipitate and prone to condemn. Instead of rushing on the impostors and comparing the evidence of sight with that of hearing, you stood aloof, or you fled. My innocence would not now have stood in need of vindication if this conduct had been pursued. That you did not pursue it, your present thoughts incontestably prove. Yet this conduct might surely have been expected from Pleyel. That he would not hastily impute the blackest of crimes, that he would not couple my name with infamy and cover me with ruin for inadequate or slight reasons, might reasonably have been expected." The sobs which convulsed my bosom would not suffer me to proceed.

Pleyel was for a moment affected. He looked at me with some expression of doubt; but this quickly gave place to a mournful solemnity. He fixed his eyes on the floor as in reverie, and spoke:—

"Two hours hence I am gone. Shall I carry away with me the sorrow that is now my guest? or shall that sorrow be accumulated tenfold? What is she that is now before me? Shall every hour supply me with new proofs of a wickedness beyond example? Already I deem her the most abandoned and detestable of human creatures. Her coming and her tears imparted a gleam of hope; but that gleam has vanished."

He now fixed his eyes upon me, and every muscle in his face trembled. His tone was hollow and terrible: —"Thou knowest that I was a witness of your interview, yet thou comest hither to upbraid me for injustice! Thou canst look me in the face and say that I am deceived! An inscrutable Providence has fashioned thee for some end. Thou wilt live, no doubt, to fulfil the purposes of thy Maker, if he repent not of his workmanship and send not his vengeance to exterminate thee ere the measure of thy days be full. Surely nothing in the shape of man can vie with thee!

"But I thought I had stifled this fury. I am not constituted thy judge. My office is to pity and amend, and not to punish and revile. I deemed myself exempt from all tempestuous passions. I had almost persuaded myself to weep over thy fall; but I am frail as dust and mutable as water: I am calm, I am compassionate, only in thy absence. Make this house, this room, thy abode as long as thou wilt, but forgive me if I prefer solitude for the short time during which I shall stay." Saying this, he motioned as if to leave the apartment.

The stormy passions of this man affected me by sympathy. I ceased to weep. I was motionless and speechless with agony. I sat with my hands clasped, mutely gazing after him as he withdrew. I desired to detain him, but was unable to make any effort for that purpose till he had passed out of the room. I then uttered an involuntary and piercing cry:—"Pleyel! Art thou gone? Gone forever?"

At this summons he hastily returned. He beheld me wild, pale, gasping for breath, and my head already sinking on my bosom. A painful dizziness seized me, and I fainted away.

When I recovered, I found myself stretched on a

bed in the outer apartment, and Pleyel, with two female servants, standing beside it. All the fury and scorn which the countenance of the former lately expressed had now disappeared, and was succeeded by the most tender anxiety. As soon as he perceived that my senses were returned to me, he clasped his hands, and exclaimed, "God be thanked! you are once more alive. I had almost despaired of your recovery. I fear I have been precipitate and unjust. My senses must have been the victims of some inexplicable and momentary frenzy. Forgive me, I beseech you; forgive my reproaches. I would purchase conviction of your purity at the price of my existence here and hereafter."

He once more, in a tone of the most fervent tenderness, besought me to be composed, and then left me to the care of the women.

CHAPTER XIII

Here was wrought a surprising change in my friend. What was it that had shaken conviction so firm? Had any thing occurred during my fit, adequate to produce so total an alteration? My attendants informed me that he had not left my apartment; that the unusual duration of my fit, and the failure for a time of all the means used for my recovery, had filled him with grief and dismay. Did he regard the effect which his reproaches had produced as a proof of my sincerity?

In this state of mind, I little regarded my languors of body. I rose and requested an interview with him before my departure, on which I was resolved, notwithstanding his earnest solicitation to spend the night at his house. He complied with my request. The tenderness which he had lately betrayed had now disappeared, and he once more relapsed into a chilling solemnity.

I told him that I was preparing to return to my brother's; that I had come hither to vindicate my innocence from the foul aspersions which he had cast upon it. My pride had not taken refuge in silence or distance. I had not relied upon time, or the suggestions of his cooler thoughts, to confute his charges. Conscious as I was that I was perfectly guiltless, and entertaining some value for his good opinion, I could not prevail upon myself to believe that my efforts to make my innocence manifest would be fruitless. Adverse appearances might be numerous and specious, but they were unquestionably false. I was willing to believe him sincere, that he made no charges which he himself did not believe; but these charges were destitute of truth. The grounds of his opinion were fallacious; and I desired an opportunity of detecting their fallacy. I entreated him to be explicit, and to give me a detail of what he had heard and what he had seen.

At these words my companion's countenance grew darker. He appeared to be struggling with his rage. He opened his lips to speak, but his accents died away ere they were formed. This conflict lasted for some minutes, but his fortitude was finally successful. He spoke as follows:—

"I would fain put an end to this hateful scene; what I shall say will be breath idly and unprofitably consumed. The clearest narrative will add nothing to your present knowledge. You are acquainted with the grounds of my opinion, and yet you avow yourself innocent; why then should I rehearse these grounds? You are apprized of the character of Carwin; why then should I enumerate the discoveries which I have made respecting him? Yet, since it is your request,—since, considering the limitedness of human faculties, some error may possibly lurk in those appearances which I have witnessed,—I will briefly relate what I know.

"Need I dwell upon the impressions which your conversation and deportment originally made upon me? We parted in childhood; but our intercourse by letter was copious and uninterrupted. How fondly did I anticipate a meeting with one whom her letters had previously taught me to consider as the first of women, and how fully realized were the expectations that I had formed!

"'Here,' said I, 'is a being after whom sages may model their transcendent intelligence and painters their ideal beauty. Here is exemplified that union between intellect and form which has hitherto existed only in the conceptions of the poet. I have watched your eyes; my attention has hung upon your lips. I have questioned whether the enchantments of your voice were more conspicuous in the intricacies of melody or the emphasis of rhetoric. I have marked the transitions of your discourse, the felicities of your expression, your refined argumentation and glowing imagery, and been forced to acknowledge that all delights were meagre and contemptible, compared with those connected with the audience and sight of you. I have contemplated your principles, and been astonished at the solidity of their foundation and the perfection of their structure. I have traced you to your home. I have viewed you in relation to your servants, to your family, to your neighbours, and to the world. I have seen by what skilful arrangements you facilitate the performance of the most arduous and complicated duties; what daily accessions of strength your judicious discipline bestowed upon your memory; what correctness and abundance of knowledge was daily experienced by your unwearied application to books and to writing. 'If she that possesses so much in the bloom of youth will go on accumulating her stores, what,' said I, 'is the picture she will display at a mature age?'

"You know not the accuracy of my observation. I was desirous that others should profit by an example so rare. I therefore noted down in writing every particular of your conduct. I was anxious to benefit by an opportunity so seldom afforded us. I laboured not to omit the slightest shade or the most petty line in your portrait. Here there was no other task incumbent on me but to copy; there was no need to exaggerate or overlook in order to produce a more unexceptionable pattern. Here was a combination of harmonies and graces incapable of diminution or accession without injury to its completeness.

"I found no end and no bounds to my task. No display of a scene like this could be chargeable with redundancy or superfluity. Even the colour of a shoe, the knot of a ribbon, or your attitude in plucking a rose, were of moment to be recorded. Even the arrangements of your breakfast-table and your toilet have been amply displayed.

"I know that mankind are more easily enticed to virtue by example than by precept. I know that the absoluteness of a model, when supplied by invention, diminishes its salutary influence, since it is useless, we think, to strive after that which we know to be beyond our reach. But the picture which I drew was not a phantom: as a model, it was devoid of imperfection; and to aspire to that height which had been really attained was by no means unreasonable. I had another and more interesting object in view. One existed who claimed all my tenderness. Here, in all its parts, was a model worthy of assiduous study and indefatigable imitation. I called upon her, as she wished to secure and enhance my esteem, to mould her thoughts, her words, her countenance, her actions, by this pattern.

"The task was exuberant of pleasure; and I was deeply engaged in it, when an imp of mischief was let loose in the form of Carwin. I admired his powers and accomplishments. I did not wonder that they were admired by you. On the rectitude of your judgment, however, I relied to keep this admiration within discreet and scrupulous bounds. I assured myself that the strangeness of his deportment and the obscurity of his life would teach you caution. Of all errors, my knowledge of your character informed me that this was least likely to befall you.

"You were powerfully affected by his first appearance; you were bewitched by his countenance and his tones. Your description was ardent and pathetic; I listened to you with some emotions of surprise. The portrait you drew in his absence, and the intensity with which you mused upon it, were new and unexpected incidents. They bespoke a sensibility somewhat too vivid, but from which, while subjected to the guidance of an understanding like yours, there was nothing to dread.

"A more direct intercourse took place between you. I need not apologize for the solicitude which I entertained for your safety. He that gifted me with perception of excellence compelled me to love it. In the midst of danger and pain, my contemplations have ever been cheered by your image. Every object in competition with you was worthless and trivial. No price was too great by which your safety could be purchased. For that end, the sacrifice of ease, of health, and even of life, would cheerfully have been made by me. What wonder, then, that I scrutinized the sentiments and deportment of this man with ceaseless vigilance, that I watched your words and your looks when he was present, and that I extracted cause for the deepest inquietude from every token which you gave of having put your happiness into this man's keeping?

"I was cautious in deciding. I recalled the various conversations in which the topics of love and marriage had been discussed. As a woman, young, beautiful, and independent, it behooved you to have fortified your mind with just principles on this subject. Your principles were eminently just. Had not their rectitude and their firmness been attested by your treatment of that specious seducer Dashwood? These principles, I was prone to believe, exempted you from danger in this new state of things. I was not the last to pay my homage to the unrivalled capacity, insinuation, and eloquence of this man. I have disguised, but could never stifle, the conviction that his eyes and voice had a witchcraft in them which rendered him truly formidable; but I reflected on the ambiguous expression of his countenance,—an ambiguity which you were the first to remark,—on the cloud which obscured his character, and on the suspicious nature of that concealment which he studied, and concluded you to be safe. I denied the obvious construction to appearances. I referred your conduct to some principle which had not been hitherto disclosed, but which was reconcilable with those already known.

"I was not suffered to remain long in this suspense. One evening, you may recollect, I came to your house, where it was my purpose, as usual, to lodge, somewhat earlier than ordinary. I spied a light in your chamber as I approached from the outside, and, on inquiring of Judith, was informed that you were writing. As your kinsman and friend and fellow-lodger, I thought I had a right to be familiar. You were in your chamber; but your employment and the time were such as to make it no infraction of decorum to follow you thither. The spirit of mischievous gayety possessed me. I proceeded on tiptoe. You did not perceive my entrance; and I advanced softly till I was able to overlook your shoulder.

"I had gone thus far in error, and had no power to recede. How cautiously should we guard against the first inroads of temptation! I knew that to pry into your papers was criminal; but I reflected that no sentiment of yours was of a nature which made it your interest to conceal it. You wrote much more than you permitted your friends to peruse. My curiosity was strong, and I had only to throw a glance upon the paper to secure its gratification. I should never have deliberately committed an act like this. The slightest obstacle would have repelled me; but my eye glanced almost spontaneously upon the paper. I caught only parts of sentences; but my eyes comprehended more at a glance, because the characters were short-hand. I lighted on the words *summer-house, midnight,* and made out a passage which spoke of the propriety and of the effects to be expected from *another* interview. All this passed in less than a moment. I then checked myself, and made myself known to you by a tap upon your shoulder.

"I could pardon and account for some trifling alarm; but your trepidation and blushes were excessive. You hurried the paper out of sight, and seemed too anxious to discover whether I knew the contents to allow yourself to make any inquiries. I wondered at these appearances of consternation, but did not reason on them until I had retired. When alone, these incidents suggested themselves to my reflections anew.

"To what scene, or what interview, I asked, did you allude? Your disappearance on a former evening, my tracing you to the recess in the bank, your silence on my first and second call, your vague answers and invincible embarrassment when you at length ascended the hill, I recollected with new surprise. Could this be the summer-house alluded to? A certain timidity and consciousness had generally attended you, when this incident and this recess had been the subjects of conversation. Nay, I imagined that the last time that adventure was mentioned, which happened in the presence of Carwin, the countenance of the latter betrayed some emotion. Could the interview have been with him?

"This was an idea calculated to rouse every faculty to contemplation. An interview at that hour, in this darksome retreat, with a man of his mysterious but formidable character!—a clandestine interview, and one which you afterwards endeavoured with so much solicitude to conceal! It was a fearful and portentous occurrence. I could not measure his power or fathom his designs. Had he rifled from you the secret of your love, and reconciled you to concealment and nocturnal meetings? I scarcely ever spent a night of more inquietude.

"I knew not how to act. The ascertainment of this man's character and views seemed to be, in the first place, necessary. Had he openly preferred his suit to you, we should have been empowered to make direct inquiries; but, since he had chosen this obscure path, it seemed reasonable to infer that his character was exceptionable. It at least subjected us to the necessity of resorting to other means of information. Yet the improbability that you should commit a deed of such rashness made me reflect anew upon the insufficiency of those grounds on which my suspicions had been built, and almost to condemn myself for harbouring them.

"Though it was mere conjecture that the interview spoken of had taken place with Carwin, yet two ideas occurred to involve me in the most painful doubts. This man's reasonings might be so specious, and his artifices so profound, that, aided by the passion which you had conceived for him, he had finally succeeded; or his situation might be such as to justify the secrecy which you maintained. In neither case did my wildest reveries suggest to me that your honour had been forfeited.

"I could not talk with you on this subject. If the imputation was false, its atrociousness would have justly drawn upon me your resentment, and I must have explained by what facts it had been suggested. If it were true, no benefit would follow from the mention of it. You had chosen to conceal it for some reasons; and, whether these reasons were true or false, it was proper to discover and remove them in the first place. Finally, I acquiesced in the least painful supposition, trammelled as it was with perplexities,—that Carwin was upright, and that, if the reasons of your silence were known, they would be found to be just.

CHAPTER XIV

"Three days have elapsed since this occurrence. I have been haunted by perpetual inquietude. To bring myself to regard Carwin without terror, and to acquiesce in the belief of your safety, was impossible. Yet to put an end to my doubts seemed to be impracticable. If some light could be reflected on the actual situation of this man, a direct path would present itself. If he were, contrary to the tenor of his conversation, cunning and malignant, to apprize you of this would be to place you in security. If he were merely unfortunate and inno-

cent, most readily would I espouse his cause; and if
his intentions were upright with regard to you, most
eagerly would I sanctify your choice by my approbation.

"It would be vain to call upon Carwin for an avowal
of his deeds. It was better to know nothing, than to be
deceived by an artful tale. What he was unwilling to
communicate (and this unwillingness had been repeatedly manifested) could never be extorted from him.
Importunity might be appeased or imposture effected
by fallacious representations. To the rest of the world
he was unknown. I had often made him the subject
of discourse; but a glimpse of his figure in the street
was the sum of their knowledge who knew most. None
had ever seen him before, and all received as new the
information which my intercourse with him in Valencia, and my present intercourse, enabled me to give.

"Wieland was your brother. If he had really made
you the object of his courtship, was not a brother authorized to interfere and demand from him the confession of his views? Yet what were the grounds on which
I had reared this supposition? Would they justify a
measure like this? Surely not.

"In the course of my restless meditations, it occurred
to me at length that my duty required me to speak to
you, to confess the indecorum of which I had been
guilty, and to state the reflections to which it had led
me. I was prompted by no mean or selfish views. The
heart within my breast was not more precious than
your safety: most cheerfully would I have interposed
my life between you and danger. Would you cherish
resentment at my conduct? When acquainted with the
motive which produced it, it would not only exempt
me from censure, but entitle me to gratitude.

"Yesterday had been selected for the rehearsal of the
newly-imported tragedy. I promised to be present. The

state of my thoughts but little qualified me for a performer or auditor in such a scene; but I reflected that
after it was finished I should return home with you,
and should then enjoy an opportunity of discoursing
with you fully on this topic. My resolution was not
formed without a remnant of doubt as to its propriety.
When I left this house to perform the visit I had promised, my mind was full of apprehension and despondency. The dubiousness of the event of our conversation, fear that my interference was too late to secure
your peace, and the uncertainty to which hope gave
birth, whether I had not erred in believing you devoted to this man, or, at least, in imagining that he had
obtained your consent to midnight conferences, distracted me with contradictory opinions and repugnant
emotions.

"I can assign no reason for calling at Mrs. Baynton's.
I had seen her in the morning, and knew her to be well.
The concerted hour had nearly arrived, and yet I
turned up the street which leads to her house and dis-
mounted at her door. I entered the parlour and threw
myself in a chair. I saw and inquired for no one. My
whole frame was overpowered by dreary and comfort-
less sensations. One idea possessed me wholly: the inexpressible importance of unveiling the designs and
character of Carwin, and the utter improbability that
this ever would be effected. Some instinct induced me
to lay my hand upon a newspaper. I had perused all
the general intelligence it contained in the morning,
and at the same spot. The act was rather mechanical
than voluntary.

"I threw a languid glance at the first column that presented itself. The first words which I read began with
the offer of a reward of three hundred guineas for the
apprehension of a convict under sentence of death,
who had escaped from Newgate prison in Dublin.

Good heaven! how every fibre of my frame tingled when I proceeded to read that the name of the criminal was Francis Carwin!

"The descriptions of his person and address were minute. His stature, hair, complexion, the extraordinary position and arrangement of his features, his awkward and disproportionate form, his gesture and gait, corresponded perfectly with those of our mysterious visitant. He had been found guilty in two indictments, —one for the murder of the Lady Jane Conway, and the other for a robbery committed on the person of the Honourable Mr. Ludloe.

"I repeatedly perused this passage. The ideas which flowed in upon my mind affected me like an instant transition from death to life. The purpose dearest to my heart was thus effected, at a time and by means the least of all others within the scope of my foresight. But what purpose? Carwin was detected. Acts of the blackest and most sordid guilt had been committed by him. Here was evidence which imparted to my understanding the most luminous certainty. The name, visage, and deportment were the same. Between the time of his escape and his appearance among us there was a sufficient agreement. Such was the man with whom I suspected you to maintain a clandestine correspondence. Should I not haste to snatch you from the talons of this vulture? Should I see you rushing to the verge of a dizzy precipice, and not stretch forth a hand to pull you back? I had no need to deliberate. I thrust the paper in my pocket, and resolved to obtain an immediate conference with you. For a time, no other image made its way to my understanding. At length it occurred to me, that though the information I possessed was, in one sense, sufficient, yet, if more could be obtained, more was desirable. This passage was copied from a British paper; part of it only, perhaps, was transcribed. The printer was in possession of the original.

"Towards his house I immediately turned my horse's head. He produced the paper, but I found nothing more than had already been seen. While busy in perusing it, the printer stood by my side. He noticed the object of which I was in search. 'Ay,' said he, 'that is a strange affair. I should never have met with it had not Mr. Hallet sent to me the paper, with a particular request to republish that advertisement.'

"Mr. Hallet! What reasons could he have for making this request? Had the paper sent to him been accompanied by any information respecting the convict? Had he personal or extraordinary reasons for desiring its republication? This was to be known only in one way. I speeded to his house. In answer to my interrogations, he told me that Ludloe had formerly been in America, and that during his residence in this city considerable intercourse had taken place between them. Hence a confidence arose, which has since been kept alive by occasional letters. He had lately received a letter from him, enclosing the newspaper from which this extract had been made. He put it into my hands, and pointed out the passages which related to Carwin.

"Ludloe confirms the facts of his conviction and escape; and adds that he had reason to believe him to have embarked for America. He describes him in general terms, as the most incomprehensible and formidable among men; as engaged in schemes reasonably suspected to be in the highest degree criminal, but such as no human intelligence is able to unravel; that his ends are pursued by means which leave it in doubt whether he be not in league with some infernal spirit; that his crimes have hitherto been perpetrated with the aid of some unknown but desperate accomplices; that he wages a perpetual war against the happiness of

mankind, and sets his engines of destruction at work
against every object that presents itself.

"This is the substance of the letter. Hallet expressed
some surprise at the curiosity which was manifested by
me on this occasion. I was too much absorbed by the
ideas suggested by this letter to pay attention to his remarks. I shuddered with the apprehension of the evil
to which our indiscreet familiarity with this man had
probably exposed us. I burned with impatience to see
you, and to do what in me lay to avert the calamity
which threatened us. It was already five o'clock. Night
was hastening, and there was no time to be lost. On
leaving Mr. Hallet's house, who should meet me in the
street but Bertrand, the servant whom I left in Germany? His appearance and accoutrements bespoke
him to have just alighted from a toilsome and long
journey. I was not wholly without expectation of seeing
him about this time, but no one was then more distant
from my thoughts. You know what reasons I have for
anxiety respecting scenes with which this man was
conversant. Carwin was for a moment forgotten. In answer to my vehement inquiries, Bertrand produced a
copious packet. I shall not at present mention its contents, nor the measures which they obliged me to
adopt. I bestowed a brief perusal on these papers, and,
having given some directions to Bertrand, resumed my
purpose with regard to you. My horse I was obliged to
resign to my servant, he being charged with a commission that required speed. The clock had struck ten, and
Mettingen was five miles distant. I was to journey
thither on foot. These circumstances only added to my
expedition.

"As I passed swiftly along, I reviewed all the incidents accompanying the appearance and deportment
of that man among us. Late events have been inexplicable and mysterious beyond any of which I have

either read or heard. These events were coeval with Carwin's introduction. I am unable to explain their origin and mutual dependence; but I do not, on that account, believe them to have a supernatural original. Is not this man the agent? Some of them seem to be propitious; but what should I think of those threats of assassination with which you were lately alarmed? Bloodshed is the trade and horror is the element of this man. The process by which the sympathies of nature are extinguished in our hearts, by which evil is made our good, and by which we are made susceptible of no activity but in the infliction and no joy but in the spectacle of woes, is an obvious process. As to alliance with evil genii, the power and the malice of demons have been a thousand times exemplified in human beings. There are no devils but those which are begotten upon selfishness and reared by cunning.

"Now, indeed, the scene was changed. It was not his secret poniard that I dreaded. It was only the success of his efforts to make you a confederate in your own destruction, to make your will the instrument by which he might bereave you of liberty and honour.

"I took, as usual, the path through your brother's ground. I ranged with celerity and silence along the bank. I approached the fence which divides Wieland's estate from yours. The recess in the bank being near this line, it being necessary for me to pass near it, my mind being tainted with inveterate suspicions concerning you, suspicions which were indebted for their strength to incidents connected with this spot, what wonder that it seized upon my thoughts?

"I leaped on the fence; but before I descended on the opposite side I paused to survey the scene. Leaves dropping with dew and glistening in the moon's rays, with no moving object to molest the deep repose, filled me with security and hope. I left the station at length, and tended forward. You were probably at rest. How should I communicate, without alarming you, the intelligence of my arrival? An immediate interview was to be procured. I could not bear to think that a minute should be lost by remissness or hesitation. Should I knock at the door? or should I stand under your chamber windows, which I perceived to be open, and awaken you by my calls?

"These reflections employed me as I passed opposite to the summer-house. I had scarcely gone by, when my ear caught a sound unusual at this time and place. It was almost too faint and too transient to allow me a distinct perception of it. I stopped to listen; presently it was heard again, and now it was somewhat in a louder key. It was laughter; and unquestionably produced by a female voice. That voice was familiar to my senses. It was yours.

"Whence it came I was at first at a loss to conjecture; but this uncertainty vanished when it was heard the third time. I threw back my eyes towards the recess. Every other organ and limb was useless to me. I did not reason on the subject. I did not, in a direct manner, draw my conclusions from the hour, the place, the hilarity which this sound betokened, and the circumstance of having a companion, which it no less incontestably proved. In an instant, as it were, my heart was invaded with cold, and the pulses of life at a stand.

"Why should I go farther? Why should I return? Should I not hurry to a distance from a sound which, though formerly so sweet and delectable, was now more hideous than the shrieks of owls?

"I had no time to yield to this impulse. The thought of approaching and listening occurred to me. I had no doubt of which I was conscious. Yet my certainty was capable of increase. I was likewise stimulated by a sentiment that partook of rage. I was governed by a half-formed and tempestuous resolution to break in upon your interview and strike you dead with my upbraiding.

"I approached with the utmost caution. When I reached the edge of the bank immediately above the summer-house, I thought I heard voices from below, as busy in conversation. The steps in the rock are clear of bushy impediments. They allowed me to descend into a cavity beside the building without being detected. Thus to lie in wait could only be justified by the momentousness of the occasion."

Here Pleyel paused in his narrative and fixed his eyes upon me. Situated as I was, my horror and astonishment at this tale gave way to compassion for the anguish which the countenance of my friend betrayed. I reflected on his force of understanding. I reflected on the powers of my enemy. I could easily divine the substance of the conversation that was overheard. Carwin had constructed his plot in a manner suited to the characters of those whom he had selected for his victims. I saw that the convictions of Pleyel were immutable. I forbore to struggle against the storm, because I saw that all struggles would be fruitless. I was calm; but my calmness was the torpor of despair, and not the tranquillity of fortitude. It was calmness invincible by any thing that his grief and his fury could suggest to Pleyel. He resumed:—

"Woman! wilt thou hear me further? Shall I go on to repeat the conversation? Is it shame that makes thee tongue-tied? Shall I go on? or art thou satisfied with what has been already said?"

I bowed my head. "Go on," said I. "I make not this request in the hope of undeceiving you. I shall no longer contend with my own weakness. The storm is let loose, and I shall peaceably submit to be driven by its fury. But go on. This conference will end only with affording me a clearer foresight of my destiny; but that will be some satisfaction, and I will not part without it."

Why, on hearing these words, did Pleyel hesitate? Did some unlooked-for doubt insinuate itself into his mind? Was his belief suddenly shaken by my looks, or my words, or by some newly-recollected circumstance? Whencesoever it arose, it could not endure the test of deliberation. In a few minutes the flame of resentment was again lighted up in his bosom. He proceeded with his accustomed vehemence:—

"I hate myself for this folly. I can find no apology for this tale. Yet I am irresistibly impelled to relate it. She that hears me is apprized of every particular. I have only to repeat to her her own words. She will listen with a tranquil air, and the spectacle of her obduracy will drive me to some desperate act. Why then should I persist? yet persist I must."

Again he paused. "No!" said he; "it is impossible to repeat your avowals of love, your appeals to former confessions of your tenderness, to former deeds of dishonour, to the circumstances of the first interview that took place between you. It was on that night when I traced you to this recess. Thither had he enticed you, and there had you ratified an unhallowed compact by admitting him——

"Great God! thou witnessedst the agonies that tore my bosom at that moment! thou witnessedst my efforts to repel the testimony of my ears! It was in vain that you dwelt upon the confusion which my unlooked-for summons excited in you; the tardiness with which a suitable excuse occurred to you; your resentment that my impertinent intrusion had put an end to that charming interview; a disappointment for which you endeavoured to compensate yourself by the frequency and duration of subsequent meetings.

"In vain you dwelt upon incidents of which you only could be conscious; incidents that occurred on occasions on which none besides your own family were witnesses. In vain was your discourse characterized by peculiarities inimitable of sentiment and language. My conviction was effected only by an accumulation of the same tokens. I yielded not but to evidence which took away the power to withhold my faith.

"My sight was of no use to me. Beneath so thick an umbrage the darkness was intense. Hearing was the only avenue to information which the circumstances allowed to be open. I was couched within three feet of you. Why should I approach nearer? I could not contend with your betrayer. What could be the purpose of a contest? You stood in no need of a protector. What could I do but retire from the spot overwhelmed with confusion and dismay? I sought my chamber, and endeavoured to regain my composure. The door of the house, which I found open, your subsequent entrance, closing, and fastening it, and going into your chamber, which had been thus long deserted, were only confirmations of the truth.

"Why should I paint the tempestuous fluctuation of my thoughts between grief and revenge, between rage and despair? Why should I repeat my vows of eternal implacability and persecution, and the speedy recantation of these vows?

"I have said enough. You have dismissed me from a place in your esteem. What I think and what I feel is of no importance in your eyes. May the duty which I owe myself enable me to forget your existence! In a few minutes I go hence. Be the maker of your fortune; and may adversity instruct you in that wisdom which education was unable to impart to you!"

Those were the last words which Pleyel uttered. He left the room, and my new emotions enabled me to wit-

ness his departure without any apparent loss of composure. As I sat alone, I ruminated on these incidents.
Nothing was more evident than that I had taken an
eternal leave of happiness. Life was a worthless thing,
separate from that good which had now been wrested
from me; yet the sentiment that now possessed me had
no tendency to palsy my exertions and overbear my
strength. I noticed that the light was declining, and
perceived the propriety of leaving this house. I placed
myself again in the chaise, and returned slowly towards the city.

CHAPTER XV

Before I reached the city it was dusk. It was my purpose to spend the night at Mettingen. I was not solicit-
ous, as long as I was attended by a faithful servant, to
be there at an early hour. My exhausted strength required me to take some refreshment. With this view,
and in order to pay respect to one whose affection for
me was truly maternal, I stopped at Mrs. Baynton's.
She was absent from home; but I had scarcely entered
the house, when one of her domestics presented me a
letter. I opened, and read as follows:—

To Clara Wieland.

What shall I say to extenuate the misconduct of
last night? It is my duty to repair it to the utmost
of my power; but the only way in which it can be
repaired you will not, I fear, be prevailed on to
adopt. It is by granting me an interview, at your
own house, at eleven o'clock this night. I have no

means of removing any fears that you may entertain of my designs, but my simple and solemn declarations. These, after what has passed between us,
you may deem unworthy of confidence. I cannot
help it. My folly and rashness have left me no other
resource. I will be at your door by that hour. If
you choose to admit me to a conference, provided
that conference has no witnesses, I will disclose to
you particulars the knowledge of which is of the
utmost importance to your happiness. Farewell.

CARWIN.

What a letter was this! A man known to be an assassin and robber, one capable of plotting against my life
and my fame, detected lurking in my chamber and
avowing designs the most flagitious and dreadful, now
solicits me to grant him a midnight interview!—to admit him alone into my presence! Could he make this request with the expectation of my compliance? What
had he seen in me that could justify him in admitting
so wild a belief? Yet this request is preferred with the
utmost gravity. It is not accompanied by an appearance of uncommon earnestness. Had the misconduct to
which he alludes been a slight incivility, and the interview requested to take place in the midst of my friends,
there would have been no extravagance in the tenor
of this letter; but, as it was, the writer had surely been
bereft of his reason.

I perused this epistle frequently. The request it contained might be called audacious or stupid, if it had
been made by a different person; but from Carwin,
who could not be unaware of the effect which it must
naturally produce, and of the manner in which it would
unavoidably be treated, it was perfectly inexplicable.
He must have counted on the success of some plot, in
order to extort my assent. None of those motives by

which I am usually governed would ever have persuaded me to meet any one of his sex at the time and place which he had prescribed. Much less would I consent to a meeting with a man tainted with the most detestable crimes, and by whose arts my own safety had been so imminently endangered and my happiness irretrievably destroyed. I shuddered at the idea that such a meeting was possible. I felt some reluctance to approach a spot which he still visited and haunted.

Such were the ideas which first suggested themselves on the perusal of the letter. Meanwhile, I resumed my journey. My thoughts still dwelt upon the same topic. Gradually, from ruminating on this epistle, I reverted to my interview with Pleyel. I recalled the particulars of the dialogue to which he had been an auditor. My heart sunk anew on viewing the inextricable complexity of this deception, and the inauspicious concurrence of events which tended to confirm him in his error. When he approached my chamber door, my terror kept me mute. He put his ear, perhaps, to the crevice, but it caught the sound of nothing human. Had I called, or made any token that denoted some one to be within, words would have ensued; and, as omnipresence was impossible, this discovery, and the artless narrative of what had just passed, would have saved me from his murderous invectives. He went into his chamber, and, after some interval, I stole across the entry and down the stairs with inaudible steps. Having secured the outer doors, I returned with less circumspection. He heard me not when I descended; but my returning steps were easily distinguished. Now, he thought, was the guilty interview at an end. In what other way was it possible for him to construe these signals?

How fallacious and precipitate was my decision! Carwin's plot owed its success to a coincidence of

events scarcely credible. The balance was swayed from
its equipoise by a hair. Had I even begun the conversation with an account of what befell me in my chamber, my previous interview with Wieland would have
taught him to suspect me of imposture; yet, if I were
discoursing with this ruffian when Pleyel touched the
lock of my chamber door, and when he shut his own
door with so much violence, how, he might ask, should
I be able to relate these incidents? Perhaps he had
withheld the knowledge of these circumstances from
my brother, from whom, therefore, I could not obtain
it, so that my innocence would have thus been irresistibly demonstrated.

The first impulse which flowed from these ideas was
to return upon my steps and demand once more an
interview. But he was gone; his parting declarations
were remembered.

"Pleyel," I exclaimed, "thou art gone forever! Are thy
mistakes beyond the reach of detection? Am I helpless
in the midst of this snare? The plotter is at hand. He
even speaks in the style of penitence. He solicits an
interview which he promises shall end in the disclosure
of something momentous to my happiness. What can
he say which will avail to turn aside this evil? But why
should his remorse be feigned? I have done him no injury. His wickedness is fertile only of despair; and the
billows of remorse will some time overbear him. Why
may not this event have already taken place? Why
should I refuse to see him?"

This idea was present, as it were, for a moment. I
suddenly recoiled from it, confounded at that frenzy
which could give even momentary harbour to such a
scheme; yet presently it returned. At length I even conceived it to deserve deliberation. I questioned whether
it was not proper to admit, at a lonely spot, in a sacred
hour, this man of tremendous and inscrutable attri-

butes, this performer of horrid deeds, and whose presence was predicted to call down unheard-of and unutterable horrors.

What was it that swayed me? I felt myself divested of the power to will contrary to the motives that determined me to seek his presence. My mind seemed to be split into separate parts, and these parts to have entered into furious and implacable contention. These tumults gradually subsided. The reasons why I should confide in that interposition which had hitherto defended me, in those tokens of compunction which this letter contained, in the efficacy of this interview to restore its spotlessness to my character and banish all illusions from the mind of my friend, continually acquired new evidence and new strength.

What should I fear in his presence? This was unlike an artifice intended to betray me into his hands. If it were an artifice, what purpose would it serve? The freedom of my mind was untouched, and that freedom would defy the assaults of blandishments or magic. Force I was not able to repel. On the former occasion my courage, it is true, had failed at the imminent approach of danger; but then I had not enjoyed opportunities of deliberation; I had foreseen nothing; I was sunk into imbecility by my previous thoughts; I had been the victim of recent disappointments and anticipated ills. Witness my infatuation in opening the closet in opposition to divine injunctions.

Now, perhaps, my courage was the offspring of a no less erring principle. Pleyel was forever lost to me. I strove in vain to assume his person and suppress my resentment; I strove in vain to believe in the assuaging influence of time, to look forward to the birthday of new hopes, and the re-exaltation of that luminary of whose effulgencies I had so long and so liberally partaken.

What had I to suffer worse than was already inflicted?

Was not Carwin my foe? I owed my untimely fate to his treason. Instead of flying from his presence, ought I not to devote all my faculties to the gaining of an interview, and compel him to repair the ills of which he has been the author? Why should I suppose him impregnable to argument? Have I not reason on my side, and the power of imparting conviction? Cannot he be made to see the justice of unravelling the maze in which Pleyel is bewildered?

He may, at least, be accessible to fear. Has he nothing to fear from the rage of an injured woman? But suppose him inaccessible to such inducements; suppose him to persist in all his flagitious purposes: are not the means of defence and resistance in my power?

In the progress of such thoughts was the resolution at last formed. I hoped that the interview was sought by him for a laudable end; but, be that as it would, I trusted that, by energy of reasoning or of action, I should render it auspicious, or at least harmless.

Such a determination must unavoidably fluctuate. The poet's chaos was no unapt emblem of the state of my mind. A torment was awakened in my bosom, which I foresaw would end only when this interview was past and its consequences fully experienced. Hence my impatience for the arrival of the hour which had been prescribed by Carwin.

Meanwhile, my meditations were tumultuously active. New impediments to the execution of the scheme were speedily suggested. I had apprized Catharine of my intention to spend this and many future nights with her. Her husband was informed of this arrangement, and had zealously approved it. Eleven o'clock exceeded their hour of retiring. What excuse should I form for changing my plan? Should I show this letter

to Wieland and submit myself to his direction? But I
knew in what way he would decide. He would fer-
vently dissuade me from going. Nay, would he not do
more? He was apprized of the offences of Carwin, and
of the reward offered for his apprehension. Would he
not seize this opportunity of executing justice on a
criminal?

This idea was new. I was plunged once more into
doubt. Did not equity enjoin me thus to facilitate his
arrest? No. I disdained the office of betrayer. Carwin
was unapprized of his danger, and his intentions were
possibly beneficent. Should I station guards about the
house, and make an act intended perhaps for my benefit instrumental to his own destruction? Wieland might
be justified in thus employing the knowledge which I
should impart; but I, by imparting it, should pollute
myself with more hateful crimes than those unde-
servedly imputed to me. This scheme, therefore, I unhesitatingly rejected. The views with which I should
return to my own house it would therefore be necessary to conceal. Yet some pretext must be invented. I
had never been initiated into the trade of lying. Yet
what but falsehood was a deliberate suppression of the
truth? To deceive by silence or by words is the same.

Yet what would a lie avail me? What pretext would
justify this change in my plan? Would it not tend to
confirm the imputations of Pleyel? That I should voluntarily return to a house in which honour and life had so
lately been endangered could be explained in no way
favourable to my integrity.

These reflections, if they did not change, at least suspended, my decision. In this state of uncertainty I
alighted at the *hut*. We gave this name to the house
tenanted by the farmer and his servants, and which
was situated on the verge of my brother's ground, and
at a considerable distance from the mansion. The path

to the mansion was planted by a double row of walnuts. Along this path I proceeded alone. I entered the parlour, in which was a light just expiring in the socket. There was no one in the room. I perceived by the clock that stood against the wall that it was near eleven. The lateness of the hour startled me. What had become of the family? They were usually retired an hour before this; but the unextinguished taper and the unbarred door were indications that they had not retired. I again returned to the hall, and passed from one room to another, but still encountered not a human being.

I imagined that perhaps the lapse of a few minutes would explain these appearances. Meanwhile, I reflected that the preconcerted hour had arrived. Carwin was perhaps waiting my approach. Should I immediately retire to my own house, no one would be apprized of my proceeding. Nay, the interview might pass, and I be enabled to return in half an hour. Hence no necessity would arise for dissimulation.

I was so far influenced by these views that I rose to execute this design; but again the unusual condition of the house occurred to me, and some vague solicitude as to the condition of the family. I was nearly certain that my brother had not retired; but by what motives he could be induced to desert his house thus unseasonably I could by no means divine. Louisa Conway, at least, was at home, and had probably retired to her chamber: perhaps she was able to impart the information I wanted.

I went to her chamber, and found her asleep. She was delighted and surprised at my arrival, and told me with how much impatience and anxiety my brother and his wife had awaited my coming. They were fearful that some mishap had befallen me, and had remained up longer than the usual period. Notwithstanding the lateness of the hour, Catharine would not resign the hope of seeing me. Louisa said she had left them both in the parlour, and she knew of no cause for their absence.

As yet I was not without solicitude on account of their personal safety. I was far from being perfectly at ease on that head, but entertained no distinct conception of the danger that impended over them. Perhaps, to beguile the moments of my long-protracted stay, they had gone to walk upon the bank. The atmosphere, though illuminated only by the starlight, was remarkably serene. Meanwhile, the desirableness of an interview with Carwin again returned, and I finally resolved to seek it.

I passed with doubting and hasty steps along the path. My dwelling, seen at a distance, was gloomy and desolate. It had no inhabitant; for my servant, in consequence of my new arrangement, had gone to Mettingen. The temerity of this attempt began to show itself in more vivid colours to my understanding. Whoever has pointed steel is not without arms; yet what must have been the state of my mind when I could meditate, without shuddering, on the use of a murderous weapon, and believe myself secure merely because I was capable of being made so by the death of another! Yet this was not my state. I felt as if I was rushing into deadly toils without the power of pausing or receding.

CHAPTER XVI

As soon as I arrived in sight of the front of the house, my attention was excited by a light from the window of my own chamber. No appearance could be less explicable. A meeting was expected with Carwin; but that he preoccupied my chamber, and had supplied himself with light, was not to be believed. What motive could influence him to adopt this conduct? Could I proceed until this was explained? Perhaps, if I should proceed to a distance in front, some one would be visible. A sidelong but feeble beam from the window fell upon the piny copse which skirted the bank. As I eyed it, it suddenly became mutable, and, after flitting to and fro for a short time, it vanished. I turned my eye again towards the window, and perceived that the light was still there; but the change which I had noticed was occasioned by a change in the position of the lamp or candle within. Hence, that some person was there was an unavoidable inference.

I paused to deliberate on the propriety of advancing. Might I not advance cautiously, and, therefore, without danger? Might I not knock at the door, or call, and be apprized of the nature of my visitant before I entered? I approached and listened at the door, but could hear nothing. I knocked at first timidly, but afterwards with loudness. My signals were unnoticed. I stepped back and looked, but the light was no longer discernible. Was it suddenly extinguished by a human agent? What purpose but concealment was intended? Why was the illumination produced, to be thus suddenly brought to an end? And why, since some one was there, had silence been observed?

These were questions the solution of which may be readily supposed to be entangled with danger. Would not this danger, when measured by a woman's fears, expand into gigantic dimensions? Menaces of death; the stunning exertions of a warning voice; the known and unknown attributes of Carwin; our recent interview in this chamber; the preappointment of a meeting at this place and hour,—all thronged into my memory. What was to be done?

Courage is no definite or steadfast principle. Let that man who shall purpose to assign motives to the actions of another blush at his folly and forbear. Not more presumptuous would it be to attempt the classification of all nature and the scanning of Supreme intelligence. I gazed for a minute at the window, and fixed my eyes, for a second minute, on the ground. I drew forth from my pocket, and opened, a penknife. "This," said I, "be my safeguard and avenger. The assailant shall perish, or myself shall fall."

I had locked up the house in the morning, but had the key of the kitchen door in my pocket. I therefore determined to gain access behind. Thither I hastened, unlocked, and entered. All was lonely, darksome, and waste. Familiar as I was with every part of my dwelling, I easily found my way to a closet, drew forth a taper, a flint, tinder, and steel, and in a moment, as it were, gave myself the guidance and protection of light.

What purpose did I meditate? Should I explore my way to my chamber, and confront the being who had dared to intrude into this recess and had laboured for concealment? By putting out the light did he seek to hide himself, or mean only to circumvent my incautious steps? Yet was it not more probable that he desired my absence by thus encouraging the supposition that the house was unoccupied? I would see this man in spite of all impediments; ere I died, I would see his face, and summon him to penitence and retribution; no matter at what cost an interview was purchased. Reputation and life might be wrested from me by another, but my rectitude and honour were in my own keeping, and were safe.

I proceeded to the foot of the stairs. At such a crisis my thoughts may be supposed at no liberty to range; yet vague images rushed into my mind of the mysterious interposition which had been experienced on the last night. My case at present was not dissimilar; and, if my angel were not weary of fruitless exertions to save, might not a new warning be expected? Who could say whether his silence were ascribable to the absence of danger, or to his own absence?

In this state of mind, no wonder that a shivering cold crept through my veins; that my pause was prolonged; and that a fearful glance was thrown backward.

Alas! my heart droops, and my fingers are enervated; my ideas are vivid, but my language is faint: now know I what it is to entertain incommunicable sentiments. The chain of subsequent incidents is drawn through my mind, and, being linked with those which forewent, by turns rouse up agonies and sink me into hopelessness.

Yet I will persist to the end. My narrative may be invaded by inaccuracy and confusion; but, if I live no longer, I will, at least, live to complete it. What but ambiguities, abruptnesses, and dark transitions, can be expected from the historian who is, at the same time, the sufferer of these disasters?

I have said that I cast a look behind. Some object was expected to be seen, or why should I have gazed in that direction? Two senses were at once assailed. The same piercing exclamation of *"Hold! hold!"* was uttered within the same distance of my ear. This it was that I heard. The airy undulation, and the shock given to my nerves, were real. Whether the spectacle which I beheld existed in my fancy or without might be doubted.

I had not closed the door of the apartment I had just

left. The staircase, at the foot of which I stood, was eight or ten feet from the door, and attached to the wall through which the door led. My view, therefore, was sidelong, and took in no part of the room.

Through this aperture was a head thrust and drawn back with so much swiftness that the immediate conviction was, that thus much of a form ordinarily invisible had been unshrouded. The face was turned towards me. Every muscle was tense; the forehead and brows were drawn into vehement expression; the lips were stretched as in the act of shrieking, and the eyes emitted sparks, which, no doubt, if I had been unattended by a light, would have illuminated like the coruscations of a meteor. The sound and the vision were present, and departed together at the same instant; but the cry was blown into my ear, while the face was many paces distant.

This face was well suited to a being whose performances exceeded the standard of humanity; and yet its features were akin to those I had before seen. The image of Carwin was blended in a thousand ways with the stream of my thoughts. This visage was, perhaps, portrayed by my fancy. If so, it will excite no surprise that some of his lineaments were now discovered. Yet affinities were few and unconspicuous, and were lost amidst the blaze of opposite qualities.

What conclusion could I form? Be the face human or not, the intimation was imparted from above. Experience had evinced the benignity of that being who gave it. Once he had interposed to shield me from harm, and subsequent events demonstrated the usefulness of that interposition. Now was I again warned to forbear. I was hurrying to the verge of the same gulf, and the same power was exerted to recall my steps. Was it possible for me not to obey? Was I capable of holding on in the same perilous career? Yes. Even of this I was capable!

The intimation was imperfect; it gave no form to my danger and prescribed no limits to my caution. I had formerly neglected it, and yet escaped. Might I not trust to the same issue? This idea might possess, though imperceptibly, some influence. I persisted; but it was not merely on this account. I cannot delineate the motives that led me on. I now speak as if no remnant of doubt existed in my mind as to the supernatural origin of these sounds; but this is owing to the imperfection of my language, for I only mean that the belief was more permanent and visited more frequently my sober meditations than its opposite. The immediate effects served only to undermine the foundations of my judgment and precipitate my resolutions.

I must either advance or return. I chose the former, and began to ascend the stairs. The silence underwent no second interruption. My chamber door was closed, but unlocked, and, aided by vehement efforts of my courage, I opened and looked in.

No hideous or uncommon object was discernible. The danger, indeed, might easily have lurked out of sight, have sprung upon me as I entered, and have rent me with his iron talons; but I was blind to this fate, and advanced, though cautiously, into the room.

Still, every thing wore its accustomed aspect. Neither lamp nor candle was to be found. Now, for the first time, suspicions were suggested as to the nature of the light which I had seen. Was it possible to have been the companion of that supernatural visage; a meteorous refulgence producible at the will of him to whom that visage belonged, and partaking of the nature of that which accompanied my father's death?

The closet was near, and I remembered the compli-

cated horrors of which it had been productive. Here,
perhaps, was enclosed the source of my peril and the
gratification of my curiosity. Should I adventure once
more to explore its recesses? This was a resolution not
easily formed. I was suspended in thought, when,
glancing my eye on a table, I perceived a written paper. Carwin's hand was instantly recognised, and,
snatching up the paper, I read as follows:—

"There was folly in expecting your compliance with
my invitation. Judge how I was disappointed in finding another in your place. I have waited, but to wait
any longer would be perilous. I shall still seek an interview, but it must be at a different time and place;
meanwhile, I will write this—How will you bear—how
inexplicable will be this transaction!—An event so unexpected,—a sight so horrible!"

Such was this abrupt and unsatisfactory script. The
ink was yet moist; the hand was that of Carwin. Hence
it was to be inferred that he had this moment left the
apartment, or was still in it. I looked back, on the sudden expectation of seeing him behind me.

What other did he mean? What transaction had
taken place adverse to my expectations? What sight
was about to be exhibited? I looked around me once
more, but saw nothing which indicated strangeness.
Again I remembered the closet, and was resolved to
seek in that the solution of these mysteries. Here, perhaps, was enclosed the scene destined to awaken my
horrors and baffle my foresight.

I have already said that the entrance into this closet
was beside my bed, which, on two sides, was closely
shrouded by curtains. On that side nearest the closet
the curtain was raised. As I passed along I cast my eye
thither. I started, and looked again. I bore a light in
my hand, and brought it nearer my eyes, in order to
dispel any illusive mists that might have hovered be-

fore them. Once more I fixed my eyes upon the bed, in hope that this more steadfast scrutiny would annihilate the object which before seemed to be there.

This, then, was the sight which Carwin had predicted! This was the event which my understanding was to find inexplicable! This was the fate which had been reserved for me, but which, by some untoward chance, had befallen another!

I had not been terrified by empty menaces. Violation and death awaited my entrance into this chamber. Some inscrutable chance had led *her* hither before me, and the merciless fangs of which I was designed to be the prey had mistaken their victim, and had fixed themselves in *her* heart. But where was my safety? Was the mischief exhausted or flown? The steps of the assassin had just been here; they could not be far off; in a moment he would rush into my presence, and I should perish under the same polluting and suffocating grasp!

My frame shook, and my knees were unable to support me. I gazed alternately at the closet door and at the door of my room. At one of these avenues would enter the exterminator of my honour and my life. I was prepared for defence; but, now that danger was imminent, my means of defence and my power to use them were gone. I was not qualified by education and experience to encounter perils like these; or perhaps I was powerless because I was again assaulted by surprise, and had not fortified my mind by foresight and previous reflection against a scene like this.

Fears for my own safety again yielded place to reflections on the scene before me. I fixed my eyes upon her countenance. My sister's well-known and beloved features could not be concealed by convulsion or lividness. What direful illusion led thee hither? Bereft of thee, what hold on happiness remains to thy offspring

and thy spouse? To lose thee by a common fate would
have been sufficiently hard; but thus suddenly to perish,—to become the prey of this ghastly death! How
will a spectacle like this be endured by Wieland? To
die beneath his grasp would not satisfy thy enemy.
This was mercy to the evils which he previously made
thee suffer! After these evils death was a boon which
thou besoughtest him to grant. He entertained no en-
mity against thee; I was the object of his treason; but
by some tremendous mistake his fury was misplaced.
But how comest thou hither? and where was Wieland
in thy hour of distress?

I approached the corpse; I lifted the still flexible
hand, and kissed the lips which were breathless. Her
flowing drapery was discomposed. I restored it to order, and, seating myself on the bed, again fixed steadfast eyes upon her countenance. I cannot distinctly
recollect the ruminations of that moment. I saw confusedly, but forcibly, that every hope was extinguished
with the life of *Catharine.* All happiness and dignity
must henceforth be banished from the house and name
of Wieland; all that remained was to linger out in agonies a short existence and leave to the world a monument of blasted hopes and changeable fortune. Pleyel
was already lost to me; yet, while Catharine lived, life
was not a detestable possession. But now, severed from
the companion of my infancy, the partaker of all my
thoughts, my cares, and my wishes, I was like one set
afloat upon a stormy sea and hanging his safety upon
a plank; night was closing upon him, and an unexpected surge had torn him from his hold and overwhelmed him forever.

CHAPTER XVII

I had no inclination nor power to move from this spot. For more than an hour my faculties and limbs seemed to be deprived of all activity. The door below creaked on its hinges, and steps ascended the stairs. My wandering and confused thoughts were instantly recalled by these sounds, and, dropping the curtain of the bed, I moved to a part of the room where any one who entered should be visible; such are the vibrations of sentiment, that, notwithstanding the seeming fulfilment of my fears and increase of my danger, I was conscious, on this occasion, to no turbulence but that of curiosity.

At length he entered the apartment, and I recognised my brother. It was the same Wieland whom I had ever seen. Yet his features were pervaded by a new expression. I supposed him unacquainted with the fate of his wife, and his appearance confirmed this persuasion. A brow expanding into exultation I had hitherto never seen in him; yet such a brow did he now wear. Not only was he unapprized of the disaster that had happened, but some joyous occurrence had betided. What a reverse was preparing to annihilate his transitory bliss! No husband ever doated more fondly, for no wife ever claimed so boundless a devotion. I was not uncertain as to the effects to flow from the discovery of her fate. I confided not at all in the efforts of his reason or his piety. There were few evils which his modes of thinking would not disarm of their sting; but here all opiates to grief and all compellers of patience were vain. This spectacle would be unavoidably followed by the outrages of desperation and a rushing to death.

For the present, I neglected to ask myself what motive brought him hither. I was only fearful of the effects to flow from the sight of the dead. Yet could it be long concealed from him? Sometime, and speedily, he would obtain this knowledge. No stratagems could considerably or usefully prolong his ignorance. All that could be sought was to take away the abruptness of the change, and shut out the confusion of despair and the inroads of madness; but I knew my brother, and knew that all exertions to console him would be fruitless.

What could I say? I was mute, and poured forth those tears on his account which my own unhappiness had been unable to extort. In the midst of my tears, I was not unobservant of his motions. These were of a nature to rouse some other sentiment than grief, or, at least, to mix with it a portion of astonishment.

His countenance suddenly became troubled. His hands were clasped with a force that left the print of his nails in his flesh. His eyes were fixed on my feet. His brain seemed to swell beyond its continent. He did not cease to breathe, but his breath was stifled into groans. I had never witnessed the hurricane of human passions. My element had, till lately, been all sunshine and calm. I was unconversant with the altitudes and energies of sentiment, and was transfixed with inexplicable horror by the symptoms which I now beheld.

After a silence and a conflict which I could not interpret, he lifted his eyes to heaven, and in broken accents exclaimed, "This is too much! any victim but this, and thy will be done. Have I not sufficiently attested my faith and my obedience? She that is gone, they that have perished, were linked with my soul by ties which only thy command would have broken; but here is sanctity and excellence surpassing human. This work-manship is thine, and it cannot be thy will to heap it into ruins."

Here, suddenly unclasping his hands, he struck one of them against his forehead, and continued:— "Wretch! who made thee quicksighted in the councils of thy Maker? Deliverance from mortal fetters is awarded to this being, and thou art the minister of this decree."

So saying, Wieland advanced towards me. His words and his motions were without meaning, except on one supposition. The death of Catharine was already known to him, and that knowledge, as might have been suspected, had destroyed his reason. I had feared noth-ing less; but, now that I beheld the extinction of a mind the most luminous and penetrating that ever dignified the human form, my sensations were fraught with new and insupportable anguish.

I had not time to reflect in what way my own safety would be effected by this revolution, or what I had to dread from the wild conceptions of a madman. He ad-vanced towards me. Some hollow noises were wafted by the breeze. Confused clamours were succeeded by many feet traversing the grass and then crowding into the piazza.

These sounds suspended my brother's purpose, and he stood to listen. The signals multiplied and grew louder; perceiving this, he turned from me, and hur-ried out of my sight. All about me was pregnant with motives to astonishment. My sister's corpse, Wieland's frantic demeanour, and, at length, this crowd of visit-ants, so little accorded with my foresight, that my men-tal progress was stopped. The impulse had ceased which was accustomed to give motion and order to my thoughts.

Footsteps thronged upon the stairs, and presently

many faces showed themselves within the door of my apartment. These looks were full of alarm and watchfulness. They pried into corners as if in search of some fugitive; next their gaze was fixed upon me, and betokened all the vehemence of terror and pity. For a time I questioned whether these were not shapes and faces like that which I had seen at the bottom of the stairs,—creatures of my fancy or airy existences.

My eye wandered from one to another, till at length it fell on a countenance which I well knew. It was that of Mr. Hallet. This man was a distant kinsman of my mother, venerable for his age, his uprightness and sagacity. He had long discharged the functions of a magistrate and good citizen. If any terrors remained, his presence was sufficient to dispel them.

He approached, took my hand with a compassionate air, and said, in a low voice, "Where, my dear Clara, are your brother and sister?" I made no answer, but pointed to the bed. His attendants drew aside the curtain, and, while their eyes glared with horror at the spectacle which they beheld, those of Mr. Hallet overflowed with tears.

After considerable pause, he once more turned to me:—"My dear girl, this sight is not for you. Can you confide in my care and that of Mrs. Baynton's? We will see all performed that circumstances require."

I made strenuous opposition to this request. I insisted on remaining near her till she was interred. His remonstrances, however, and my own feelings, showed me the propriety of a temporary dereliction. Louisa stood in need of a comforter, and my brother's children of a nurse. My unhappy brother was himself an object of solicitude and care. At length I consented to relinquish the corpse, and go to my brother's, whose house, I said, would need a mistress, and his children a parent.

During this discourse, my venerable friend struggled with his tears, but my last intimation called them forth with fresh violence. Meanwhile, his attendants stood round in mournful silence, gazing on me and at each other. I repeated my resolution, and rose to execute it; but he took my hand to detain me. His countenance betrayed irresolution and reluctance. I requested him to state the reason of his opposition to this measure. I entreated him to be explicit. I told him that my brother had just been there, and that I knew his condition. This misfortune had driven him to madness, and his offspring must want a protector. If he chose, I would resign Wieland to his care; but his innocent and helpless babes stood in instant need of nurse and mother, and these offices I would by no means allow another to perform while I had life.

Every word that I uttered seemed to augment his perplexity and distress. At last he said, "I think, Clara, I have entitled myself to some regard from you. You have professed your willingness to oblige me. Now I call upon you to confer upon me the highest obligation in your power. Permit Mrs. Baynton to have the management of your brother's house for two or three days; then it shall be yours to act in it as you please. No matter what are my motives in making this request; perhaps I think your age, your sex, or the distress which this disaster must occasion, incapacitates you for the office. Surely you have no doubt of Mrs. Baynton's tenderness or discretion."

New ideas now rushed into my mind. I fixed my eyes steadfastly on Mr. Hallet. "Are they well?" said I. "Is Louisa well? Are Benjamin, and William, and Constantine, and little Clara, are they safe? Tell me truly, I beseech you!"

"They are well," he replied; "they are perfectly safe."

"Fear no effeminate weakness in me; I can bear to hear the truth. Tell me truly, are they well?"

He again assured me that they were well.

"What, then," resumed I, "do you fear? Is it possible for any calamity to disqualify me for performing my duty to these helpless innocents? I am willing to divide the care of them with Mrs. Baynton; I shall be grateful for her sympathy and aid; but what should I be to desert them at an hour like this?"

I will cut short this distressful dialogue. I still persisted in my purpose, and he still persisted in his opposition. This excited my suspicions anew; but these were removed by solemn declarations of their safety. I could not explain this conduct in my friend, but at length consented to go to the city, provided I should see them for a few minutes at present, and should return on the morrow.

Even this arrangement was objected to. At length he told me they were removed to the city. Why were they removed, I asked, and whither? My importunities would not now be eluded. My suspicions were roused, and no evasion or artifice was sufficient to allay them. Many of the audience began to give vent to their emotions in tears. Mr. Hallet himself seemed as if the conflict were too hard to be longer sustained. Something whispered to my heart that havoc had been wider than I now witnessed. I suspected this concealment to arise from apprehensions of the effects which a knowledge of the truth would produce in me. I once more entreated him to inform me truly of their state. To enforce my entreaties, I put on an air of insensibility. "I can guess," said I, "what has happened: they are indeed beyond the reach of injury, for they are dead? Is it not so?" My voice faltered in spite of my courageous efforts.

"Yes," said he, "they are dead! Dead by the same fate, and by the same hand, with their mother!"

"Dead!" replied I; "what! all?"

"All!" replied he; "he spared *not one!*"

Allow me, my friends, to close my eyes upon the after-scene. Why should I protract a tale which I already begin to feel is too long? Over this scene, at least, let me pass lightly. Here, indeed, my narrative would be imperfect. All was tempestuous commotion in my heart and in my brain. I have no memory for aught but unconscious transitions and rueful sights. I was ingenious and indefatigable in the invention of torments. I would not dispense with any spectacle adapted to exasperate my grief. Each pale and mangled form I crushed to my bosom. Louisa, whom I loved with so ineffable a passion, was denied to me at first, but my obstinacy conquered their reluctance.

They led the way into a darkened hall. A lamp pendant from the ceiling was uncovered, and they pointed to a table. The assassin had defrauded me of my last and miserable consolation. I sought not in her visage for the tinge of the morning and the lustre of heaven. These had vanished with life; but I hoped for liberty to print a last kiss upon her lips. This was denied me; for such had been the merciless blow that destroyed her, that not a *lineament remained!*

I was carried hence to the city. Mrs. Hallet was my companion and my nurse. Why should I dwell upon the rage of fever and the effusions of delirium? Carwin was the phantom that pursued my dreams, the giant oppressor under whose arm I was forever on the point of being crushed. Strenuous muscles were required to hinder my flight, and hearts of steel to withstand the eloquence of my fears. In vain I called upon them to look upward, to mark his sparkling rage and scowling contempt. All I sought was to fly from the stroke that was lifted. Then I heaped upon my guards the most vehement reproaches, or betook myself to wailings on the helplessness of my condition.

This malady at length declined, and my weeping friends began to look for my restoration. Slowly, and with intermitted beams, memory revisited me. The scenes that I had witnessed were revived, became the theme of deliberation and deduction, and called forth the effusions of more rational sorrow.

CHAPTER XVIII

I had imperfectly recovered my strength, when I was informed of the arrival of my mother's brother, Thomas Cambridge. Ten years since, he went to Europe, and was a surgeon in the British forces in Germany during the whole of the late war. After its conclusion, some connection that he had formed with an Irish officer made him retire into Ireland. Intercourse had been punctually maintained by letters with his sister's children, and hopes were given that he would shortly return to his native country and pass his old age in our society. He was now in an evil hour arrived.

I desired an interview with him for numerous and urgent reasons. With the first returns of my understanding I had anxiously sought information of the fate of my brother. During the course of my disease I had never seen him; and vague and unsatisfactory answers were returned to all my inquiries. I had vehemently interrogated Mrs. Hallet and her husband, and solicited an interview with this unfortunate man; but they mysteriously insinuated that his reason was still unsettled, and that his circumstances rendered an interview impossible. Their reserve on the particulars of this destruction and the author of it was equally invincible.

For some time, finding all my efforts fruitless, I had desisted from direct inquiries and solicitations, determined, as soon as my strength was sufficiently renewed, to pursue other means of dispelling my uncertainty. In this state of things, my uncle's arrival and intention to visit me were announced. I almost shuddered to behold the face of this man. When I reflected on the disasters that had befallen us, I was half unwilling to witness that dejection and grief which would be disclosed in his countenance. But I believed that all transactions had been thoroughly disclosed to him, and confided in my importunity to extort from him the knowledge that I sought.

I had no doubt as to the person of our enemy; but the motives that urged him to perpetrate these horrors, the means that he used, and his present condition, were totally unknown. It was reasonable to expect some information on this head from my uncle. I therefore waited his coming with impatience. At length, in the dusk of the evening, and in my solitary chamber, this meeting took place.

This man was our nearest relation, and had ever treated us with the affection of a parent. Our meeting, therefore, could not be without overflowing tenderness and gloomy joy. He rather encouraged than restrained the tears that I poured out in his arms, and took upon himself the task of comforter. Allusions to recent disasters could not be long omitted. One topic facilitated the admission of another. At length I mentioned and deplored the ignorance in which I had been kept respecting my brother's destiny and the circumstances of our misfortunes. I entreated him to tell me what was Wieland's condition, and what progress had been

made in detecting or punishing the author of this unheard-of devastation.

"The author!" said he; "do you know the author?"

"Alas!" I answered, "I am too well acquainted with
him. The story of the grounds of my suspicions would
be painful and too long. I am not apprized of the extent of your present knowledge. There are none but
Wieland, Pleyel, and myself, who are able to relate
certain facts."

"Spare yourself the pain," said he. "All that Wieland and Pleyel can communicate I know already. If
any thing of moment has fallen within your own exclusive knowledge, and the relation be not too arduous
for your present strength, I confess I am desirous of
hearing it. Perhaps you allude to one by the name of
Carwin. I will anticipate your curiosity by saying that
since these disasters no one has seen or heard of him.
His agency is, therefore, a mystery still unsolved."

I readily complied with his request, and related as
distinctly as I could, though in general terms, the
events transacted in the summer-house and my chamber. He listened without apparent surprise to the tale
of Pleyel's errors and suspicions, and with augmented
seriousness to my narrative of the warnings and inexplicable vision, and the letter found upon the table. I
waited for his comments.

"You gather from this," said he, "that Carwin is the
author of all this misery?"

"Is it not," answered I, "an unavoidable inference?
But what know you respecting it? Was it possible to
execute this mischief without witness or coadjutor? I
beseech you to relate to me when and why Mr. Hallet
was summoned to the scene, and by whom this disaster
was first suspected or discovered. Surely, suspicion
must have fallen upon some one, and pursuit was
made."

My uncle rose from his seat, and traversed the floor with hasty steps. His eyes were fixed upon the ground, and he seemed buried in perplexity. At length he paused, and said, with an emphatic tone, "It is true; the instrument is known. Carwin may have plotted, but the execution was another's. That other is found, and his deed is ascertained."

"Good heaven!" I exclaimed; "what say you? Was not Carwin the assassin? Could any hand but his have carried into act this dreadful purpose?"

"Have I not said," returned he, "that the performance was another's? Carwin, perhaps, or heaven, or insanity, prompted the murderer; but Carwin is unknown. The actual performer has long since been called to judgment and convicted, and is, at this moment, at the bottom of a dungeon loaded with chains."

I lifted my hands and eyes. "Who then is this assassin? By what means and whither was he traced? What is the testimony of his guilt?"

"His own, corroborated with that of a servant-maid who spied the murder of the children from a closet where she was concealed. The magistrate returned from your dwelling to your brother's. He was employed in hearing and recording the testimony of the only witness, when the criminal himself, unexpected, unsolicited, unsought, entered the hall, acknowledged his guilt, and rendered himself up to justice.

"He has since been summoned to the bar. The audience was composed of thousands whom rumours of this wonderful event had attracted from the greatest distance. A long and impartial examination was made, and the prisoner was called upon for his defence. In compliance with this call, he delivered an ample relation of his motives and actions." There he stopped.

I besought him to say who this criminal was, and what the instigations that compelled him. My uncle was silent. I urged this inquiry with new force. I reverted to my own knowledge, and sought in this some basis to conjecture. I ran over the scanty catalogue of the men whom I knew; I lighted on no one who was qualified for ministering to malice like this. Again I resorted to importunity. Had I ever seen the criminal? Was it sheer cruelty or diabolical revenge that produced this overthrow?

He surveyed me for a considerable time, and listened to my interrogations in silence. At length he spoke:— "Clara, I have known thee by report, and in some degree by observation. Thou art a being of no vulgar sort. Thy friends have hitherto treated thee as a child. They meant well, but perhaps they were unacquainted with thy strength. I assure myself that nothing will surpass thy fortitude.

"Thou art anxious to know the destroyer of thy family, his actions, and his motives. Shall I call him to thy presence, and permit him to confess before thee? Shall I make him the narrator of his own tale?"

I started on my feet, and looked round me with fearful glances, as if the murderer was close at hand. "What do you mean?" said I. "Put an end, I beseech you, to this suspense."

"Be not alarmed; you will never more behold the face of this criminal, unless he be gifted with supernatural strength, and sever like threads the constraint of links and bolts. I have said that the assassin was arraigned at the bar, and that the trial ended with a summons from the judge to confess or to vindicate his actions. A reply was immediately made with significance of gesture and a tranquil majesty which denoted less of humanity than godhead. Judges, advocates, and auditors were panic-struck and breathless with attention. One of the hearers faithfully recorded the speech.

"There it is," continued he, putting a roll of papers in my hand: "you may read it at your leisure."

With these words, my uncle left me alone. My curiosity refused me a moment's delay. I opened the papers, and read as follows.

CHAPTER XIX

"Theodore Wieland, the prisoner at the bar, was now called upon for his defence. He looked around him for some time in silence, and with a mild countenance. At length he spoke:—

"It is strange: I am known to my judges and my auditors. Who is there present a stranger to the character of Wieland? who knows him not as a husband,—as a father,—as a friend? yet here am I arraigned as a criminal. I am charged with diabolical malice; I am accused of the murder of my wife and my children!

"It is true, they were slain by me: they all perished by my hand. The task of vindication is ignoble. What is it that I am called to vindicate? and before whom?

"You know that they are dead, and that they were killed by me. What more would you have? Would you extort from me a statement of my motives? Have you failed to discover them already? You charge me with malice; but your eyes are not shut; your reason is still vigorous; your memory has not forsaken you. You know whom it is that you thus charge. The habits of his life are known to you; his treatment of his wife and his offspring is known to you; the soundness of his integrity, and the unchangeableness of his principles, are familiar to your apprehension; yet you persist in this charge! You lead me hither manacled as a felon; you deem me worthy of a vile and tormenting death!

"Who are they whom I have devoted to death? My wife—the little ones, that drew their being from me— that creature who, as she surpassed them in excellence, claimed a larger affection than those whom natural affinities bound to my heart. Think ye that malice could have urged me to this deed? Hide your audacious fronts from the scrutiny of heaven. Take refuge in some cavern unvisited by human eyes. Ye may deplore your wickedness or folly, but ye cannot expiate it.

"Think not that I speak for your sakes. Hug to your hearts this detestable infatuation. Deem me still a murderer, and drag me to untimely death. I make not an effort to dispel your illusion; I utter not a word to cure you of your sanguinary folly; but there are probably some in this assembly who have come from far; for their sakes, whose distance has disabled them from knowing me, I will tell what I have done, and why.

"It is needless to say that God is the object of my supreme passion. I have cherished in his presence a single and upright heart. I have thirsted for the knowledge of his will. I have burnt with ardour to approve my faith and my obedience.

"My days have been spent in searching for the revelation of that will; but my days have been mournful, because my search failed. I solicited direction; I turned on every side where glimmerings of light could be discovered. I have not been wholly uninformed; but my knowledge has always stopped short of certainty. Dissatisfaction has insinuated itself into all my thoughts. My purposes have been pure, my wishes indefatigable; but not till lately were these purposes thoroughly accomplished and these wishes fully gratified.

"I thank thee, my Father, for thy bounty; that thou didst not ask a less sacrifice than this; that thou placedst me in a condition to testify my submission to thy will! What have I withheld which it was thy pleasure to exact? Now may I, with dauntless and erect eye, claim my reward, since I have given thee the treasure of my soul.

"I was at my own house; it was late in the evening; my sister had gone to the city, but proposed to return. It was in expectation of her return that my wife and I delayed going to bed beyond the usual hour; the rest of the family, however, were retired.

"My mind was contemplative and calm,—not wholly devoid of apprehension on account of my sister's safety. Recent events, not easily explained, had suggested the existence of some danger; but this danger was without a distinct form in our imagination, and scarcely ruffled our tranquillity.

"Time passed, and my sister did not arrive. Her house is at some distance from mine, and, though her arrangements had been made with a view to residing with us, it was possible that, through forgetfulness, or the occurrence of unforeseen emergencies, she had returned to her own dwelling.

"Hence it was conceived proper that I should ascertain the truth by going thither. I went. On my way my mind was full of those ideas which related to my intellectual condition. In the torrent of fervid conceptions, I lost sight of my purpose. Sometimes I stood still; sometimes I wandered from my path, and experienced some difficulty, on recovering from my fit of musing, to regain it.

"The series of my thoughts is easily traced. At first every vein beat with raptures known only to the man whose parental and conjugal love is without limits, and the cup of whose desires, immense as it is, overflows with gratification. I know not why emotions that were perpetual visitants should now have recurred with unusual energy. The transition was not new from sensations of joy to a consciousness of gratitude. The Author of my being was likewise the dispenser of every gift with which that being was embellished. The service to which a benefactor like this was entitled could not be circumscribed. My social sentiments were indebted to their alliance with devotion for all their value. All passions are base, all joys feeble, all energies malignant, which are not drawn from this source.

"For a time my contemplations soared above earth and its inhabitants. I stretched forth my hands; I lifted my eyes, and exclaimed, 'Oh that I might be admitted to thy presence! that mine were the supreme delight of knowing thy will, and of performing it!—the blissful privilege of direct communication with thee, and of listening to the audible enunciation of thy pleasure!

"'What task would I not undertake, what privation would I not cheerfully endure, to testify my love of thee? Alas! thou hidest thyself from my view; glimpses only of thy excellence and beauty are afforded me. Would that a momentary emanation from thy glory would visit me! that some unambiguous token of thy presence would salute my senses!'

"In this mood I entered the house of my sister. It was vacant. Scarcely had I regained recollection of the purpose that brought me hither. Thoughts of a different tendency had such absolute possession of my mind, that the relations of time and space were almost obliterated from my understanding. These wanderings, however, were restrained, and I ascended to her chamber.

"I had no light, and might have known by external observation that the house was without any inhabitant. With this, however, I was not satisfied. I entered the room, and, the object of my search not appearing, I prepared to return.

"The darkness required some caution in descending the stair. I stretched my hand to seize the balustrade by which I might regulate my steps. How shall I describe the lustre which at that moment burst upon my vision?

"I was dazzled. My organs were bereaved of their activity. My eyelids were half-closed, and my hands withdrawn from the balustrade. A nameless fear chilled my veins, and I stood motionless. This irradiation did not retire or lessen. It seemed as if some powerful effulgence covered me like a mantle.

"I opened my eyes and found all about me luminous and glowing. It was the element of heaven that flowed around. Nothing but a fiery stream was at first visible; but, anon, a shrill voice from behind called upon me to attend.

"I turned. It is forbidden to describe what I saw: words, indeed, would be wanting to the task. The lineaments of that being whose veil was now lifted and whose visage beamed upon my sight, no hues of pencil or of language can portray.

"As it spoke, the accents thrilled to my heart:—'Thy prayers are heard. In proof of thy faith, render me thy wife. This is the victim I choose. Call her hither, and here let her fall.' The sound, and visage, and light vanished at once.

"What demand was this? The blood of Catharine was to be shed! My wife was to perish by my hand! I sought opportunity to attest my virtue. Little did I expect that a proof like this would have been demanded.

"'My wife!' I exclaimed; 'O God! subsitute some other victim. Make me not the butcher of my wife. My own blood is cheap. This will I pour out before thee with a willing heart; but spare, I beseech thee, this precious life, or commission some other than her husband to perform the bloody deed.'

"In vain. The conditions were prescribed; the decree had gone forth, and nothing remained but to execute it. I rushed out of the house and across the intermediate fields, and stopped not till I entered my own parlour.

"My wife had remained here during my absence, in anxious expectation of my return with some tidings of her sister. I had none to communicate. For a time I was breathless with my speed. This, and the tremors that shook my frame, and the wildness of my looks, alarmed her. She immediately suspected some disaster to have happened to her friend, and her own speech was as much overpowered by emotion as mine.

"She was silent, but her looks manifested her impatience to hear what I had to communicate. I spoke, but with so much precipitation as scarcely to be understood; catching her, at the same time, by the arm, and forcibly pulling her from her seat.

"'Come along with me; fly; waste not a moment; time will be lost, and the deed will be omitted. Tarry not; question not; but fly with me!'

"This deportment added afresh to her alarms. Her eyes pursued mine, and she said, 'What is the matter? For God's sake, what is the matter? Where would you have me go?'

"My eyes were fixed upon her countenance while she spoke. I thought upon her virtues; I viewed her as the mother of my babes; as my wife. I recalled the purpose for which I thus urged her attendance. My heart faltered, and I saw that I must rouse to this work all my faculties. The danger of the least delay was imminent.

"I looked away from her, and, again exerting my

force, drew her towards the door:—'You must go with me; indeed you must.'

"In her fright she half resisted my efforts, and again exclaimed, 'Good heaven! what is it you mean? Where go? What has happened? Have you found Clara?'

"'Follow me, and you will see,' I answered, still urging her reluctant steps forward.

"'What frenzy has seized you? Something must needs have happened. Is she sick? Have you found her?'

"'Come and see. Follow me, and know for yourself.'

"Still she expostulated, and besought me to explain this mysterious behaviour. I could not trust myself to answer her, to look at her; but, grasping her arm, I drew her after me. She hesitated, rather through confusion of mind than from unwillingness to accompany me. This confusion gradually abated, and she moved forward, but with irresolute footsteps and continual exclamations of wonder and terror. Her interrogations of 'what was the matter?' and 'whither was I going?' were ceaseless and vehement.

"It was the scope of my efforts not to think; to keep up a conflict and uproar in my mind in which all order and distinctness should be lost; to escape from the sensations produced by her voice. I was therefore silent. I strove to abridge this interval by my haste, and to waste all my attention in furious gesticulations.

"In this state of mind we reached my sister's door. She looked at the windows and saw that all was desolate. 'Why come we here? There is nobody here. I will not go in.'

"Still I was dumb; but, opening the door, I drew her into the entry. This was the allotted scene; here she was to fall. I let go her hand, and, pressing my palms against my forehead, made one mighty effort to work up my soul to the deed.

"In vain; it would not be; my courage was appalled, my arms nerveless. I muttered prayers that my strength might be aided from above. They availed nothing.

"Horror diffused itself over me. This conviction of my cowardice, my rebellion, fastened upon me, and I stood rigid and cold as marble. From this state I was somewhat relieved by my wife's voice, who renewed her supplications to be told why we came hither and what was the fate of my sister.

"What could I answer? My words were broken and inarticulate. Her fears naturally acquired force from the observation of these symptoms; but these fears were misplaced. The only inference she deduced from my conduct was that some terrible mishap had befallen Clara.

"She wrung her hands, and exclaimed, in an agony, 'Oh, tell me, where is she? What has become of her? Is she sick? Dead? Is she in her chamber? Oh, let me go thither and know the worst!'

"This proposal set my thoughts once more in motion. Perhaps what my rebellious heart refused to perform here, I might obtain strength enough to execute else-where.

" 'Come, then,' said I; 'let us go.'

" 'I will, but not in the dark. We must first procure a light.'

" 'Fly, then, and procure it; but, I charge you, linger not. I will await for your return.'

"While she was gone, I strode along the entry. The fellness of a gloomy hurricane but faintly resembled the discord that reigned in my mind. To omit this sacri-fice must not be; yet my sinews had refused to perform it. No alternative was offered. To rebel against the mandate was impossible; but obedience would render me the executioner of my wife. My will was strong, but my limbs refused their office.

"She returned with a light. I led the way to the chamber: she looked round her; she lifted the curtain of the bed; she saw nothing.

"At length she fixed inquiring eyes upon me. The light now enabled her to discover in my visage what darkness had hitherto concealed. Her cares were now transferred from my sister to myself, and she said, in a tremulous voice, 'Wieland, you are not well: what ails you? Can I do nothing for you?'

"That accents and looks so winning should disarm me of my resolution, was to be expected. My thoughts were thrown anew into anarchy. I spread my hand before my eyes that I might not see her, and answered only by groans. She took my other hand between hers, and, pressing it to her heart, spoke with that voice which had ever swayed my will and wafted away sorrow:—

"'My friend! my soul's friend! tell me thy cause of grief. Do I not merit to partake with thee in thy cares? Am I not thy wife?'

"This was too much. I broke from her embrace, and retired to a corner of the room. In this pause, courage was once more infused into me. I resolved to execute my duty. She followed me, and renewed her passionate entreaties to know the cause of my distress.

"I raised my head and regarded her with steadfast looks. I muttered something about death, and the injunctions of my duty. At these words she shrunk back, and looked at me with a new expression of anguish. After a pause, she clasped her hands, and exclaimed,—

"'Oh, Wieland! Wieland! God grant that I am mistaken! but something surely is wrong. I see it; it is too plain; thou art undone,—lost to me and to thyself.' At the same time she gazed on my features with intensest anxiety, in hope that different symptoms would take place. I replied to her with vehemence,—

"'Undone! No; my duty is known, and I thank my God that my cowardice is now vanquished, and I have power to fulfil it. Catharine, I pity the weakness of thy nature; I pity thee, but must not spare. Thy life is claimed from my hands; thou must die!'

"Fear was now added to her grief. 'What mean you? Why talk you of death? Bethink yourself, Wieland; bethink yourself, and this fit will pass. Oh, why came I hither? Why did you drag me hither?'

"'I brought thee hither to fulfil a divine command. I am appointed thy destroyer, and destroy thee I must.' Saying this, I seized her wrists. She shrieked aloud, and endeavoured to free herself from my grasp; but her efforts were vain.

"'Surely, surely, Wieland, thou dost not mean it. Am I not thy wife? and wouldst thou kill me? Thou wilt not; and yet—I see—thou art Wieland no longer! A fury resistless and horrible possesses thee:—spare me —spare—help—help—'

"Till her breath was stopped she shrieked for help, —for mercy. When she could speak no longer, her gestures, her looks, appealed to my compassion. My accursed hand was irresolute and tremulous. I meant thy death to be sudden, thy struggles to be brief. Alas! my heart was infirm, my resolves mutable. Thrice I slackened my grasp, and life kept its hold, though in the midst of pangs. Her eyeballs started from their sockets. Grimness and distortion took place of all that used to bewitch me into transport and subdue me into reverence.

"I was commissioned to kill thee, but not to torment thee with the foresight of thy death; not to multiply thy fears and prolong thy agonies. Haggard, and pale, and lifeless, at length thou ceasedst to contend with thy destiny.

"This was a moment of triumph. Thus had I successfully subdued the stubbornness of human passions: the victim which had been demanded was given; the deed was done past recall.

"I lifted the corpse in my arms and laid it on the bed. I gazed upon it with delight. Such was the elation of my thoughts, that I even broke into laughter. I clapped my hands and exclaimed, 'It is done! My sacred duty is fulfilled! To that I have sacrificed, O my God! thy last and best gift, my wife!'

"For a while I thus soared above frailty. I imagined I had set myself forever beyond the reach of selfishness; but my imaginations were false. This rapture quickly subsided. I looked again at my wife. My joyous ebullitions vanished, and I asked myself who it was whom I saw. Methought it could not be Catharine. It could not be the woman who had lodged for years in my heart; who had slept nightly in my bosom; who had borne in her womb, who had fostered at her breast, the beings who called me father; whom I had watched with delight, and cherished with a fondness ever new and perpetually growing: it could not be the same.

"Where was her bloom? These deadly and blood-suffused orbs but ill resemble the azure and ecstatic tenderness of her eyes. The lucid stream that meandered over that bosom, the glow of love that was wont to sit upon that cheek, are much unlike these livid stains and this hideous deformity. Alas! these were the traces of agony; the gripe of the assassin had been here!

"I will not dwell upon my lapse into desperate and outrageous sorrow. The breath of heaven that sustained me was withdrawn, and I sunk into *mere man.* I leaped from the floor; I dashed my head against the wall; I uttered screams of horror; I panted after torment and pain. Eternal fire, and the bickerings of hell, compared with what I felt, were music and a bed of roses.

"I thank my God that this degeneracy was transient,

—that he deigned once more to raise me aloft. I thought upon what I had done as a sacrifice to duty, and *was calm*. My wife was dead; but I reflected that though this source of human consolation was closed, yet others were still open. If the transports of a husband were no more, the feelings of a father had still scope for exercise. When remembrance of their mother should excite too keen a pang, I would look upon them and *be comforted*.

"While I revolved these ideas, new warmth flowed in upon my heart—I was wrong. These feelings were the growth of selfishness. Of this I was not aware, and, to dispel the mist that obscured my perceptions, a new effulgence and a new mandate were necessary.

"From these thoughts I was recalled by a ray that was shot into the room. A voice spake like that which I had before heard:—'Thou hast done well. But all is not done—the sacrifice is incomplete—thy children must be offered—they must perish with their mother!——'"

CHAPTER XX

Will you wonder that I read no further? Will you not rather be astonished that I read thus far? What power supported me through such a task I know not. Perhaps the doubt from which I could not disengage my mind —that the scene here depicted was a dream—contributed to my perseverance. In vain the solemn introduction of my uncle, his appeals to my fortitude, and allusions to something monstrous in the events he was about to disclose,—in vain the distressful perplexity, the mysterious silence and ambiguous answers,

of my attendants, especially when the condition of my
brother was the theme of my inquiries,—were remembered. I recalled the interview with Wieland in my
chamber, his preternatural tranquillity succeeded by
bursts of passion and menacing actions. All these coin-
cided with the tenor of this paper.

Catharine and her children, and Louisa, were dead.
The act that destroyed them was in the highest degree
inhuman. It was worthy of savages trained to murder
and exulting in agonies.

Who was the performer of the deed? Wieland! My
brother! The husband and the father! That man of gen-
tle virtues and invincible benignity! placable and mild,
—an idolater of peace! "Surely," said I, "it is a dream.
For many days have I been vexed with frenzy. Its do-
minion is still felt; but new forms are called up to di-
versify and augment my torments."

The paper dropped from my hand, and my eyes followed it. I shrunk back, as if to avoid some petrifying
influence that approached me. My tongue was mute;
all the functions of nature were at a stand, and I sunk
upon the floor lifeless.

The noise of my fall, as I afterwards heard, alarmed
my uncle, who was in a lower apartment, and whose
apprehensions had detained him. He hastened to my
chamber, and administered the assistance which my
condition required. When I opened my eyes I beheld
him before me. His skill as a reasoner as well as a physician was exerted to obviate the injurious effects of
this disclosure; but he had wrongly estimated the
strength of my body or of my mind. This new shock
brought me once more to the brink of the grave, and
my malady was much more difficult to subdue than at
first.

I will not dwell upon the long train of dreary sensations, and the hideous confusion of my understanding.

Time slowly restored its customary firmness to my frame and order to my thoughts. The images impressed upon my mind by this fatal paper were somewhat effaced by my malady. They were obscure and disjointed, like the parts of a dream. I was desirous of freeing my imagination from this chaos. For this end I questioned my uncle, who was my constant companion. He was intimidated by the issue of his first experiment, and took pains to elude or discourage my inquiry. My impetuosity sometimes compelled him to have resort to misrepresentations and untruths.

Time effected that end, perhaps, in a more beneficial manner. In the course of my meditations the recollections of the past gradually became more distinct. I revolved them, however, in silence, and, being no longer accompanied with surprise, they did not exercise a death-dealing power. I had discontinued the perusal of the paper in the midst of the narrative; but what I read, combined with information elsewhere obtained, threw, perhaps, a sufficient light upon these detestable transactions; yet my curiosity was not inactive. I desired to peruse the remainder.

My eagerness to know the particulars of this tale was mingled and abated by my antipathy to the scene which would be disclosed. Hence I employed no means to effect my purpose. I desired knowledge, and, at the same time, shrunk back from receiving the boon.

One morning, being left alone, I rose from my bed, and went to a drawer where my finer clothing used to be kept. I opened it, and this fatal paper saluted my sight. I snatched it involuntarily, and withdrew to a chair. I debated, for a few minutes, whether I should open and read. Now that my fortitude was put to trial, it failed. I felt myself incapable of deliberately surveying a scene of so much horror. I was prompted to return it to its place; but this resolution gave way, and I determined to peruse some part of it. I turned over the leaves till I came near the conclusion. The narrative of the criminal was finished, the verdict of *guilty* reluctantly pronounced by the jury, and the accused interrogated why sentence of death should not pass. The answer was brief, solemn, and emphatical.

"No. I have nothing to say. My tale has been told. My motives have been truly stated. If my judges are unable to discern the purity of my intentions, or to credit the statement of them which I have just made; if they see not that my deed was enjoined by heaven, that obedience was the test of perfect virtue, and the extinction of selfishness and error, they must pronounce me a murderer.

"They refuse to credit my tale; they impute my acts to the influence of demons; they account me an example of the highest wickedness of which human nature is capable; they doom me to death and infamy. Have I power to escape this evil? If I have, be sure I will exert it. I will not accept evil at their hand, when I am entitled to good; I will suffer only when I cannot elude suffering.

"You say that I am guilty. Impious and rash! thus to usurp the prerogatives of your Maker! to set up your bounded views and halting reason as the measure of truth!

"Thou, Omnipotent and Holy! Thou knowest that my actions were conformable to thy will. I know not what is crime; what actions are evil in their ultimate and comprehensive tendency, or what are good. Thy knowledge, as thy power, is unlimited. I have taken thee for my guide, and cannot err. To the arms of thy protection I intrust my safety. In the awards of thy justice I confide for my recompense.

"Come death when it will, I am safe. Let calumny and abhorrence pursue me among men; I shall not be defrauded of my dues. The peace of virtue, and the glory of obedience, will be my portion hereafter."

Here ended the speaker. I withdrew my eyes from the page; but, before I had time to reflect on what I had read, Mr. Cambridge entered the room. He quickly perceived how I had been employed, and betrayed some solicitude respecting the condition of my mind.

His fears, however, were superfluous. What I had read threw me into a state not easily described. Anguish and fury, however, had no part in it. My faculties were chained up in wonder and awe. Just then, I was unable to speak. I looked at my friend with an air of inquisitiveness, and pointed at the roll. He comprehended my inquiry, and answered me with looks of gloomy acquiescence. After some time, my thoughts found their way to my lips.

Such, then, were the acts of my brother. Such were his words. For this he was condemned to die; to die upon the gallows! A fate cruel and unmerited! "And is it so?" continued I, struggling for utterance, which this new idea made difficult; "is he—dead?"

"No. He is alive. There could be no doubt as to the cause of these excesses. They originated in sudden madness; but that madness continues, and he is condemned to perpetual imprisonment."

"Madness, say you? Are you sure? Were not these sights and these sounds really seen and heard?"

My uncle was surprised at my question. He looked at me with apparent inquietude. "Can you doubt," said he, "that these were illusions? Does heaven, think you, interfere for such ends?"

"Oh, no; I think it not. Heaven cannot stimulate to such unheard-of outrage. The agent was not good, but evil."

"Nay, my dear girl," said my friend, "lay aside these

fancies. Neither angel nor devil had any part in this affair."

"You misunderstand me," I answered; "I believe the agency to be external and real, but not supernatural."

"Indeed!" said he, in an accent of surprise. "Whom do you then suppose to be the agent?"

"I know not. All is wildering conjecture. I cannot forget Carwin. I cannot banish the suspicion that he was the setter of these snares. But how can we suppose it to be madness? Did insanity ever before assume this form?"

"Frequently. The illusion, in this case, was more dreadful in its consequences than any that has come to my knowledge; but I repeat that similar illusions are not rare. Did you never hear of an instance which occurred in your mother's family?"

"No. I beseech you, relate it. My grandfather's death I have understood to have been extraordinary, but I know not in what respect. A brother, to whom he was much attached, died in his youth; and this, as I have heard, influenced, in some remarkable way, the fate of my grandfather; but I am unacquainted with particulars."

"On the death of that brother," resumed my friend, "my father was seized with dejection, which was found to flow from two sources. He not only grieved for the loss of a friend, but entertained the belief that his own death would be inevitably consequent on that of his brother. He waited from day to day in expectation of the stroke which he predicted was speedily to fall upon him. Gradually, however, he recovered his cheerfulness and confidence. He married, and performed his part in the world with spirit and activity. At the end of twenty-one years it happened that he spent the summer with his family at a house which he possessed on the sea-coast in Cornwall. It was at no great distance from a cliff which overhung the ocean and rose into the air to a great height. The summit was level and secure, and easily ascended on the land side. The company frequently repaired hither in clear weather, invited by its pure airs and extensive prospects. One evening in June my father, with his wife and some friends, chanced to be on this spot. Every one was happy, and my father's imagination seemed particularly alive to the grandeur of the scenery.

"Suddenly, however, his limbs trembled and his features betrayed alarm. He threw himself into the attitude of one listening. He gazed earnestly in a direction in which nothing was visible to his friends. This lasted for a minute; then, turning to his companions, he told them that his brother had just delivered to him a summons, which must be instantly obeyed. He then took a hasty and solemn leave of each person, and, before their surprise would allow them to understand the scene, he rushed to the edge of the cliff, threw himself headlong, and was seen no more.

"In the course of my practice in the German army, many cases equally remarkable have occurred. Unquestionably the illusions were maniacal, though the vulgar thought otherwise. They are all reducible to one class,* and are not more difficult of explication and cure than most affections of our frame."

This opinion my uncle endeavoured, by various means, to impress upon me. I listened to his reasonings and illustrations with silent respect. My astonishment was great on finding proofs of an influence of which I had supposed there were no examples; but I was far from accounting for appearances in my uncle's manner. Ideas thronged into my mind which I was unable to disjoin or to regulate. I reflected that this madness,

* Mania mutabilis. See Darwin's Zoonomia, vol. ii. Class III. 1, 2, where similar cases are stated.

if madness it were, had affected Pleyel and myself as well as Wieland. Pleyel had heard a mysterious voice. I had seen and heard. A form had showed itself to me as well as to Wieland. The disclosure had been made in the same spot. The appearance was equally complete and equally prodigious in both instances. Whatever supposition I should adopt, had I not equal reason to tremble? What was my security against influences equally terrific and equally irresistible?

It would be vain to attempt to describe the state of mind which this idea produced. I wondered at the change which a moment had effected in my brother's condition. Now was I stupefied with tenfold wonder in contemplating myself. Was I not likewise transformed from rational and human into a creature of nameless and fearful attributes? Was I not transported to the brink of the same abyss? Ere a new day should come, my hands might be imbrued in blood, and my remaining life be consigned to a dungeon and chains.

With moral sensibility like mine, no wonder that this new dread was more insupportable than the anguish I had lately endured. Grief carries its own antidote along with it. When thought becomes merely a vehicle of pain, its progress must be stopped. Death is a cure which nature or ourselves must administer. To this cure I now looked forward with gloomy satisfaction.

My silence could not conceal from my uncle the state of my thoughts. He made unwearied efforts to divert my attention from views so pregnant with danger. His efforts, aided by time, were in some measure successful. Confidence in the strength of my resolution and in the healthful state of my faculties was once more revived. I was able to devote my thoughts to my brother's state and the causes of this disastrous proceeding.

My opinions were the sport of eternal change. Sometimes I conceived the apparition to be more than human. I had no grounds on which to build a disbelief. I could not deny faith to the evidence of my religion; the testimony of men was loud and unanimous: both these concurred to persuade me that evil spirits existed, and that their energy was frequently exerted in the system of the world.

These ideas connected themselves with the image of Carwin. "Where is the proof," said I, "that demons may not be subjected to the control of men? This truth may be distorted and debased in the minds of the ignorant. The dogmas of the vulgar with regard to this subject are glaringly absurd; but, though these may justly be neglected by the wise, we are scarcely justified in totally rejecting the possibility that men may obtain supernatural aid.

"The dreams of superstition are worthy of contempt. Witchcraft, its instruments and miracles, the compact ratified by a bloody signature, the apparatus of sulphureous smells and thundering explosions, are monstrous and chimerical. These have no part in the scene over which the genius of Carwin presides. That conscious beings, dissimilar from human, but moral and voluntary agents as we are, somewhere exist, can scarcely be denied. That their aid may be employed to benign or malignant purposes cannot be disproved.

"Darkness rests upon the designs of this man. The extent of his power is unknown: but is there not evidence that it has been now exerted?"

I recurred to my own experience. Here Carwin had actually appeared upon the stage; but this was in a human character. A voice and a form were discovered; but one was apparently exerted, and the other disclosed, not to befriend, but to counteract, Carwin's designs. There were tokens of hostility, and not of alliance between them. Carwin was the miscreant whose projects were resisted by a minister of heaven. How can this be reconciled to the stratagem which ruined my brother? There the agency was at once preternatural and malignant.

The recollection of this fact led my thoughts into a new channel. The malignity of that influence which governed my brother had hitherto been no subject of doubt. His wife and children were destroyed; they had expired in agony and fear: yet was it indisputably certain that their murderer was criminal? He was acquitted at the tribunal of his own conscience; his behaviour at his trial, and since, was faithfully reported to me; appearances were uniform; not for a moment did he lay aside the majesty of virtue; he repelled all invectives by appealing to the Deity and to the tenor of his past life. Surely there was truth in this appeal: none but a command from heaven could have swayed his will; and nothing but unerring proof of divine approbation could sustain his mind in its present elevation.

CHAPTER XXI

Such, for some time, was the course of my meditations. My weakness, and my aversion to be pointed out as an object of surprise or compassion, prevented me from going into public. I studiously avoided the visits of those who came to express their sympathy or gratify their curiosity. My uncle was my principal companion. Nothing more powerfully tended to console me than his conversation.

With regard to Pleyel, my feelings seemed to have

undergone a total revolution. It often happens that one passion supplants another. Late disasters had rent my heart, and, now that the wound was in some degree closed, the love which I had cherished for this man seemed likewise to have vanished.

Hitherto, indeed, I had had no cause for despair. I was innocent of that offence which had estranged him from my presence. I might reasonably expect that my innocence would at some time be irresistibly demonstrated, and his affection for me be revived with his esteem. Now my aversion to be thought culpable by him continued, but was unattended with the same impatience. I desired the removal of his suspicions, not for the sake of regaining his love, but because I delighted in the veneration of so excellent a man, and because he himself would derive pleasure from conviction of my integrity.

My uncle had early informed me that Pleyel and he had seen each other since the return of the latter from Europe. Amidst the topics of their conversation, I discovered that Pleyel had carefully omitted the mention of those events which had drawn upon me so much abhorrence. I could not account for his silence on this subject. Perhaps time or some new discovery had altered or shaken his opinion. Perhaps he was unwilling, though I were guilty, to injure me in the opinion of my venerable kinsman. I understood that he had frequently visited me during my disease, had watched many successive nights by my bedside, and manifested the utmost anxiety on my account.

The journey which he was preparing to take, at the termination of our last interview, the catastrophe of the ensuing night induced him to delay. The motives of this journey I had till now totally mistaken. They were explained to me by my uncle, whose tale excited my astonishment without awakening my regret. In a different state of mind, it would have added unspeakably to my distress, but now it was more a source of pleasure than pain. This, perhaps, is not the least extraordinary of the facts contained in this narrative. It will excite less wonder when I add that my indifference was temporary, and that the lapse of a few days showed me that my feelings were deadened for a time, rather than finally extinguished.

Theresa de Stolberg was alive. She had conceived the resolution of seeking her lover in America. To conceal her flight, she had caused the report of her death to be propagated. She put herself under the conduct of Bertrand, the faithful servant of Pleyel. The packet which the latter received from the hands of his servant contained the tidings of her safe arrival at Boston, and to meet her there was the purpose of his journey.

This discovery had set this man's character in a new light. I had mistaken the heroism of friendship for the frenzy of love. He who had gained my affections may be supposed to have previously entitled himself to my reverence; but the levity which had formerly characterized the behaviour of this man tended to obscure the greatness of his sentiments. I did not fail to remark that, since this lady was still alive, the voice in the temple which asserted her death must either have been intended to deceive, or have been itself deceived. The latter supposition was inconsistent with the notion of a spiritual, and the former with that of a benevolent, being.

When my disease abated, Pleyel had forborne his visits, and had lately set out upon this journey. This amounted to a proof that my guilt was still believed by him. I was grieved for his errors, but trusted that my vindication would, sooner or later, be made.

Meanwhile, tumultuous thoughts were again set afloat by a proposal made to me by my uncle. He imagined that new airs would restore my languishing constitution, and a varied succession of objects tend to repair the shock which my mind had received. For this end, he proposed to me to take up my abode with him in France or Italy.

At a more prosperous period, this scheme would have pleased for its own sake. Now my heart sickened at the prospect of nature. The world of man was shrouded in misery and blood, and constituted a loathsome spectacle. I willingly closed my eyes in sleep, and regretted that the respite it afforded me was so short. I marked with satisfaction the progress of decay in my frame, and consented to live, merely in the hope that the course of nature would speedily relieve me from the burden. Nevertheless, as he persisted in his scheme, I concurred in it merely because he was entitled to my gratitude, and because my refusal gave him pain.

No sooner was he informed of my consent, than he told me I must make immediate preparation to embark, as the ship in which he had engaged a passage would be ready to depart in three days. This expedition was unexpected. There was an impatience in his manner, when he urged the necessity of despatch, that excited my surprise. When I questioned him as to the cause of this haste, he generally stated reasons which, at that time, I could not deny to be plausible, but which, on the review, appeared insufficient. I suspected that the true motives were concealed, and believed that these motives had some connection with my brother's destiny.

I now recollected that the information respecting Wieland which had from time to time been imparted to me was always accompanied with airs of reserve and mysteriousness. What had appeared sufficiently explicit at the time it was uttered, I now remembered to have been faltering and ambiguous. I was resolved to remove my doubts by visiting the unfortunate man in his dungeon. Heretofore the idea of this visit had occurred to me; but the horrors of his dwelling-place, his wild yet placid physiognomy, his neglected locks, the fetters which constrained his limbs, terrible as they were in description, how could I endure to behold?

Now, however, that I was preparing to take an everlasting farewell of my country, now that an ocean was henceforth to separate me from him, how could I part without an interview? I would examine his situation with my own eyes. I would know whether the representations which had been made to me were true. Perhaps the sight of the sister whom he was wont to love with a passion more than fraternal might have an auspicious influence on his malady.

Having formed this resolution, I waited to communicate it to Mr. Cambridge. I was aware that without his concurrence I could not hope to carry it into execution, and could discover no objection to which it was liable. If I had not been deceived as to his condition, no inconvenience could arise from this proceeding. His consent, therefore, would be the test of his sincerity.

I seized this opportunity to state my wishes on this head. My suspicions were confirmed by the manner in which my request affected him. After some pause, in which his countenance betrayed every mark of perplexity, he said to me, "Why would you pay this visit? What useful purpose can it serve?"

"We are preparing," said I, "to leave the country forever. What kind of being should I be to leave behind me a brother in calamity without even a parting interview? Indulge me for three minutes in the sight of him. My heart will be much easier after I have looked at him and shed a few tears in his presence."

"I believe otherwise. The sight of him would only

augment your distress, without contributing, in any degree, to his benefit."

"I know not that," returned I. "Surely the sympathy of his sister, proofs that her tenderness is as lively as ever, must be a source of satisfaction to him. At present he must regard all mankind as his enemies and calumniators. His sister he, probably, conceives to partake in the general infatuation, and to join in the cry of abhorrence that is raised against him. To be undeceived in this respect, to be assured that, however I may impute his conduct to delusion, I still retain all my former affection for his person and veneration for the purity of his motives, cannot but afford him pleasure. When he hears that I have left the country without even the ceremonious attention of a visit, what will he think of me? His magnanimity may hinder him from repining, but he will surely consider my behaviour as savage and unfeeling. Indeed, dear sir, I must pay this visit. To embark with you without paying it will be impossible. It may be of no service to him, but will enable me to acquit myself of what I cannot but esteem a duty. Besides," continued I, "if it be a mere fit of insanity that has seized him, may not my presence chance to have a salutary influence? The mere sight of me, it is not impossible, may rectify his perceptions."

"Ay," said my uncle, with some eagerness; "it is by no means impossible that your interview may have that effect; and for that reason, beyond all others, would I dissuade you from it."

I expressed my surprise at this declaration. "Is it not to be desired that an error so fatal as this should be rectified?"

"I wonder at your question. Reflect on the consequences of this error. Has he not destroyed the wife whom he loved, the children whom he idolized? What is it that enables him to bear the remembrance but the belief that he acted as his duty enjoined? Would you rashly bereave him of this belief? Would you restore him to himself, and convince him that he was instigated to this dreadful outrage by a perversion of his organs, or a delusion from hell?

"Now his visions are joyous and elate. He conceives himself to have reached a loftier degree of virtue than any other human being. The merit of his sacrifice is only enhanced, in the eyes of superior beings, by the detestation that pursues him here, and the sufferings to which he is condemned. The belief that even his sister has deserted him, and gone over to his enemies, adds to his sublimity of feelings, and his confidence in divine approbation and future recompense.

"Let him be undeceived in this respect, and what floods of despair and of horror will overwhelm him! Instead of glowing approbation and serene hope, will he not hate and torture himself? Self-violence, or a frenzy far more savage and destructive than this, may be expected to succeed. I beseech you, therefore, to relinquish this scheme. If you calmly reflect upon it, you will discover that your duty lies in carefully shunning him."

Mr. Cambridge's reasonings suggested views to my understanding that had not hitherto occurred. I could not but admit their validity; but they showed in a new light the depth of that misfortune in which my brother was plunged. I was silent and irresolute.

Presently I considered that whether Wieland was a maniac, a faithful servant of his God, the victim of hellish illusions, or the dupe of human imposture, was by no means certain. In this state of my mind, it became me to be silent during the visit that I projected. This visit should be brief; I should be satisfied merely to snatch a look at him. Admitting that a change in his opinions were not to be desired, there was no danger, from the conduct which I should pursue, that this change should be wrought.

But I could not conquer my uncle's aversion to this scheme. Yet I persisted; and he found that, to make me voluntarily relinquish it, it was necessary to be more explicit than he had hitherto been. He took both my hands, and, anxiously examining my countenance as he spoke, "Clara," said he, "this visit must not be paid. We must hasten with the utmost expedition from this shore. It is folly to conceal the truth from you; and, since it is only by disclosing the truth that you can be prevailed upon to lay aside this project, the truth shall be told.

"Oh, my dear girl!" continued he, with increasing energy in his accent, "your brother's frenzy is, indeed, stupendous and frightful. The soul that formerly actuated his frame has disappeared. The same form remains; but the wise and benevolent Wieland is no more. A fury that is rapacious of blood, that lifts his strength almost above that of mortals, that bends all his energies to the destruction of whatever was once dear to him, possesses him wholly.

"You must not enter his dungeon; his eyes will no sooner be fixed upon you than an exertion of his force will be made. He will shake off his fetters in a moment and rush upon you. No interposition will then be strong or quick enough to save you.

"The phantom that has urged him to the murder of Catharine and her children is not yet appeased. Your life, and that of Pleyel, are exacted from him by this imaginary being. He is eager to comply with this demand. Twice he has escaped from his prison. The first time, he no sooner found himself at liberty than he hasted to Pleyel's house. It being midnight, the latter was in bed. Wieland penetrated unobserved to his chamber, and opened his curtain. Happily, Pleyel awoke at the critical moment, and escaped the fury of his kinsman by leaping from his chamber-window into the court. Happily he reached the ground without injury. Alarms were given, and, after diligent search, your brother was found in a chamber of your house, whither, no doubt, he had sought you.

"His chains, and the watchfulness of his guards, were redoubled; but again, by some miracle, he restored himself to liberty. He was now incautiously apprized of the place of your abode; and, had not information of his escape been instantly given, your death would have been added to the number of his atrocious acts.

"You now see the danger of your project. You must not only forbear to visit him, but, if you would save him from the crime of imbruing his hands in your blood, you must leave the country. There is no hope that his malady will end but with his life, and no precaution will insure your safety but that of placing the ocean between you.

"I confess I came over with an intention to reside among you; but these disasters have changed my views. Your own safety and my happiness require that you should accompany me in my return, and I entreat you to give your cheerful concurrence to this measure."

After these representations from my uncle, it was impossible to retain my purpose. I readily consented to seclude myself from Wieland's presence. I likewise acquiesced in the proposal to go to Europe; not that I ever expected to arrive there, but because, since my principles forbade me to assail my own life, change had some tendency to make supportable the few days which disease should spare to me.

What a tale had thus been unfolded! I was hunted to death, not by one whom my misconduct had exasperated, who was conscious of illicit motives, and who sought his end by circumvention and surprise; but by

one who deemed himself commissioned for this act by
heaven; who regarded this career of horror as the last
refinement of virtue; whose implacability was proportioned to the reverence and love which he felt for me,
and who was inaccessible to the fear of punishment
and ignominy.

In vain should I endeavour to stay his hand by urging the claims of a sister or friend: these were his only
reasons for pursuing my destruction. Had I been a
stranger to his blood; had I been the most worthless of
human kind; my safety had not been endangered.

"Surely," said I, "my fate is without example. The
frenzy which is charged upon my brother must belong
to myself. My foe is manacled and guarded; but I derive no security from these restraints. I live not in a
community of savages; yet, whether I sit or walk, go
into crowds or hide myself in solitude, my life is
marked for a prey to inhuman violence; I am in perpetual danger of perishing; of perishing under the
grasp of a brother."

I recollected the omens of this destiny; I remembered the gulf to which my brother's invitation had
conducted me; I remembered that, when on the brink
of danger, the author of my peril was depicted by my
fears in his form. Thus realized were the creatures of
prophetic sleep and of wakeful terror!

These images were unavoidably connected with that
of Carwin. In this paroxysm of distress, my attention
fastened on him as the grand deceiver; the author of
this black conspiracy; the intelligence that governed in
this storm.

Some relief is afforded in the midst of suffering,
when its author is discovered or imagined, and an object found on which we may pour out our indignation
and our vengeance. I ran over the events that had
taken place since the origin of our intercourse with

him, and reflected on the tenor of that description which was received from Ludloe. Mixed up with notions of supernatural agency were the vehement suspicions which I entertained, that Carwin was the enemy whose machinations had destroyed us.

I thirsted for knowledge and for vengeance. I regarded my hasty departure with reluctance, since it would remove me from the means by which this knowledge might be obtained and this vengeance gratified. This departure was to take place in two days. At the end of two days I was to bid an eternal adieu to my native country. Should I not pay a parting visit to the scene of these disasters? Should I not bedew with my tears the graves of my sister and her children? Should I not explore their desolate habitation, and gather from the sight of its walls and furniture food for my eternal melancholy?

This suggestion was succeeded by a secret shuddering. Some disastrous influence appeared to overhang the scene. How many memorials should I meet with serving to recall the images of those I had lost!

I was tempted to relinquish my design, when it occurred to me that I had left among my papers a journal of transactions in short-hand. I was employed in this manuscript on that night when Pleyel's incautious curiosity tempted him to look over my shoulder. I was then recording my adventure in *the recess*, an imperfect sight of which led him into such fatal errors.

I had regulated the disposition of all my property. This manuscript, however, which contained the most secret transactions of my life, I was desirous of destroying. For this end I must return to my house, and this I immediately determined to do.

I was not willing to expose myself to opposition from my friends, by mentioning my design; I therefore bespoke the use of Mr. Hallet's chaise, under pretence of enjoying an airing, as the day was remarkably bright.

This request was gladly complied with, and I directed the servant to conduct me to Mettingen. I dismissed him at the gate, intending to use, in returning, a carriage belonging to my brother.

CHAPTER XXII

The inhabitants of the HUT received me with a mixture of joy and surprise. Their homely welcome, and their artless sympathy, were grateful to my feelings. In the midst of their inquiries as to my health, they avoided all allusions to the source of my malady. They were honest creatures, and I loved them well. I participated in the tears which they shed when I mentioned to them my speedy departure for Europe, and promised to acquaint them with my welfare during my long absence.

They expressed great surprise when I informed them of my intention to visit my cottage. Alarm and foreboding overspread their features, and they attempted to dissuade me from visiting a house which they firmly believed to be haunted by a thousand ghostly apparitions.

These apprehensions, however, had no power over my conduct. I took an irregular path which led me to my own house. All was vacant and forlorn. A small enclosure near which the path led was the burying-ground belonging to the family. This I was obliged to pass. Once I had intended to enter it, and ponder on the emblems and inscriptions which my uncle had caused to be made on the tombs of Catharine and her children; but now my heart faltered as I approached, and I hastened forward that distance might conceal it from my view.

When I approached the recess, my heart again sunk. I averted my eyes, and left it behind me as quickly as possible. Silence reigned through my habitation, and a darkness which closed doors and shutters produced. Every object was connected with mine or my brother's history. I passed the entry, mounted the stair, and unlocked the door of my chamber. It was with difficulty that I curbed my fancy and smothered my fears. Slight movements and casual sounds were transformed into beckoning shadows and calling shapes.

I proceeded to the closet. I opened and looked round it with fearfulness. All things were in their accustomed order. I sought and found the manuscript where I was used to deposit it. This being secured, there was nothing to detain me; yet I stood and contemplated a while the furniture and walls of my chamber. I remembered how long this apartment had been a sweet and tranquil asylum; I compared its former state with its present dreariness, and reflected that I now beheld it for the last time.

Here it was that the incomprehensible behaviour of Carwin was witnessed; this the stage on which that enemy of man showed himself for a moment unmasked. Here the menaces of murder were wafted to my ear; and here these menaces were executed.

These thoughts had a tendency to take from me my self-command. My feeble limbs refused to support me, and I sunk upon a chair. Incoherent and half-articulate exclamations escaped my lips. The name of Carwin was uttered, and eternal woes—woes like that which his malice had entailed upon us—were heaped upon him. I invoked all-seeing heaven to drag to light and punish this betrayer, and accused its providence for having thus long delayed the retribution that was due to so enormous a guilt.

I have said that the window-shutters were closed. A feeble light, however, found entrance through the crevices. A small window illuminated the closet, and, the door being closed, a dim ray streamed through the keyhole. A kind of twilight was thus created, sufficient for the purposes of vision, but, at the same time, involving all minuter objects in obscurity.

This darkness suited the colour of my thoughts. I sickened at the remembrance of the past. The prospect of the future excited my loathing. I muttered, in a low voice, "Why should I live longer? Why should I drag a miserable being? All for whom I ought to live have perished. Am I not myself hunted to death?"

At that moment my despair suddenly became vigorous. My nerves were no longer unstrung. My powers, that had long been deadened, were revived. My bosom swelled with a sudden energy, and the conviction darted through my mind, that to end my torments was, at once, practicable and wise.

I knew how to find way to the recesses of life. I could use a lancet with some skill, and could distinguish between vein and artery. By piercing deep into the latter, I should shun the evils which the future had in store for me, and take refuge from my woes in quiet death.

I started on my feet, for my feebleness was gone, and hasted to the closet. A lancet and other small instruments were preserved in a case which I had deposited here. Inattentive as I was to foreign considerations, my ears were still open to any sound of mysterious import that should occur. I thought I heard a step in the entry. My purpose was suspended, and I cast an eager glance at my chamber door, which was open. No one appeared, unless the shadow which I discerned upon the floor was the outline of a man. If it were, I was authorized to suspect that some one was posted close to the entrance, who possibly had overheard my exclamations.

My teeth chattered, and a wild confusion took the place of my momentary calm. Thus it was when a terrific visage had disclosed itself on a former night. Thus it was when the evil destiny of Wieland assumed the lineaments of something human. What horrid apparition was preparing to blast my sight?

Still I listened and gazed. Not long, for the shadow moved; a foot, unshapely and huge, was thrust forward; a form advanced from its concealment, and stalked into the room. It was Carwin!

While I had breath, I shrieked. While I had power over my muscles, I motioned with my hand that he should vanish. My exertions could not last long: I sunk into a fit.

Oh that this grateful oblivion had lasted forever! Too quickly I recovered my senses. The power of distinct vision was no sooner restored to me, than this hateful form again presented itself, and I once more relapsed.

A second time, untoward nature recalled me from the sleep of death. I found myself stretched upon the bed. When I had power to look up, I remembered only that I had cause to fear. My distempered fancy fashioned to itself no distinguishable image. I threw a languid glance round me: once more my eyes lighted upon Carwin.

He was seated on the floor, his back rested against the wall; his knees were drawn up, and his face was buried in his hands. That his station was at some distance, that his attitude was not menacing, that his ominous visage was concealed, may account for my now escaping a shock violent as those which were past. I withdrew my eyes, but was not again deserted by my senses.

On perceiving that I had recovered my sensibility, he lifted his head. This motion attracted my attention. His countenance was mild, but sorrow and astonishment sat upon his features. I averted my eyes and feebly exclaimed, "Oh, fly!—fly far and forever!—I cannot behold you and live!"

He did not rise upon his feet, but clasped his hands, and said, in a tone of deprecation, "I will fly. I am become a fiend, the sight of whom destroys. Yet tell me my offence! You have linked curses with my name; you ascribe to me a malice monstrous and infernal. I look around: all is loneliness and desert! This house and your brother's are solitary and dismantled! You die away at the sight of me! My fear whispers that some deed of horror has been perpetrated; that I am the undesigning cause."

What language was this? Had he not avowed himself a ravisher? Had not this chamber witnessed his atrocious purposes? I besought him with new vehemence to go.

He lifted his eyes:—"Great heaven! what have I done? I think I know the extent of my offences. I have acted, but my actions have possibly effected more than I designed. This fear has brought me back from my retreat. I come to repair the evil of which my rashness was the cause, and to prevent more evil. I come to confess my errors."

"Wretch!" I cried, when my suffocating emotions would permit me to speak, "the ghosts of my sister and her children,—do they not rise to accuse thee? Who was it that blasted the intellect of Wieland? Who was it that urged him to fury and guided him to murder? Who, but thou and the devil, with whom thou art confederated?"

At these words a new spirit pervaded his countenance. His eyes once more appealed to heaven. "If I have memory—if I have being—I am innocent. I intended no ill; but my folly, indirectly and remotely, may have caused it. But what words are these? Your brother lunatic! His children dead!"

What should I infer from this deportment? Was the ignorance which these words implied real or pretended? Yet how could I imagine a mere human agency in these events? But, if the influence was preternatural or maniacal in my brother's case, they must be equally so in my own. Then I remembered that the voice exerted was to save me from Carwin's attempts. These ideas tended to abate my abhorrence of this man, and to detect the absurdity of my accusations.

"Alas!" said I, "I have no one to accuse. Leave me to my fate. Fly from a scene stained with cruelty, devoted to despair."

Carwin stood for a time musing and mournful. At length he said, "What has happened? I came to expiate my crimes: let me know them in their full extent. I have horrible forebodings! What has happened?"

I was silent; but, recollecting the intimation given by this man when he was detected in my closet, which implied some knowledge of that power which interfered in my favour, I eagerly inquired, "What was that voice which called upon me to hold when I attempted to open the closet? What face was that which I saw at the bottom of the stairs? Answer me truly."

"I came to confess the truth. Your allusions are horrible and strange. Perhaps I have but faint conceptions of the evils which my infatuation has produced; but what remains I will perform. It was *my voice* that you heard! It was *my face* that you saw!"

For a moment I doubted whether my remembrance of events were not confused. How could he be at once

stationed at my shoulder and shut up in my closet?
How could he stand near me and yet be invisible? But
if Carwin's were the thrilling voice and the fiery image
which I had heard and seen, then was he the prompter
of my brother, and the author of these dismal outrages.

Once more I averted my eyes and struggled for
speech:—"Begone! thou man of mischief! Remorseless
and implacable miscreant, begone!"

"I will obey," said he, in a disconsolate voice; "yet,
wretch as I am, am I unworthy to repair the evils that
I have committed? I came as a repentant criminal. It
is you whom I have injured, and at your bar am I willing to appear and confess and expiate my crimes. I
have deceived you; I have sported with your terrors;
I have plotted to destroy your reputation. I come now
to remove your terrors; to set you beyond the reach of
similar fears; to rebuild your fame as far as I am able.

"This is the amount of my guilt, and this the fruit of
my remorse. Will you not hear me? Listen to my confession, and then denounce punishment. All I ask is a
patient audience."

"What!" I replied; "was not thine the voice that commanded my brother to imbrue his hands in the blood
of his children?—to strangle that angel of sweetness, his
wife? Has he not vowed my death, and the death of
Pleyel, at thy bidding? Hast thou not made him the
butcher of his family?—changed him who was the glory
of his species into worse than brute?—robbed him of
reason and consigned the rest of his days to fetters and
stripes?"

Carwin's eyes glared and his limbs were petrified at
this intelligence. No words were requisite to prove him
guiltless of these enormities: at the time, however, I
was nearly insensible to these exculpatory tokens. He
walked to the farther end of the room, and, having recovered some degree of composure, he spoke:—

"I am not this villain. I have slain no one; I have prompted none to slay; I have handled a tool of wonderful efficacy without malignant intentions, but without caution. Ample will be the punishment of my temerity, if my conduct has contributed to this evil." He paused.

I likewise was silent. I struggled to command myself so far as to listen to the tale which he should tell. Observing this, he continued:—

"You are not apprized of the existence of a power which I possess. I know not by what name to call it.* It enables me to mimic exactly the voice of another, and to modify the sound so that it shall appear to come from what quarter and be uttered at what distance I please.

"I know not that every one possesses this power. Perhaps, though a casual position of my organs in my

* *Biloquium*, or ventrilocution. Sound is varied according to the variations of direction and distance. The art of the ventriloquist consists in modifying his voice according to all these variations, without changing his place. See the work of the Abbé de la Chappelle, in which are accurately recorded the performances of one of these artists, and some ingenious though unsatisfactory speculations are given on the means by which the effects are produced. This power is, perhaps, given by nature, but is doubtless improvable, if not acquirable, by art. It may, possibly, consist in an unusual flexibility or extension of the bottom of the tongue and the uvula. That speech is producible by these alone must be granted, since anatomists mention two instances of persons speaking without a tongue. In one case the organ was originally wanting, but its place was supplied by a small tubercle, and the uvula was perfect. In the other the tongue was destroyed by disease, but probably a small part of it remained.

This power is difficult to explain, but the fact is undeniable. Experience shows that the human voice can imitate the voice of all men and of all inferior animals. The sound of musical instruments, and even noises from the contact of inanimate substances, have been accurately imitated. The mimicry of animals is notorious; and Dr. Burney ("Musical Travels") mentions one who imitated a flute and violin, so as to deceive even his ears.

youth showed me that I possessed it, it is an art which may be taught to all. Would to God I had died unknowing of the secret! It has produced nothing but degradation and calamity.

"For a time the possession of so potent and stupendous an endowment elated me with pride. Unfortified by principle, subjected to poverty, stimulated by headlong passions, I made this powerful engine subservient to the supply of my wants and the gratification of my vanity. I shall not mention how diligently I cultivated this gift, which seemed capable of unlimited improvement; nor detail the various occasions on which it was successfully exerted to lead superstition, conquer avarice, or excite awe.

"I left America, which is my native soil, in my youth. I have been engaged in various scenes of life, in which my peculiar talent has been exercised with more or less success. I was finally betrayed, by one who called himself my friend, into acts which cannot be justified, though they are susceptible of apology.

"The perfidy of this man compelled me to withdraw from Europe. I returned to my native country, uncertain whether silence and obscurity would save me from his malice. I resided in the purlieus of the city. I put on the garb and assumed the manners of a clown.

"My chief recreation was walking. My principal haunts were the lawns and gardens of Mettingen. In this delightful region the luxuriances of nature had been chastened by judicious art, and each successive contemplation unfolded new enchantments.

"I was studious of seclusion; I was satiated with the intercourse of mankind, and discretion required me to shun their intercourse. For these reasons I long avoided the observation of your family, and chiefly visited these precincts at night.

"I was never weary of admiring the position and

ornaments of *the temple*. Many a night have I passed under its roof, revolving no pleasing meditations. When, in my frequent rambles, I perceived this apartment was occupied, I gave a different direction to my steps. One evening, when a shower had just passed, judging by the silence that no one was within, I ascended to this building. Glancing carelessly round, I perceived an open letter on the pedestal. To read it was doubtless an offence against politeness. Of this offence, however, I was guilty.

"Scarcely had I gone half through when I was alarmed by the approach of your brother. To scramble down the cliff on the opposite side was impracticable. I was unprepared to meet a stranger. Besides the awkwardness attending such an interview in these circumstances, concealment was necessary to my safety. A thousand times had I vowed never again to employ the dangerous talent which I possessed; but such was the force of habit and the influence of present convenience, that I used this method of arresting his progress and leading him back to the house, with his errand, whatever it was, unperformed. I had often caught parts, from my station below, of your conversation in this place, and was well acquainted with the voice of your sister.

"Some weeks after this I was again quietly seated in this recess. The lateness of the hour secured me, as I thought, from all interruption. In this, however, I was mistaken; for Wieland and Pleyel, as I judged by their voices, earnest in dispute, ascended the hill.

"I was not sensible that any inconvenience could possibly have flowed from my former exertion; yet it was followed with compunction, because it was a deviation from a path which I had assigned to myself. Now my aversion to this means of escape was enforced by an unauthorized curiosity, and by the knowledge of a

bushy hollow on the edge of the hill, where I should be
safe from discovery. Into this hollow I thrust myself.

"The propriety of removal to Europe was the question eagerly discussed. Pleyel intimated that his anxiety to go was augmented by the silence of Theresa de
Stolberg. The temptation to interfere in this dispute
was irresistible. In vain I contended with inveterate
habits. I disguised to myself the impropriety of my conduct, by recollecting the benefits which it might produce. Pleyel's proposal was unwise, yet it was enforced
with plausible arguments and indefatigable zeal. Your
brother might be puzzled and wearied, but could not
be convinced. I conceived that to terminate the controversy in favour of the latter was conferring a benefit
on all parties. For this end I profited by an opening in
the conversation, and assured them of Catharine's irreconcilable aversion to the scheme, and of the death
of the Saxon baroness. The latter event was merely a
conjecture, but rendered extremely probable by Pleyel's representations. My purpose, you need not be
told, was effected.

"My passion for mystery, and a species of imposture,
which I deemed harmless, was thus awakened afresh.
This second lapse into error made my recovery more
difficult. I cannot convey to you an adequate idea of
the kind of gratification which I derived from these
exploits; yet I meditated nothing. My views were
bounded to the passing moment, and commonly suggested by the momentary exigence.

"I must not conceal any thing. Your principles teach
you to abhor a voluptuous temper; but, with whatever
reluctance, I acknowledge this temper to be mine. You
imagine your servant Judith to be innocent as well as
beautiful; but you took her from a family where hypocrisy, as well as licentiousness, was wrought into a sys-

tem. My attention was captivated by her charms, and her principles were easily seen to be flexible.

"Deem me not capable of the iniquity of seduction. Your servant is not destitute of feminine and virtuous qualities; but she was taught that the best use of her charms consists in the sale of them. My nocturnal visits to Mettingen were now prompted by a double view, and my correspondence with your servant gave me, at all times, access to your house.

"The second night after our interview, so brief and so little foreseen by either of us, some demon of mischief seized me. According to my companion's report, your perfections were little less than divine. Her uncouth but copious narratives converted you into an object of worship. She chiefly dwelt upon your courage, because she herself was deficient in that quality. You held apparitions and goblins in contempt. You took no precautions against robbers. You were just as tranquil and secure in this lonely dwelling as if you were in the midst of a crowd.

"Hence a vague project occurred to me to put this courage to the test. A woman capable of recollection in danger, of warding off groundless panics, of discerning the true mode of proceeding and profiting by her best resources, is a prodigy. I was desirous of ascertaining whether you were such a one.

"My expedient was obvious and simple. I was to counterfeit a murderous dialogue; but this was to be so conducted that another, and not yourself, should appear to be the object. I was not aware of the possibility that you should appropriate these menaces to yourself. Had you been still and listened, you would have heard the struggles and prayers of the victim, who would likewise have appeared to be shut up in the closet, and whose voice would have been Judith's. This scene would have been an appeal to your compassion; and

the proof of cowardice or courage which I expected
from you would have been your remaining inactive in
your bed, or your entering the closet with a view to
assist the sufferer. Some instances which Judith related
of your fearlessness and promptitude made me adopt
the latter supposition with some degree of confidence.

"By the girl's direction I found a ladder, and
mounted to your closet window. This is scarcely large
enough to admit the head, but it answered my purpose
too well.

"I cannot express my confusion and surprise at your
abrupt and precipitate flight. I hastily removed the
ladder; and, after some pause, curiosity and doubts of
your safety induced me to follow you. I found you
stretched on the turf before your brother's door without
sense or motion. I felt the deepest regret at this unlooked-for consequence of my scheme. I knew not
what to do to procure you relief. The idea of awakening the family naturally presented itself. This emer-
gency was critical, and there was no time to deliberate.
It was a sudden thought that occurred. I put my lips to
the keyhole, and sounded an alarm which effectually
roused the sleepers. My organs were naturally forcible,
and had been improved by long and assiduous exercise.

"Long and bitterly did I repent of my scheme. I was
somewhat consoled by reflecting that my purpose had
not been evil, and renewed my fruitless vows never to
attempt such dangerous experiments. For some time I
adhered, with laudable forbearance, to this resolution.

"My life has been a life of hardship and exposure.
In the summer I prefer to make my bed of the smooth
turf, or, at most, the shelter of a summer-house suffices.
In all my rambles I never found a spot in which so
many picturesque beauties and rural delights were assembled as at Mettingen. No corner of your little do-

main unites fragrance and secrecy in so perfect a degree as the recess in the bank. The odour of its leaves, the coolness of its shade, and the music of its waterfall, had early attracted my attention. Here my sadness was converted into peaceful melancholy; here my slumbers were sound, and my pleasures enhanced.

"As most free from interruption, I chose this as the scene of my midnight interviews with Judith. One evening, as the sun declined, I was seated here, when I was alarmed by your approach. It was with difficulty that I effected my escape unnoticed by you.

"At the customary hour I returned to your habitation, and was made acquainted by Judith with your unusual absence. I half suspected the true cause, and felt uneasiness at the danger there was that I should be deprived of my retreat, or, at least, interrupted in the possession of it. The girl likewise informed me that, among your other singularities, it was not uncommon for you to leave your bed and walk forth for the sake of night-airs and starlight contemplations.

"I desired to prevent this inconvenience. I found you easily swayed by fear. I was influenced in my choice of means by the facility and certainty of that to which I had been accustomed. All that I foresaw was, that, in future, this spot would be cautiously shunned by you.

"I entered the recess with the utmost caution, and discovered, by your breathings, in what condition you were. The unexpected interpretation which you placed upon my former proceeding suggested my conduct on the present occasion. The mode in which heaven is said by the poet to interfere for the prevention of crimes* was somewhat analogous to my province, and never failed to occur to me at seasons like this. It was requisite to break your slumbers; and for this end I uttered the

---

* ——"Peeps through the blanket of the dark, and cries
Hold! hold!" SHAKSPEARE.

powerful monosyllable, 'Hold! hold!' My purpose was
not prescribed by duty, yet surely it was far from being
atrocious and inexpiable. To effect it, I uttered what
was false; but it was well suited to my purpose. Nothing less was intended than to injure you. Nay, the evil
resulting from my former act was partly removed by
assuring you that in all places but this you were safe.

CHAPTER XXIII

"My morals will appear to you far from rigid, yet my
conduct will fall short of your suspicions. I am now to
confess actions less excusable; and yet surely they will
not entitle me to the name of a desperate or sordid
criminal.

"Your house was rendered, by your frequent and
long absences, easily accessible to my curiosity. My
meeting with Pleyel was the prelude to direct intercourse with you. I had seen much of the world; but
your character exhibited a specimen of human powers
that was wholly new to me. My intercourse with your
servant furnished me with curious details of your domestic management. I was of a different sex; I was not
your husband; I was not even your friend; yet my
knowledge of you was of that kind which conjugal in-
timacies can give, and, in some respects, more accurate. The observation of your domestic was guided by
me.

"You will not be surprised that I should sometimes
profit by your absence, and adventure to examine with
my own eyes the interior of your chamber. Upright and
sincere, you used no watchfulness, and practised no

precautions. I scrutinized every thing and pried everywhere. Your closet was usually locked; but it was once my fortune to find the key on a bureau. I opened and found new scope for my curiosity in your books. One of these was manuscript, and written in characters which essentially agreed with a short-hand system which I had learned from a Jesuit missionary.

"I cannot justify my conduct; yet my only crime was curiosity. I perused this volume with eagerness. The intellect which it unveiled was brighter than my limited and feeble organs could bear. I was naturally inquisitive as to your ideas respecting my deportment and the mysteries that had lately occurred.

"You know what you have written. You know that in this volume the key to your inmost soul was contained. If I had been a profound and malignant impostor, what plenteous materials were thus furnished me of stratagems and plots!

"The coincidence of your dream in the summerhouse with my exclamation was truly wonderful. The voice which warned you to forbear was, doubtless, mine, but mixed, by a common process of the fancy, with the train of visionary incidents.

"I saw in a stronger light than ever the dangerousness of that instrument which I employed, and renewed my resolutions to abstain from the use of it in future; but I was destined perpetually to violate my resolutions. By some perverse fate, I was led into circumstances in which the exertion of my powers was the sole or the best means of escape.

"On that memorable night on which our last interview took place, I came as usual to Mettingen. I was apprized of your engagement at your brother's, from which you did not expect to return till late. Some incident suggested the design of visiting your chamber. Among your books which I had not examined might be something tending to illustrate your character or the history of your family. Some intimation had been dropped by you in discourse, respecting a performance of your father, in which some important transaction in his life was recorded.

"I was desirous of seeing this book; and such was my habitual attachment to mystery, that I preferred the clandestine perusal of it. Such were the motives that induced me to make this attempt. Judith had disappeared, and, finding the house unoccupied, I supplied myself with a light and proceeded to your chamber.

"I found it easy, on experiment, to lock and unlock your closet door without the aid of a key. I shut myself in this recess, and was busily exploring your shelves, when I heard some one enter the room below. I was at a loss who it could be,—whether you or your servant. Doubtful, however, as I was, I conceived it prudent to extinguish the light. Scarcely was this done, when some one entered the chamber. The footsteps were easily distinguished to be yours.

"My situation was now full of danger and perplexity. For some time I cherished the hope that you would leave the room so long as to afford me an opportunity of escaping. As the hours passed, this hope gradually deserted me. It was plain that you had retired for the night.

"I knew not how soon you might find occasion to enter the closet. I was alive to all the horrors of detection, and ruminated without ceasing on the behaviour which it would be proper, in case of detection, to adopt. I was unable to discover any consistent method of accounting for my being thus immured.

"It occurred to me that I might withdraw you from your chamber for a few minutes by counterfeiting a voice from without. Some message from your brother might be delivered, requiring your presence at his house. I was deterred from this scheme by reflecting on the resolution I had formed, and on the possible evils that might result from it. Besides, it was not improbable that you would speedily retire to bed, and then, by the exercise of sufficient caution, I might hope to escape unobserved.

"Meanwhile I listened with the deepest anxiety to every motion from without. I discovered nothing which betokened preparation for sleep. Instead of this, I heard deep-drawn sighs, and occasionally a half-expressed and mournful ejaculation. Hence I inferred that you were unhappy. The true state of your mind with regard to Pleyel your own pen had disclosed; but I supposed you to be framed of such materials, that, though a momentary sadness might affect you, you were impregnable to any permanent and heartfelt grief. Inquietude for my own safety was for a moment suspended by sympathy with your distress.

"To the former consideration I was quickly recalled by a motion of yours which indicated I knew not what. I fostered the persuasion that you would now retire to bed; but presently you approached the closet, and detection seemed to be inevitable. You put your hand upon the lock. I had formed no plan to extricate myself from the dilemma in which the opening of the door would involve me. I felt an irreconcilable aversion to detection. Thus situated, I involuntarily seized the door, with a resolution to resist your efforts to open it.

"Suddenly you receded from the door. This deportment was inexplicable; but the relief it afforded me was quickly gone. You returned, and I once more was thrown into perplexity. The expedient that suggested itself was precipitate and inartificial. I exerted my organs and called upon you *to hold*.

"That you should persist in spite of this admonition

was a subject of astonishment. I again resisted your
efforts; for, the first expedient having failed, I knew
not what other to resort to. In this state, how was
my astonishment increased when I heard your exclamations!

"It was now plain that you knew me to be within.
Further resistance was unavailing and useless. The
door opened, and I shrunk backward. Seldom have I
felt deeper mortification and more painful perplexity.
I did not consider that the truth would be less injurious
than any lie which I could hastily frame. Conscious as
I was of a certain degree of guilt, I conceived that you
would form the most odious suspicions. The truth
would be imperfect, unless I were likewise to explain
the mysterious admonition which had been given; but
that explanation was of too great moment, and involved too extensive consequences, to make me suddenly resolve to give it.

"I was aware that this discovery would associate itself in your mind with the dialogue formerly heard in
this closet. Thence would your suspicions be aggravated, and to escape from these suspicions would be
impossible. But the mere truth would be sufficiently
opprobrious, and deprive me forever of your good
opinion.

"Thus was I rendered desperate, and my mind rapidly passed to the contemplation of the use that might
be made of previous events. Some good genius would
appear to you to have interposed to save you from injury intended by me. 'Why,' I said, 'since I must sink in
her opinion, should I not cherish this belief? Why not
personate an enemy, and pretend that celestial interference has frustrated my schemes? I must fly; but let
me leave wonder and fear behind me. Elucidation of
the mystery will always be practicable. I shall do no

injury, but merely talk of evil that was designed, but is now past.'

"Thus I extenuated my conduct to myself; but I scarcely expect that this will be to you a sufficient explication of the scene that followed. Those habits which I have imbibed, the rooted passion which possesses me for scattering around me amazement and fear, you enjoy no opportunities of knowing. That a man should wantonly impute to himself the most flagitious designs will hardly be credited, even though you reflect that my reputation was already, by my own folly, irretrievably ruined; and that it was always in my power to communicate the truth and rectify the mistake.

"I left you to ponder on this scene. My mind was full of rapid and incongruous ideas. Compunction, self-upbraiding, hopelessness, satisfaction at the view of those effects likely to flow from my new scheme, misgivings as to the beneficial result of this scheme, took possession of my mind, and seemed to struggle for the mastery.

"I had gone too far to recede. I had painted myself to you as an assassin and ravisher, withheld from guilt only by a voice from heaven. I had thus reverted into the path of error, and now, having gone thus far, my progress seemed to be irrevocable. I said to myself, 'I must leave these precincts forever. My acts have blasted my fame in the eyes of the Wielands. For the sake of creating a mysterious dread, I have made myself a villain. I may complete this mysterious plan by some new imposture, but I cannot aggravate my supposed guilt.'

"My resolution was formed, and I was swiftly ruminating on the means for executing it, when Pleyel appeared in sight. This incident decided my conduct. It was plain that Pleyel was a devoted lover, but he was, at the same time, a man of cold resolves and exquisite

sagacity. To deceive him would be the sweetest triumph I had ever enjoyed. The deception would be
momentary, but it would likewise be complete. That
his delusion would so soon be rectified was a recom-
mendation to my scheme; for I esteemed him too much
to desire to entail upon him lasting agonies.

"I had no time to reflect further, for he proceeded,
with a quick step, towards the house. I was hurried
onward involuntarily and by a mechanical impulse. I
followed him as he passed the recess in the bank, and,
shrouding myself in that spot, I counterfeited sounds
which I knew would arrest his steps.

"He stopped, turned, listened, approached, and overheard a dialogue whose purpose was to vanquish his
belief in a point where his belief was most difficult to
vanquish. I exerted all my powers to imitate your voice,
your general sentiments, and your language. Being
master, by means of your journal, of your personal history and most secret thoughts, my efforts were the
more successful. When I review the tenor of this dialogue, I cannot believe but that Pleyel was deluded.
When I think of your character, and of the inferences
which this dialogue was intended to suggest, it seems
incredible that this delusion should be produced.

"I spared not myself. I called myself murderer, thief,
guilty of innumerable perjuries and misdeeds. That
you had debased yourself to the level of such a one, no
evidence, methought, would suffice to convince him
who knew you so thoroughly as Pleyel; and yet the imposture amounted to proof which the most jealous scrutiny would find to be unexceptionable.

"He left his station precipitately and resumed his
way to the house. I saw that the detection of his error
would be instantaneous, since, not having gone to bed,
an immediate interview would take place between
you. At first this circumstance was considered with re-

gret; but, as time opened my eyes to the possible consequences of this scene, I regarded it with pleasure.

"In a short time the infatuation which had led me thus far began to subside. The remembrance of former reasonings and transactions was renewed. How often I had repented this kind of exertion; how many evils were produced by it which I had not foreseen; what occasions for the bitterest remorse it had administered, now passed through my mind. The black catalogue of stratagems was now increased. I had inspired you with the most vehement terrors; I had filled your mind with faith in shadows and confidence in dreams; I had depraved the imagination of Pleyel; I had exhibited you to his understanding as devoted to brutal gratifications and consummate in hypocrisy. The evidence which accompanied this delusion would be irresistible to one whose passion had perverted his judgment, whose jealousy with regard to me had already been excited, and who, therefore, would not fail to overrate the force of this evidence. What fatal act of despair or of vengeance might not this error produce?

"With regard to myself, I had acted with a frenzy that surpassed belief. I had warred against my peace and my fame; I had banished myself from the fellowship of vigorous and pure minds; I was self-expelled from a scene which the munificence of nature had adorned with unrivalled beauties, and from haunts in which all the muses and humanities had taken refuge.

"I was thus torn by conflicting fears and tumultuous regrets. The night passed away in this state of confusion; and the next morning, in the gazette left at my obscure lodging, I read a description and an offer of reward for the apprehension of my person. I was said to have escaped from an Irish prison, in which I was confined as an offender convicted of enormous and complicated crimes.

"This was the work of an enemy, who, by falsehood and stratagem, had procured my condemnation. I was, indeed, a prisoner, but escaped, by the exertion of my powers, the fate to which I was doomed, but which I did not deserve. I had hoped that the malice of my foe was exhausted; but I now perceived that my precautions had been wise, for that the intervention of an ocean was insufficient for my security.

"Let me not dwell on the sensations which this discovery produced. I need not tell by what steps I was induced to seek an interview with you, for the purpose of disclosing the truth, and repairing, as far as possible, the effects of my misconduct. It was unavoidable that this gazette would fall into your hands, and that it would tend to confirm every erroneous impression.

"Having gained this interview, I purposed to seek some retreat in the wilderness, inaccessible to your inquiry and to the malice of my foe, where I might henceforth employ myself in composing a faithful narrative of my actions. I designed it as my vindication from the aspersions that had rested on my character, and as a lesson to mankind on the evils of credulity on the one hand, and of imposture on the other.

"I wrote you a billet, which was left at the house of your friend, and which I knew would, by some means, speedily come to your hands. I entertained a faint hope that my invitation would be complied with. I knew not what use you would make of the opportunity which this proposal afforded you of procuring the seizure of my person; but this fate I was determined to avoid, and I had no doubt but due circumspection, and the exercise of the faculty which I possessed, would enable me to avoid it.

"I lurked through the day in the neighbourhood of Mettingen; I approached your habitation at the appointed hour: I entered it in silence, by a trap-door which led into the cellar. This had formerly been bolted on the inside, but Judith had, at an early period in our intercourse, removed this impediment. I ascended to the first floor, but met with no one, nor any thing that indicated the presence of a human being.

"I crept softly up-stairs, and at length perceived your chamber door to be opened and a light to be within. It was of moment to discover by whom this light was accompanied. I was sensible of the inconveniences to which my being discovered at your chamber door by any one within would subject me; I therefore called out in my own voice, but so modified that it should appear to ascend from the court below, 'Who is in the chamber? Is it Miss Wieland?'

"No answer was returned to this summons. I listened, but no motion could be heard. After a pause I repeated my call, but no less ineffectually.

"I now approached nearer to the door, and adventured to look in. A light stood on the table, but nothing human was discernible. I entered cautiously, but all was solitude and stillness.

"I knew not what to conclude. If the house were inhabited, my call would have been noticed; yet some suspicion insinuated itself that silence was studiously kept by persons who intended to surprise me. My approach had been wary, and the silence that ensued my call had likewise preceded it; a circumstance that tended to dissipate my fears.

"At length it occurred to me that Judith might possibly be in her own room. I turned my steps thither; but she was not to be found. I passed into other rooms, and was soon convinced that the house was totally deserted. I returned to your chamber, agitated by vain surmises and opposite conjectures. The appointed hour had passed, and I dismissed the hope of an interview.

"In this state of things I determined to leave a few

lines on your toilet, and prosecute my journey to the mountains. Scarcely had I taken the pen when I laid it aside, uncertain in what manner to address you. I rose from the table and walked across the floor. A glance thrown upon the bed acquainted me with a spectacle to which my conceptions of horror had not yet reached.

"In the midst of shuddering and trepidation, the signal of your presence in the court below recalled me to myself. The deed was newly done; I only was in the house; what had lately happened justified any suspicions, however enormous. It was plain that this catastrophe was unknown to you; I thought upon the wild commotion which the discovery would awaken in your breast; I found the confusion of my own thoughts unconquerable, and perceived that the end for which I sought an interview was not now to be accomplished.

"In this state of things, it was likewise expedient to conceal my being within. I put out the light and hurried down the stairs. To my unspeakable surprise, notwithstanding every motive to fear, you lighted a candle and proceeded to your chamber.

"I retired to that room below from which a door leads into the cellar. This door concealed me from your view as you passed. I thought upon the spectacle which was about to present itself. In an exigence so abrupt and so little foreseen, I was again subjected to the empire of mechanical and habitual impulses. I dreaded the effects which this shocking exhibition, bursting on your unprepared senses, might produce.

"Thus actuated, I stepped swiftly to the door, and, thrusting my head forward, once more pronounced the mysterious interdiction. At that moment, by some untoward fate, your eyes were cast back, and you saw me in the very act of utterance. I fled through the darksome avenue at which I entered, covered with the shame of this detection.

"With diligence, stimulated by a thousand ineffable emotions, I pursued my intended journey. I have a brother whose farm is situated in the bosom of a fertile desert, near the sources of the Lehigh; and thither I now repaired.

CHAPTER XXIV

"Deeply did I ruminate on the occurrences that had just passed. Nothing excited my wonder so much as the means by which you discovered my being in the closet. This discovery appeared to be made at the moment when you attempted to open it. How could you have otherwise remained so long in the chamber apparently fearless and tranquil? And yet, having made this discovery, how could you persist in dragging me forth?— persist in defiance of an interdiction so emphatical and solemn?

"But your sister's death was an event detestable and ominous. She had been the victim of the most dreadful species of assassination. How, in a state like yours, the murderous intention could be generated, was wholly inconceivable.

"I did not relinquish my design of confessing to you the part which I had sustained in your family; but I was willing to defer it till the task which I had set myself was finished. That being done, I resumed the resolution. The motives to incite me to this continually acquired force. The more I revolved the events happening at Mettingen, the more insupportable and omi-

nous my terrors became. My waking hours and my
sleep were vexed by dismal presages and frightful inti-
mations.

"Catharine was dead by violence. Surely my malignant stars had not made me the cause of her death; yet
had I not rashly set in motion a machine over whose
progress I had no control, and which experience had
shown me was infinite in power? Every day might add
to the catalogue of horrors of which this was the source,
and a seasonable disclosure of the truth might prevent
numberless ills.

"Fraught with this conception, I have turned my
steps hither. I find your brother's house desolate; the
furniture removed, and the walls stained with damps.
Your own is in the same situation. Your chamber is dismantled and dark, and you exhibit an image of incurable grief and of rapid decay.

"I have uttered the truth. This is the extent of my
offences. You tell me a horrid tale of Wieland being
led to the destruction of his wife and children by some
mysterious agent. You charge me with the guilt of this
agency; but I repeat that the amount of my guilt has
been truly stated. The perpetrator of Catharine's death
was unknown to me till now; nay, it is still unknown
to me."

At that moment, the closing of a door in the kitchen
was distinctly heard by us. Carwin started and paused.
"There is some one coming. I must not be found here
by my enemies, and need not, since my purpose is
answered."

I had drunk in, with the most vehement attention,
every word that he had uttered. I had no breath to
interrupt his tale by interrogations or comments. The
power that he spoke of was hitherto unknown to me;
its existence was incredible; it was susceptible of no
direct proof.

He owns that his were the voice and face which I heard and saw. He attempts to give a human explanation of these phantasms; but it is enough that he owns himself to be the agent: his tale is a lie, and his nature devilish. As he deceived me, he likewise deceived my brother, and now do I behold the author of all our calamities!

Such were my thoughts when his pause allowed me to think. I should have bade him begone if the silence had not been interrupted; but now I feared no more for myself; and the milkiness of my nature was curdled into hatred and rancour. Some one was near, and this enemy of God and man might possibly be brought to justice. I reflected not that the preternatural power which he had hitherto exerted would avail to rescue him from any toils in which his feet might be entangled. Meanwhile, looks, and not words, of menace and abhorrence, were all that I could bestow.

He did not depart. He seemed dubious whether by passing out of the house, or by remaining somewhat longer where he was, he should most endanger his safety. His confusion increased when steps of one barefoot were heard upon the stairs. He threw anxious glances sometimes at the closet, sometimes at the window, and sometimes at the chamber door; yet he was detained by some inexplicable fascination. He stood as if rooted to the spot.

As to me, my soul was bursting with detestation and revenge. I had no room for surmises and fears respecting him that approached. It was doubtless a human being, and would befriend me so far as to aid me in arresting this offender.

The stranger quickly entered the room. My eyes and the eyes of Carwin were at the same moment darted upon him. A second glance was not needed to inform us who he was. His locks were tangled, and fell con-

fusedly over his forehead and ears. His shirt was of
coarse stuff, and open at the neck and breast. His coat
was once of bright and fine texture, but now torn and
tarnished with dust. His feet, his legs, and his arms,
were bare. His features were the seat of a wild and
tranquil solemnity, but his eyes bespoke inquietude
and curiosity.

He advanced with a firm step, and looking as in
search of some one. He saw me and stopped. He bent
his sight on the floor, and, clenching his hands, appeared suddenly absorbed in meditation. Such were
the figure and deportment of Wieland! Such, in his
fallen state, were the aspect and guise of my brother!

Carwin did not fail to recognise the visitant. Care
for his own safety was apparently swallowed up in the
amazement which this spectacle produced. His station
was conspicuous, and he could not have escaped the
roving glances of Wieland; yet the latter seemed totally unconscious of his presence.

Grief at this scene of ruin and blast was at first the
only sentiment of which I was conscious. A fearful stillness ensued. At length Wieland, lifting his hands,
which were locked in each other, to his breast, exclaimed, "Father! I thank thee. This is thy guidance.
Hither thou hast led me, that I might perform thy will.
Yet let me not err; let me hear again thy messenger!"

He stood for a minute as if listening; but, recovering
from his attitude, he continued, "It is not needed. Das-
tardly wretch! thus eternally questioning the behests of
thy Maker! weak in resolution, wayward in faith!"

He advanced to me, and, after another pause, resumed:—"Poor girl! a dismal fate has set its mark upon
thee. Thy life is demanded as a sacrifice. Prepare thee
to die. Make not my office difficult by fruitless opposition. Thy prayers might subdue stones; but none but
he who enjoined my purpose can shake it."

These words were a sufficient explication of the scene. The nature of his frenzy, as described by my uncle, was remembered. I, who had sought death, was now thrilled with horror because it was near. Death in this form, death from the hand of a brother, was thought upon with indescribable repugnance.

In a state thus verging upon madness, my eye glanced upon Carwin. His astonishment appeared to have struck him motionless and dumb. My life was in danger, and my brother's hand was about to be imbrued in my blood. I firmly believed that Carwin's was the instigation. I could rescue myself from this abhorred fate; I could dissipate this tremendous illusion; I could save my brother from the perpetration of new horrors, by pointing out the devil who seduced him. To hesitate a moment was to perish. These thoughts gave strength to my limbs and energy to my accents; I started on my feet:—

"Oh, brother! spare me! spare thyself! There is thy betrayer. He counterfeited the voice and face of an angel, for the purpose of destroying thee and me. He has this moment confessed it. He is able to speak where he is not. He is leagued with hell, but will not avow it; yet he confesses that the agency was his."

My brother turned slowly his eyes, and fixed them upon Carwin. Every joint in the frame of the latter trembled. His complexion was paler than a ghost's. His eye dared not meet that of Wieland, but wandered with an air of distraction from one space to another.

"Man," said my brother, in a voice totally unlike that which he had used to me, "what art thou? The charge has been made. Answer it. The visage—the voice—at the bottom of these stairs—at the hour of eleven—to whom did they belong? To thee?"

Twice did Carwin attempt to speak, but his words

died away upon his lips. My brother resumed, in a tone
of greater vehemence:—

"Thou falterest. Faltering is ominous. Say yes or no;
one word will suffice; but beware of falsehood. Was it
a stratagem of hell to overthrow my family? Wast thou
the agent?"

I now saw that the wrath which had been prepared
for me was to be heaped upon another. The tale that I
heard from him, and his present trepidations, were
abundant testimonies of his guilt. But what if Wieland
should be undeceived! What if he shall find his act to
have proceeded not from a heavenly prompter, but
from human treachery! Will not his rage mount into
whirlwind? Will not he tear limb from limb this devoted wretch?

Instinctively I recoiled from this image; but it gave
place to another. Carwin may be innocent, but the impetuosity of his judge may misconstrue his answers into
a confession of guilt. Wieland knows not that mysterious voices and appearances were likewise witnessed
by me. Carwin may be ignorant of those which misled
my brother. Thus may his answers unwarily betray
himself to ruin.

Such might be the consequences of my frantic precipitation, and these it was necessary, if possible, to
prevent. I attempted to speak; but Wieland, turning
suddenly upon me, commanded silence, in a tone furious and terrible. My lips closed, and my tongue refused
its office.

"What art thou?" he resumed, addressing himself to
Carwin. "Answer me: whose form—whose voice,—was
it thy contrivance? Answer me."

The answer was now given, but confusedly and
scarcely articulated. "I meant nothing—I intended no
ill—if I understand—if I do not mistake you—it is too

true—I did appear—in the entry—did speak. The contrivance was mine, but——"

These words were no sooner uttered, than my brother ceased to wear the same aspect. His eyes were downcast; he was motionless; his respiration became hoarse, like that of a man in the agonies of death. Carwin seemed unable to say more. He might have easily escaped; but the thought which occupied him related to what was horrid and unintelligible in this scene, and not to his own danger.

Presently the faculties of Wieland, which, for a time, were chained up, were seized with restlessness and trembling. He broke silence. The stoutest heart would have been appalled by the tone in which he spoke. He addressed himself to Carwin:—

"Why art thou here? Who detains thee? Go and learn better. I will meet thee, but it must be at the bar of thy Maker. There shall I bear witness against thee."

Perceiving that Carwin did not obey, he continued, "Dost thou wish me to complete the catalogue by thy death? Thy life is a worthless thing. Tempt me no more. I am but a man, and thy presence may awaken a fury which may spurn my control. Begone!"

Carwin, irresolute, striving in vain for utterance, his complexion pallid as death, his knees beating one against another, slowly obeyed the mandate and withdrew.

CHAPTER XXV

A few words more and I lay aside the pen forever. Yet why should I not relinquish it now? All that I have said is preparatory to this scene, and my fingers, tremulous and cold as my heart, refuse any further exertion. This must not be. Let my last energies support me in the finishing of this task. Then will I lay down my head in the lap of death. Hushed will be all my murmurs in the sleep of the grave.

Every sentiment has perished in my bosom. Even friendship is extinct. Your love for me has prompted me to this task; but I would not have complied if it had not been a luxury thus to feast upon my woes. I have justly calculated upon my remnant of strength. When I lay down the pen the taper of life will expire; my existence will terminate with my tale.

Now that I was left alone with Wieland, the perils of my situation presented themselves to my mind. That this paroxysm should terminate in havoc and rage it was reasonable to predict. The first suggestion of my fears had been disproved by my experience. Carwin had acknowledged his offences, and yet had escaped. The vengeance which I had harboured had not been admitted by Wieland; and yet the evils which I had endured, compared with those inflicted on my brother, were as nothing. I thirsted for his blood, and was tormented with an insatiable appetite for his destruction; but my brother was unmoved, and had dismissed him in safety. Surely thou wast more than man, while I am sunk below the beasts.

Did I place a right construction on the conduct of Wieland? Was the error that misled him so easily rectified? Were views so vivid and faith so strenuous thus liable to fading and to change? Was there not reason to doubt the accuracy of my perceptions? With images like these was my mind thronged, till the deportment of my brother called away my attention.

I saw his lips move and his eyes cast up to heaven. Then would he listen and look back, as if in expectation of some one's appearance. Thrice he repeated these gesticulations and this inaudible prayer. Each time the mist of confusion and doubt seemed to grow darker and to settle on his understanding. I guessed at the meaning of these tokens. The words of Carwin had shaken his belief, and he was employed in summoning the messenger who had formerly communed with him, to attest the value of those new doubts. In vain the summons was repeated, for his eye met nothing but vacancy, and not a sound saluted his ear.

He walked to the bed, gazed with eagerness at the pillow which had sustained the head of the breathless Catharine, and then returned to the place where I sat. I had no power to lift my eyes to his face: I was dubious of his purpose; this purpose might aim at my life.

Alas! nothing but subjection to danger and exposure to temptation can show us what we are. By this test was I now tried, and found to be cowardly and rash. Men can deliberately untie the thread of life, and of this I had deemed myself capable. It was now that I stood upon the brink of fate, that the knife of the sacrificer was aimed at my heart, I shuddered, and betook myself to any means of escape, however monstrous.

Can I bear to think—can I endure to relate the outrage which my heart meditated? Where were my means of safety? Resistance was vain. Not even the energy of despair could set me on a level with that strength which his terrific prompter had bestowed upon Wieland. Terror enables us to perform incredible feats; but terror was not then the state of my mind: where then were my hopes of rescue?

Methinks it is too much. I stand aside, as it were, from myself; I estimate my own deservings; a hatred, immortal and inexorable, is my due. I listen to my own pleas, and find them empty and false: yes, I acknowledge that my guilt surpasses that of mankind; I confess

that the curses of a world and the frowns of a Deity
are inadequate to my demerits. Is there a thing in the
world worthy of infinite abhorrence? It is I.

What shall I say? I was menaced, as I thought, with
death, and, to elude this evil, my hand was ready to
inflict death upon the menacer. In visiting my house, I
had made provision against the machinations of Carwin. In a fold of my dress an open penknife was concealed. This I now seized and drew forth. It lurked out
of view; but I now see that my state of mind would
have rendered the deed inevitable if my brother had
lifted his hand. This instrument of my preservation
would have been plunged into his heart.

O insupportable remembrance! hide thee from my
view for a time; hide it from me that my heart was
black enough to meditate the stabbing of a brother!
a brother thus supreme in misery; thus towering in
virtue!

He was probably unconscious of my design, but
presently drew back. This interval was sufficient to restore me to myself. The madness, the iniquity, of that
act which I had purposed rushed upon my apprehension. For a moment I was breathless with agony. At the
next moment I recovered my strength, and threw the
knife with violence on the floor.

The sound awoke my brother from his reverie. He
gazed alternately at me and at the weapon. With a
movement equally solemn he stooped and took it up.
He placed the blade in different positions, scrutinizing
it accurately, and maintaining, at the same time, a profound silence.

Again he looked at me; but all that vehemence and
loftiness of spirit which had so lately characterized his
features were flown. Fallen muscles, a forehead contracted into folds, eyes dim with unbidden drops, and

a ruefulness of aspect which no words can describe, were now visible.

His looks touched into energy the same sympathies in me, and I poured forth a flood of tears. This passion was quickly checked by fear, which had now no longer my own but his safety for their object. I watched his deportment in silence. At length he spoke:—

"Sister," said he, in an accent mournful and mild, "I have acted poorly my part in this world. What thinkest thou? Shall I not do better in the next?"

I could make no answer. The mildness of his tone astonished and encouraged me. I continued to regard him with wistful and anxious looks.

"I think," resumed he, "I will try. My wife and my babes have gone before. Happy wretches! I have sent you to repose, and ought not to linger behind."

These words had a meaning sufficiently intelligible. I looked at the open knife in his hand and shuddered, but knew not how to prevent the deed which I dreaded. He quickly noticed my fears, and comprehended them. Stretching towards me his hand, with an air of increasing mildness, "Take it," said he; "fear not for thy own sake, nor for mine. The cup is gone by, and its transient inebriation is succeeded by the soberness of truth.

"Thou angel whom I was wont to worship! fearest thou, my sister, for thy life? Once it was the scope of my labours to destroy thee, but I was prompted to the deed by heaven; such, at least, was my belief. Thinkest thou that thy death was sought to gratify malevolence? No. I am pure from all stain. I believed that my God was my mover!

"Neither thee nor myself have I cause to injure. I have done my duty; and surely there is merit in having sacrificed to that all that is dear to the heart of man. If a devil has deceived me, he came in the habit of an angel. If I erred, it was not my judgment that deceived me, but my senses. In thy sight, Being of beings! I am still pure. Still will I look for my reward in thy justice!"

Did my ears truly report these sounds? If I did not err, my brother was restored to just perceptions. He knew himself to have been betrayed to the murder of his wife and children, to have been the victim of infernal artifice; yet he found consolation in the rectitude of his motives. He was not devoid of sorrow, for this was written on his countenance; but his soul was tranquil and sublime.

Perhaps this was merely a transition of his former madness into a new shape. Perhaps he had not yet awakened to the memory of the horrors which he had perpetrated. Infatuated wretch that I was! To set myself up as a model by which to judge of my heroic brother! My reason taught me that his conclusions were right; but, conscious of the impotence of reason over my own conduct, conscious of my cowardly rashness and my criminal despair, I doubted whether any one could be steadfast and wise.

Such was my weakness, that even in the midst of these thoughts my mind glided into abhorrence of Carwin, and I uttered, in a low voice, "O Carwin! Carwin! what hast thou to answer for?"

My brother immediately noticed the involuntary exclamation. "Clara!" said he, "be thyself. Equity used to be a theme for thy eloquence. Reduce its lessons to practice, and be just to that unfortunate man. The instrument has done its work, and I am satisfied.

"I thank thee, my God, for this last illumination! My enemy is thine also. I deemed him to be man,—the man with whom I have often communed; but now thy goodness has unveiled to me his true nature. As the performer of thy behests, he is my friend."

My heart began now to misgive me. His mournful

aspect had gradually yielded place to a serene brow. A new soul appeared to actuate his frame, and his eyes to beam with preternatural lustre. These symptoms did not abate, and he continued:—

"Clara, I must not leave thee in doubt. I know not what brought about thy interview with the being whom thou callest Carwin. For a time I was guilty of thy error, and deduced from his incoherent confessions that I had been made the victim of human malice. He left us at my bidding, and I put up a prayer that my doubts should be removed. Thy eyes were shut and thy ears sealed to the vision that answered my prayer.

"I was indeed deceived. The form thou hast seen was the incarnation of a demon. The visage and voice which urged me to the sacrifice of my family were his. Now he personates a human form; then he was environed with the lustre of heaven.

"Clara," he continued, advancing closer to me, "thy death must come. This minister is evil, but he from whom his commission was received is God. Submit then with all thy wonted resignation to a decree that cannot be reversed or resisted. Mark the clock. Three minutes are allowed to thee, in which to call up thy fortitude and prepare thee for thy doom." There he stopped.

Even now, when this scene exists only in memory, when life and all its functions have sunk into torpor, my pulse throbs, and my hairs uprise; my brows are knit, as then, and I gaze around me in distraction. I was unconquerably averse to death; but death, imminent and full of agony as that which was threatened, was nothing. This was not the only or chief inspirer of my fears.

For him, not for myself, was my soul tormented. I might die, and no crime, surpassing the reach of mercy, would pursue me to the presence of my Judge; but my assassin would survive to contemplate his deed, and that assassin was Wieland!

Wings to bear me beyond his reach I had not. I could not vanish with a thought. The door was open, but my murderer was interposed between that and me. Of self-defence I was incapable. The frenzy that lately prompted me to blood was gone: my state was desperate; my rescue was impossible.

The weight of these accumulated thoughts could not be borne. My sight became confused; my limbs were seized with convulsion; I spoke, but my words were half formed:—

"Spare me, my brother! Look down, righteous Judge! snatch me from this fate! take away this fury from him, or turn it elsewhere!"

Such was the agony of my thoughts that I noticed not steps entering my apartment. Supplicating eyes were cast upward; but when my prayer was breathed I once more wildly gazed at the door. A form met my sight; I shuddered as if the God whom I invoked were present. It was Carwin that again intruded, and who stood before me, erect in attitude and steadfast in look!

The sight of him awakened new and rapid thoughts. His recent tale was remembered; his magical transitions and mysterious energy of voice. Whether he were infernal or miraculous or human, there was no power and no need to decide. Whether the contriver or not of this spell, he was able to unbind it, and to check the fury of my brother. He had ascribed to himself intentions not malignant. Here now was afforded a test of his truth. Let him interpose, as from above; revoke the savage decree which the madness of Wieland has assigned to heaven, and extinguish forever this passion for blood!

My mind detected at a glance this avenue to safety. The recommendations it possessed thronged as it were together, and made but one impression on my intellect. Remoter effects and collateral dangers I saw not. Perhaps the pause of an instant had sufficed to call them up. The improbability that the influence which governed Wieland was external or human; the tendency of this stratagem to sanction so fatal an error or substitute a more destructive rage in place of this; the insufficiency of Carwin's mere muscular forces to counteract the efforts and restrain the fury of Wieland, might, at a second glance, have been discovered; but no second glance was allowed. My first thought hurried me to action, and, fixing my eyes upon Carwin, I exclaimed,—

"O wretch! once more hast thou come? Let it be to abjure thy malice; to counterwork this hellish stratagem; to turn from me and from my brother this desolating rage!

"Testify thy innocence or thy remorse; exert the powers which pertain to thee, whatever they be, to turn aside this ruin. Thou art the author of these horrors! What have I done to deserve thus to die? How have I merited this unrelenting persecution? I adjure thee, by that God whose voice thou hast dared to counterfeit, to save my life!

"Wilt thou then go?—leave me! Succourless!"

Carwin listened to my entreaties unmoved, and turned from me. He seemed to hesitate a moment,— then glided through the door. Rage and despair stifled my utterance. The interval of respite was past; the pangs reserved for me by Wieland were not to be endured; my thoughts rushed again into anarchy. Having received the knife from his hand, I held it loosely and without regard; but now it seized again my attention, and I grasped it with force.

He seemed to notice not the entrance or exit of Carwin. My gesture and the murderous weapon appeared to have escaped his notice. His silence was unbroken;

his eye, fixed upon the clock for a time, was now withdrawn; fury kindled in every feature; all that was human in his face gave way to an expression supernatural
and tremendous. I felt my left arm within his grasp.

Even now I hesitated to strike. I shrunk from his
assault, but in vain.

Here let me desist. Why should I rescue this event
from oblivion? Why should I paint this detestable conflict? Why not terminate at once this series of horrors?
—Hurry to the verge of the precipice, and cast myself
forever beyond remembrance and beyond hope?

Still I live; with this load upon my breast; with this
phantom to pursue my steps; with adders lodged in my
bosom, and stinging me to madness; still I consent to
live!

Yes! I will rise above the sphere of mortal passions;
I will spurn at the cowardly remorse that bids me seek
impunity in silence, or comfort in forgetfulness. My
nerves shall be new-strung to the task. Have I not resolved? I will die. The gulf before me is inevitable and
near. I will die, but then only when my tale is at an
end.

CHAPTER XXVI

My right hand, grasping the unseen knife, was still dis-
engaged. It was lifted to strike. All my strength was
exhausted but what was sufficient to the performance
of this deed. Already was the energy awakened and
the impulse given that should bear the fatal steel to his
heart, when——Wieland shrunk back; his hand was
withdrawn. Breathless with affright and desperation, I
stood, freed from his grasp; unassailed; untouched.

Thus long had the power which controlled the scene forborne to interfere: but now his might was irresistible; and Wieland in a moment was disarmed of all his purposes. A voice, louder than human organs could produce, shriller than language can depict, burst from the ceiling and commanded him—*to hold!*

Trouble and dismay succeeded to the steadfastness that had lately been displayed in the looks of Wieland. His eyes roved from one quarter to another, with an expression of doubt. He seemed to wait for a further intimation.

Carwin's agency was here easily recognised. I had besought him to interpose in my defence. He had flown. I had imagined him deaf to my prayer, and resolute to see me perish; yet he disappeared merely to devise and execute the means of my relief.

Why did he not forbear when this end was accomplished? Why did his misjudging zeal and accursed precipitation overpass that limit? Or meant he thus to crown the scene, and conduct his inscrutable plots to this consummation?

Such ideas were the fruit of subsequent contemplation. This moment was pregnant with fate. I had no power to reason. In the career of my tempestuous thoughts, rent into pieces as my mind was by accumulating horrors, Carwin was unseen and unsuspected. I partook of Wieland's credulity, shook with his amazement, and panted with his awe.

Silence took place for a moment: so much as allowed the attention to recover its post. Then new sounds were uttered from above:—

"Man of errors! cease to cherish thy delusion; not heaven or hell, but thy senses, have misled thee to commit these acts. Shake off thy frenzy, and ascend into rational and human. Be lunatic no longer."

My brother opened his lips to speak. His tone was

terrific and faint. He muttered an appeal to heaven. It was difficult to comprehend the theme of his inquiries. They implied doubt as to the nature of the impulse that hitherto had guided him, and questioned whether he had acted in consequence of insane perceptions.

To these interrogatories the voice, which now seemed to hover at his shoulder, loudly answered in the affirmative. Then uninterrupted silence ensued.

Fallen from his lofty and heroic station; now finally restored to the perception of truth; weighed to earth by the recollection of his own deeds; consoled no longer by a consciousness of rectitude for the loss of off-spring and wife,—a loss for which he was indebted to his own misguided hand,—Wieland was transformed at once into the *man of sorrows!*

He reflected not that credit should be as reasonably denied to the last as to any former intimation; that one might as justly be ascribed to erring or diseased senses as the other. He saw not that this discovery in no degree affected the integrity of his conduct; that his motives had lost none of their claims to the homage of mankind; that the preference of supreme good, and the boundless energy of duty, were undiminished in his bosom.

It is not for me to pursue him through the ghastly changes of his countenance. Words he had none. Now he sat upon the floor, motionless in all his limbs, with his eyes glazed and fixed, a monument of woe.

Anon a spirit of tempestuous but undesigning activity seized him. He rose from his place and strode across the floor, tottering and at random. His eyes were without moisture, and gleamed with the fire that consumed his vitals. The muscles of his face were agitated by convulsions. His lips moved, but no sound escaped him.

That nature should long sustain this conflict was not to be believed. My state was little different from that of my brother. I entered, as it were, into his thoughts. My heart was visited and rent by his pangs. "Oh that thy frenzy had never been cured! that thy madness, with its blissful visions, would return! or, if that must not be, that thy scene would hasten to a close!—that death would cover thee with his oblivion!

"What can I wish for thee? Thou who hast vied with the great Preacher of thy faith in sanctity of motives, and in elevation above sensual and selfish! Thou whom thy fate has changed into parricide and savage! Can I wish for the continuance of thy being? No."

For a time his movements seemed destitute of purpose. If he walked; if he turned; if his fingers were entwined with each other; if his hands were pressed against opposite sides of his head with a force sufficient to crush it into pieces; it was to tear his mind from self-contemplation; to waste his thoughts on external objects.

Speedily this train was broken. A beam appeared to be darted into his mind which gave a purpose to his efforts. An avenue to escape presented itself; and now he eagerly gazed about him. When my thoughts became engaged by his demeanour, my fingers were stretched as by a mechanical force, and the knife, no longer heeded or of use, escaped from my grasp and fell unperceived on the floor. His eye now lighted upon it; he seized it with the quickness of thought.

I shrieked aloud, but it was too late. He plunged it to the hilt in his neck; and his life instantly escaped with the stream that gushed from the wound. He was stretched at my feet; and my hands were sprinkled with his blood as he fell.

Such was thy last deed, my brother! For a spectacle like this was it my fate to be reserved! Thy eyes were closed—thy face ghastly with death—thy arms, and the spot where thou lyedst, floated in thy life's blood!

These images have not for a moment forsaken me. Till I am breathless and cold, they must continue to hover in my sight.

Carwin, as I said, had left the room; but he still lingered in the house. My voice summoned him to my aid; but I scarcely noticed his re-entrance, and now faintly recollect his terrified looks, his broken exclamations, his vehement avowals of innocence, the effusions of his pity for me, and his offers of assistance.

I did not listen—I answered him not—I ceased to upbraid or accuse. His guilt was a point to which I was indifferent. Ruffian or devil, black as hell or bright as angels, thenceforth he was nothing to me. I was incapable of sparing a look or a thought from the ruin that was spread at my feet.

When he left me, I was scarcely conscious of any variation in the scene. He informed the inhabitants of the hut of what had passed, and they flew to the spot. Careless of his own safety, he hasted to the city to inform my friends of my condition.

My uncle speedily arrived at the house. The body of Wieland was removed from my presence, and they supposed that I would follow it; but no, my home is ascertained; here I have taken up my rest, and never will I go hence, till, like Wieland, I am borne to my grave.

Importunity was tried in vain. They threatened to remove me by violence,—nay, violence was used; but my soul prizes too dearly this little roof to endure to be bereaved of it. Force should not prevail when the hoary locks and supplicating tears of my uncle were ineffectual. My repugnance to move gave birth to ferociousness and frenzy when force was employed, and they were obliged to consent to my return.

They besought me—they remonstrated—they appealed to every duty that connected me with Him that made me and with my fellow-men—in vain. While I live I will not go hence. Have I not fulfilled my destiny?

Why will ye torment me with your reasonings and reproofs? Can ye restore to me the hope of my better days? Can ye give me back Catharine and her babes? Can ye recall to life him who died at my feet?

I will eat—I will drink—I will lie down and rise up—at your bidding; all I ask is the choice of my abode. What is there unreasonable in this demand? Shortly will I be at peace. This is the spot which I have chosen in which to breathe my last sigh. Deny me not, I beseech you, so slight a boon.

Talk not to me, O my reverend friend! of Carwin. He has told thee his tale, and thou exculpatest him from all direct concern in the fate of Wieland. This scene of havoc was produced by an illusion of the senses. Be it so; I care not from what source these disasters have flowed; it suffices that they have swallowed up our hopes and our existence.

What his agency began, his agency conducted to a close. He intended, by the final effort of his power, to rescue me and to banish his illusions from my brother. Such is his tale, concerning the truth of which I care not. Henceforth I foster but one wish: I ask only quick deliverance from life and all the ills that attend it.

Go, wretch! torment me not with thy presence and thy prayers.—Forgive thee? Will that avail thee when thy fateful hour shall arrive? Be thou acquitted at thy own tribunal, and thou needest not fear the verdict of others. If thy guilt be capable of blacker hues, if hitherto thy conscience be without stain, thy crime will be made more flagrant by thus violating my retreat. Take thyself away from my sight if thou wouldst not behold my death!

Thou art gone! murmuring and reluctant! And now my repose is coming—my work is done!

CHAPTER XXVII

[Written three years after the foregoing,
and dated at Montpellier.]

I imagined that I had forever laid aside the pen; and
that I should take up my abode in this part of the world
was of all events the least probable. My destiny I
believed to be accomplished, and I looked forward
to a speedy termination of my life with the fullest
confidence.

Surely I had reason to be weary of existence, to be
impatient of every tie which held me from the grave.
I experienced this impatience in its fullest extent. I was
not only enamoured of death, but conceived, from the
condition of my frame, that to shun it was impossible,
even though I had ardently desired it; yet here am I,
a thousand leagues from my native soil, in full possession of life and of health, and not destitute of happiness.

Such is man. Time will obliterate the deepest impressions. Grief the most vehement and hopeless will
gradually decay and wear itself out. Arguments may
be employed in vain; every moral prescription may be
ineffectually tried; remonstrances, however cogent or
pathetic, shall have no power over the attention, or
shall be repelled with disdain; yet, as day follows day,
the turbulence of our emotions shall subside, and our
fluctuations be finally succeeded by a calm.

Perhaps, however, the conquest of despair was
chiefly owing to an accident which rendered my continuance in my own house impossible. At the conclu-

sion of my long, and, as I then supposed, my last, letter to you, I mentioned my resolution to wait for death in the very spot which had been the principal scene of my misfortunes. From this resolution my friends exerted themselves with the utmost zeal and perseverance to make me depart. They justly imagined that to be thus surrounded by memorials of the fate of my family would tend to foster my disease. A swift succession of new objects, and the exclusion of every thing calculated to remind me of my loss, was the only method of cure.

I refused to listen to their exhortations. Great as my calamity was, to be torn from this asylum was regarded by me as an aggravation of it. By a perverse constitution of mind, he was considered as my greatest enemy who sought to withdraw me from a scene which supplied eternal food to my melancholy, and kept my despair from languishing.

In relating the history of these disasters I derived a similar species of gratification. My uncle earnestly dissuaded me from this task; but his remonstrances were as fruitless on this head as they had been on others. They would have withheld from me the implements of writing; but they quickly perceived that to withstand would be more injurious than to comply with my wishes. Having finished my tale, it seemed as if the scene were closing. A fever lurked in my veins, and my strength was gone. Any exertion, however slight, was attended with difficulty, and, at length, I refused to rise from my bed.

I now see the infatuation and injustice of my conduct in its true colours. I reflect upon the sensations and reasonings of that period with wonder and humiliation. That I should be insensible to the claims and tears of my friends; that I should overlook the suggestions of duty, and fly from that post in which only I could be instrumental to the benefit of others; that the exercise of the social and beneficent affections, the contemplation of nature, and the acquisition of wisdom, should not be seen to be means of happiness still within my reach, is, at this time, scarcely credible.

It is true that I am now changed; but I have not the consolation to reflect that my change was owing to my fortitude or to my capacity for instruction. Better thoughts grew up in my mind imperceptibly. I cannot but congratulate myself on the change, though, perhaps, it merely argues a fickleness of temper and a defect of sensibility.

After my narrative was ended, I betook myself to my bed, in the full belief that my career in this world was on the point of finishing. My uncle took up his abode with me, and performed for me every office of nurse, physician, and friend. One night, after some hours of restlessness and pain, I sunk into deep sleep. Its tranquillity, however, was of no long duration. My fancy became suddenly distempered, and my brain was turned into a theatre of uproar and confusion. It would not be easy to describe the wild and fantastical incongruities that pestered me. My uncle, Wieland, Pleyel, and Carwin were successively and momently discerned amidst the storm. Sometimes I was swallowed up by whirlpools, or caught up in the air by half-seen and gigantic forms, and thrown upon pointed rocks or cast among the billows. Sometimes gleams of light were shot into a dark abyss, on the verge of which I was standing, and enabled me to discover, for a moment, its enormous depth and hideous precipices. Anon, I was transported to some ridge of Etna, and made a terrified spectator of its fiery torrents and its pillars of smoke.

However strange it may seem, I was conscious, even during my dream, of my real situation. I knew myself to be asleep, and struggled to break the spell by muscular exertions. These did not avail, and I continued to suffer these abortive creations till a loud voice at my bedside, and some one shaking me with violence, put an end to my reverie. My eyes were unsealed, and I started from my pillow.

My chamber was filled with smoke, which, though in some degree luminous, would permit me to see nothing, and by which I was nearly suffocated. The crackling of flames, and the deafening clamour of voices without, burst upon my ears. Stunned as I was by this hubbub, scorched with heat, and nearly choked by the accumulating vapours, I was unable to think or act for my own preservation; I was incapable, indeed, of comprehending my danger.

I was caught up, in an instant, by a pair of sinewy arms, borne to the window, and carried down a ladder which had been placed there. My uncle stood at the bottom and received me. I was not fully aware of my situation till I found myself sheltered in the *hut* and surrounded by its inhabitants.

By neglect of the servant, some unextinguished embers had been placed in a barrel in the cellar of the building. The barrel had caught fire; this was communicated to the beams of the lower floor, and thence to the upper part of the structure. It was first discovered by some persons at a distance, who hastened to the spot and alarmed my uncle and the servants. The flames had already made considerable progress, and my condition was overlooked till my escape was rendered nearly impossible.

My danger being known, and a ladder quickly procured, one of the spectators ascended to my chamber, and effected my deliverance in the manner before related.

This incident, disastrous as it may at first seem, had,

in reality, a beneficial effect upon my feelings. I was, in some degree, roused from the stupor which had seized my faculties. The monotonous and gloomy series of my thoughts was broken. My habitation was levelled with the ground, and I was obliged to seek a new one. A new train of images, disconnected with the fate of my family, forced itself on my attention; and a belief insensibly sprung up that tranquillity, if not happiness, was still within my reach. Notwithstanding the shocks which my frame had endured, the anguish of my thoughts no sooner abated than I recovered my health.

I now willingly listened to my uncle's solicitations to be the companion of his voyage. Preparations were easily made, and, after a tedious passage, we set our feet on the shore of the ancient world. The memory of the past did not forsake me; but the melancholy which it generated, and the tears with which it filled my eyes, were not unprofitable. My curiosity was revived, and I contemplated with ardour the spectacle of living manners and the monuments of past ages.

In proportion as my heart was reinstated in the possession of its ancient tranquillity, the sentiment which I had cherished with regard to Pleyel returned. In a short time he was united to the Saxon woman, and made his residence in the neighbourhood of Boston. I was glad that circumstances would not permit an interview to take place between us. I could not desire their misery; but I reaped no pleasure from reflecting on their happiness. Time, and the exertions of my fortitude, cured me, in some degree, of this folly. I continued to love him, but my passion was disguised to myself; I considered it merely as a more tender species of friendship, and cherished it without compunction.

Through my uncle's exertions, a meeting was brought about between Carwin and Pleyel, and explanations took place which restored me at once to the good opinion of the latter. Though separated so widely, our correspondence was punctual and frequent, and paved the way for that union which can only end with the death of one of us.

In my letters to him I made no secret of my former sentiments. This was a theme on which I could talk without painful though not without delicate emotions. That knowledge which I should never have imparted to a lover, I felt little scruple to communicate to a friend.

A year and a half elapsed when Theresa was snatched from him by death, in the hour in which she gave him the first pledge of their mutual affection. This event was borne by him with his customary fortitude. It induced him, however, to make a change in his plans. He disposed of his property in America, and joined my uncle and me, who had terminated the wanderings of two years at Montpellier, which will henceforth, I believe, be our permanent abode.

If you reflect upon that entire confidence which had subsisted from our infancy between Pleyel and myself, on the passion that I had contracted, and which was merely smothered for a time, and on the esteem which was mutual, you will not, perhaps, be surprised that the renovation of our intercourse should give birth to that union which at present subsists. When the period had elapsed necessary to weaken the remembrance of Theresa, to whom he had been bound by ties more of honour than of love, he tendered his affections to me. I need not add that the tender was eagerly accepted.

Perhaps you are somewhat interested in the fate of Carwin. He saw, when too late, the danger of imposture. So much affected was he by the catastrophe to which he was a witness, that he laid aside all regard to his own safety. He sought my uncle, and confided to him the tale which he had just related to me. He found a more impartial and indulgent auditor in Mr. Cambridge, who imputed to maniacal illusion the conduct of Wieland, though he conceived the previous and unseen agency of Carwin to have indirectly but powerfully predisposed to this deplorable perversion of mind.

It was easy for Carwin to elude the persecutions of Ludloe. It was merely requisite to hide himself in a remote district of Pennsylvania. This, when he parted from us, he determined to do. He is now probably engaged in the harmless pursuits of agriculture, and may come to think, without insupportable remorse, on the evils to which his fatal talents have given birth. The innocence and usefulness of his future life may, in some degree, atone for the miseries so rashly or so thoughtlessly inflicted.

More urgent considerations hindered me from mentioning, in the course of my former mournful recital, any particulars respecting the unfortunate father of Louisa Conway. That man surely was reserved to be a monument of capricious fortune. His southern journeys being finished, he returned to Philadelphia. Before he reached the city he left the highway, and alighted at my brother's door. Contrary to his expectation, no one came forth to welcome him or hail his approach. He attempted to enter the house; but bolted doors, barred windows, and a silence broken only by unanswered calls, showed him that the mansion was deserted.

He proceeded thence to my habitation, which he found, in like manner, gloomy and tenantless. His surprise may be easily conceived. The rustics who occupied the hut told him an imperfect and incredible tale. He hasted to the city, and extorted from Mrs. Baynton a full disclosure of late disasters.

He was inured to adversity, and recovered, after no long time, from the shocks produced by the disappointment of his darling scheme. Our intercourse did not terminate with his departure from America. We have since met with him in France, and light has at length been thrown upon the motives which occasioned the disappearance of his wife in the manner which I formerly related to you.

I have dwelt upon the ardour of their conjugal attachment, and mentioned that no suspicion had ever glanced upon her purity. This, though the belief was long cherished, recent discoveries have shown to be questionable. No doubt her integrity would have survived to the present moment if an extraordinary fate had not befallen her.

Major Stuart had been engaged, while in Germany, in a contest of honour with an aide-de-camp of the Marquis of Granby. His adversary had propagated a rumour injurious to his character. A challenge was sent; a meeting ensued; and Stuart wounded and disarmed the calumniator. The offence was atoned for, and his life secured by suitable concessions.

Maxwell (that was his name) shortly after, in consequence of succeeding to a rich inheritance, sold his commission and returned to London. His fortune was speedily augmented by an opulent marriage. Interest was his sole inducement to this marriage, though the lady had been swayed by a credulous affection. The true state of his heart was quickly discovered, and a separation, by mutual consent, took place. The lady withdrew to an estate in a distant county, and Maxwell continued to consume his time and fortune in the dissipation of the capital.

Maxwell, though deceitful and sensual, possessed great force of mind and specious accomplishments. He contrived to mislead the generous mind of Stuart, and to regain the esteem which his misconduct for a time had forfeited. He was recommended by her husband to the confidence of Mrs. Stuart. Maxwell was stimu-

lated by revenge, and by a lawless passion, to convert
this confidence into a source of guilt.

The education and capacity of this woman, the
worth of her husband, the pledge of their alliance
which time had produced, her maturity in age and
knowledge of the world,—all combined to render this
attempt hopeless. Maxwell, however, was not easily
discouraged. The most perfect being, he believed, must
owe his exemption from vice to the absence of temptation. The impulses of love are so subtle, and the influence of false reasoning, when enforced by eloquence
and passion, so unbounded, that no human virtue is secure from degeneracy. All arts being tried, every temptation being summoned to his aid, dissimulation being
carried to its utmost bound, Maxwell, at length, nearly
accomplished his purpose. The lady's affections were
withdrawn from her husband and transferred to him.
She could not, as yet, be reconciled to dishonour. All
efforts to induce her to elope with him were ineffectual.
She permitted herself to love, and to avow her love;
but at this limit she stopped, and was immovable.

Hence this revolution in her sentiments was productive only of despair. Her rectitude of principle preserved her from actual guilt, but could not restore to
her her ancient affection, or save her from being the
prey of remorseful and impracticable wishes. Her husband's absence produced a state of suspense. This,
however, approached to a period, and she received
tidings of his intended return. Maxwell, being likewise
apprized of this event, and having made a last and un-
successful effort to conquer her reluctance to accompany him in a journey to Italy, whither he pretended
an invincible necessity of going, left her to pursue the
measures which despair might suggest. At the same
time she received a letter from the wife of Maxwell,
unveiling the true character of this man, and revealing

facts which the artifices of her seducer had hitherto concealed from her. Mrs. Maxwell had been prompted to this disclosure by a knowledge of her husband's practices, with which his own impetuosity had made her acquainted.

This discovery, joined to the delicacy of her scruples and the anguish of remorse, induced her to abscond. This scheme was adopted in haste, but effected with consummate prudence. She fled, on the eve of her husband's arrival, in the disguise of a boy, and embarked at Falmouth in a packet bound for America.

The history of her disastrous intercourse with Maxwell, the motives inducing her to forsake her country, and the measures she had taken to effect her design, were related to Mrs. Maxwell, in reply to her communication. Between these women an ancient intimacy and considerable similitude of character subsisted. This disclosure was accompanied with solemn injunctions of secrecy, and these injunctions were, for a long time, faithfully observed.

Mrs. Maxwell's abode was situated on the banks of the Wey. Stuart was her kinsman; their youth had been spent together; and Maxwell was in some degree indebted to the man whom he betrayed for his alliance with this unfortunate lady. Her esteem for the character of Stuart had never been diminished. A meeting between them was occasioned by a tour which the latter had undertaken, in the year after his return from America, to Wales and the western counties. This interview produced pleasure and regret in each. Their own transactions naturally became the topics of their conversation; and the untimely fate of his wife and daughter were related by the guest.

Mrs. Maxwell's regard for her friend, as well as for the safety of her husband, persuaded her to concealment; but, the former being dead and the latter being out of the kingdom, she ventured to produce Mrs. Stuart's letter, and to communicate her own knowledge of the treachery of Maxwell. She had previously extorted from her guest a promise not to pursue any scheme of vengeance; but this promise was made while ignorant of the full extent of Maxwell's depravity, and his passion refused to adhere to it.

At this time my uncle and I resided at Avignon. Among the English resident there, and with whom we maintained a social intercourse, was Maxwell. This man's talents and address rendered him a favourite both with my uncle and myself. He had even tendered me his hand in marriage; but, this being refused, he had sought and obtained permission to continue with us the intercourse of friendship. Since a legal marriage was impossible, no doubt his views were flagitious. Whether he had relinquished these views I was unable to judge.

He was one in a large circle at a villa in the environs, to which I had likewise been invited, when Stuart abruptly entered the apartment. He was recognised with genuine satisfaction by me, and with seeming pleasure by Maxwell. In a short time, some affair of moment being pleaded, which required an immediate and exclusive interview, Maxwell and he withdrew together. Stuart and my uncle had been known to each other in the German army; and the purpose contemplated by the former in this long and hasty journey was confided to his old friend.

A defiance was given and received, and the banks of a rivulet, about a league from the city, was selected as the scene of this contest. My uncle, having exerted himself in vain to prevent a hostile meeting, consented to attend them as a surgeon. Next morning, at sunrise, was the time chosen.

I returned early in the evening to my lodgings.

Preliminaries being settled between the combatants, Stuart had consented to spend the evening with us, and did not retire till late. On the way to his hotel he was exposed to no molestation; but just as he stepped within the portico, a swarthy and malignant figure started from behind a column and plunged a stiletto into his body.

The author of this treason could not certainly be discovered; but the details communicated by Stuart respecting the history of Maxwell naturally pointed him out as an object of suspicion. No one expressed more concern on account of this disaster than he; and he pretended an ardent zeal to vindicate his character from the aspersions that were cast upon it. Thenceforth, however, I denied myself to his visits; and shortly after he disappeared from this scene.

Few possessed more estimable qualities, and a better title to happiness and the tranquil honours of long life, than the mother and the father of Louisa Conway; yet they were cut off in the bloom of their days, and their destiny was thus accomplished by the same hand. Maxwell was the instrument of their destruction, though the instrument was applied to this end in so different a manner.

I leave you to moralize on this tale. That virtue should become the victim of treachery is, no doubt, a mournful consideration; but it will not escape your notice, that the evils of which Carwin and Maxwell were the authors owed their existence to the errors of the sufferers. All efforts would have been ineffectual to subvert the happiness or shorten the existence of the Stuarts, if their own frailty had not seconded these efforts. If the lady had crushed her disastrous passion in the bud, and driven the seducer from her presence when the tendency of his artifices was seen; if Stuart had not admitted the spirit of absurd revenge, we should not have had to deplore this catastrophe. If Wieland had framed juster notions of moral duty and of the divine attributes, or if I had been gifted with ordinary equanimity or foresight, the double-tongued deceiver would have been baffled and repelled.

THE END.